T0129541

AUF WIEDERSEHEN

A NOVEL

Laura Otis

AUF WIEDERSEHEN
A NOVEL

iUniverse books may be ordered through booksellers or by contacting:

iUniverse
1663 Liberty Drive
Bloomington, IN 47403
www.iuniverse.com
1-800-Authors (1-800-288-4677)

Because of the dynamic nature of the internet, any web addresses or links contained in this book may have changed since publication and may no longer be valid. The views expressed in this work are solely those of the author and do not necessarily reflect the views of the publisher, and the publisher hereby disclaims any responsibility for them.

Any people depicted in stock imagery provided by Getty Images are models, and such images are being used for illustrative purposes only. Certain stock imagery © Getty Images.

ISBN: 978-1-5320-9227-5 (sc)
ISBN: 978-1-5320-9226-8 (e)

Print information available on the last page.

iUniverse rev. date: 05/21/2020

For my inspiration and my love:

Broken-tusked, big-bodied, with the light of a thousand suns,
Remove all obstacles from my performance of good tasks always.

All hail to Ganesha, mover of obstacles!

CHAPTER 1

SPINNING

THE PARTY AT 1317 EAST Fiftieth was notorious. Like the house, it had outlived generations of Chicago students and pulsed with a heartbeat all its own. Each year it created casualties, women who collapsed on coat-strewn beds, men who reeled out to be slammed by the sidewalk. The party crowned the quarter like a fool's cap, jingling as it slid down over people's eyes.

As Jack Mannheim's feet crunched up the steps, the house was throbbing with glee. His wife, Bea, hadn't wanted to come. She was finishing the Christmas cards, but he should go, she said—the chance to see people would do him good. His daughter, Jessie, was out, as usual—no one knew where. He hoped she would make it to family therapy tomorrow, a humiliation she had accepted after weeks of arguing.

The door swung open to reveal groups of students narrating anxiously, laughing wildly. Jack smiled and waved at the ones he knew: girls with cropped hair; twitchy, angular boys. Even when these skinny wits celebrated, they dressed in black. Giddy with excitement, they talked of their Modern Language Association interviews, where some of them would be finding their first jobs.

Several rooms back, Sam Loeb was dancing so that his bulk rocked in and out of a doorframe. He removed one hand from a curvy girl's hip to wave at Jack through the distant door.

"Hey, Jack, all right! C'mon, get out heah!" he roared in rambunctious Brooklynese.

Before Jack could respond, Sam lurched forward and disappeared. Jack added his coat to a quilted mound and picked his way around two frizzy-haired girls on the stairs.

"Brandeis," said one. "Pomona. Nacogdoches. I've got five so far."

"Don't ask Lucy—she doesn't have any. Hey, where is Nacogdoches anyway?"

In three weeks, professors from these far-flung colleges would be testing Jack's students' minds. Like pinballs, they would be shot into the academic world, where they would bounce around and light up campuses until they rolled into their permanent positions. Noisy Sam would lead the assault, advising job seekers with loving aggression. Each year he and his flock descended on the MLA like Mrs. Bennet with her daughters.

"Hey, glad to see you, Jack!" called Tony, one of the hosts. "Faculty hardly ever come."

A red-haired girl crumpled softly onto the couch, holding it in a confused embrace.

"Can't imagine why!" continued Tony. "Want a drink?"

Jack found a cup that didn't look wet and dipped it into a steaming, fragrant bowl. The punch burned the back of his throat pleasantly, and he frowned into the cup, trying to identify the flavor.

"Ooh, that's bad stuff," said a mischievous voice. "Don't look too hard at that."

Jack looked into the playful eyes of Ellie LaSalle, a graduate student in French. Ellie hovered and rotated on the balls of her feet, her long brown hair swinging as she moved. Ellie's short black skirt quivered as she laughed, and her fuzzy red sweater slid off one shoulder. Last semester, she had sat in on Jack's Thomas Mann seminar and had surprised him by blurting out what it had taken him years to realize. His students had been arguing about Gustav Aschenbach's obsessive pursuit of the fourteen-year-old boy Tadzio.

"But Aschenbach doesn't want to have sex with Tadzio," exclaimed Ellie.

There was a second of dead silence. No one ever said anything that crude.

"What do you think he wants?" asked Jack.

"To suffer," she replied.

From that moment, Ellie had held Jack's attention. The students had resumed jousting, now debating the causes of Aschenbach's masochism. As their words grew long and their subject minute, Jack had found himself meeting her laughing eyes. How could she, at twenty-six, have known that Aschenbach wanted to suffer?

Jack asked Ellie how many interviews she had, but a sweaty student grabbed her forearm.

"C'mon, El, we need you out there!" he spluttered.

Ellie laughed apologetically as the tall boy dragged her off. Jack started to follow, but an anxious voice called him. A first-year student wanted to know about Theodor Adorno's politics. He had heard that Adorno was secretly a fascist, and he couldn't get over it. How did he, Jack, define fascism? Jack was just the person he needed to talk to, someone who knew twentieth-century German culture. As the celebration bubbled around him, Jack submerged himself in the familiar vocabulary of the classroom. He sipped the steaming punch and talked to one student after another, yielding to the flow of their voices.

The music seemed to be growing louder, and he realized he had drifted close to the dance room. Sam was dancing with two adoring, wriggling girls who took turns popping rum balls into his mouth. In hedonistic ecstasy, Sam sighed after each morsel and ran his hand softly over the girl's waist. Jack looked around for the rum balls but didn't see any.

"Hey," he called. "Can I have one of those?"

"Which one ya want?" Sam laughed deep and low and squeezed both girls against him.

Jack laughed, shook his head, and raised his hand in refusal. "I'll just watch."

On the floor, Ellie turned like a poinsettia petal in an ocean of black. As she spun, her skirt twirled all the way out to reveal her taut white thighs.

Jack dipped his cup into the spicy bowl and leaned back against the wall. Its cool, uneven surface grudgingly supported his shoulders. The music never stopped, but by some form of communication, the dancers knew when to change partners. Jack tried to remember how dancing had felt but could recall only broken sounds.

Ellie sauntered up to Sam, who gave a tired grin of assent. On his forehead, the sweat ran in streams. As Ellie danced with Sam, her posture changed, her chest pressing forward, her shoulders back. Whereas Ellie tightened, electrified, Sam unfolded and relaxed. His eyelids drooped, and he released his breath in a long sigh. How daring she was—rolling her shoulders into him, spinning and nudging him with her behind. Never one to refuse a dare, Sam caught her hips and shifted her weight from hand to hand so that she slid back and forth against him.

From his spot on the wall, Jack played a maddening virtual reality game. He followed Sam's hands over Ellie's body so that he could almost feel the soft red wool and the firm flesh beneath. Sam's broad fingers obeyed Jack's mental commands only part of the time. They released the prize when Jack least expected it, only to pull the girl closer than he would have dared.

Jack's pulse had long since adjusted to the music, a jouncy tune that tossed bodies across the floor. The song's teasing dissonance resolved into a good-natured plea: "Lay down, Sally!" He hadn't heard this one in a long time. Jack leaned into the wall and watched the dancers writhe. Down they went, bodies twisting, chests nearly touching, the bass line poking them with happy jabs. When they rose, Ellie reached for Sam's shoulders and shook in a parody of lascivious abandon. Jack laughed, wondering how this virtual reality game was going to end.

When the music faded, Sam ambled over and draped his arm around Jack. Sam was barely tall enough to reach his friend's shoulders, and Jack marveled that anyone could touch another human being so easily.

"Oh, man," moaned Sam. "I'm gettin' too old for this."

"You looked good out there."

Sam shook his head and glanced around quickly. "She gives me such a hard-on."

"You ever—"

"Nah." Sam shifted his focus downward.

"Ever think about it?"

"About sixty-seven times a day. Can't do it, though. Couldn't ever do that." He smiled tiredly as his dark eyes returned to Jack's.

Jack never tired of the timbre of Sam's voice. Despite all Sam's years in Chicago, his Brooklyn accent hung over him like the teasing aroma of a chocolate factory whose location one can't pin down. Sam's wife, Ruth, spoke just the same way, so that they reinforced each other in a feedback loop. Jack had lost his own Bronx accent years ago, without knowing when or where. Neither Sam nor Jack had lived in New York for two decades, but they shared their origin as a warm current in an ocean of dubious aspirations.

Sam squeezed Jack's arm. "Watch her for me, will ya? I gotta go take a piss."

Jack nodded, leaned forward from the wall, and lost his balance for a moment.

Ellie was dancing with Tony now, who was twirling her ecstatically. The new song seemed made for turning, a Doors tune with a hypnotic pull.

"Don't ya love her madly?"

Ellie's hair splayed out in the soft curve of the Liberty Bell.

"Don't ya need her badly?"

Each breath filled Jack and left him in a slow, sad beat. The room faded in and out as though he were inhaling it and blowing the pieces back in place.

"Don't ya love her as she's walkin' out the door?"

"Jack!" Sam was shaking his arm. "I gotta go. Ruth just called. Jerry had a seizure."

His friend looked twenty years older than he had out on the floor. Sam had condensed from aromatic mist back into his round, solid shape, and his eyes had withdrawn into the shadows around them. He spoke with tired, knowing strength.

"Half an hour ago. Bad one. Ya never know when they're comin'. Ruth's with him, but he keeps askin' for me."

"I'm sorry," said Jack. "God, that must be rough."

"He's a tough kid. He knows what he's dealin' with, and he makes sure he has a life. Couple more years and I'll give him Dostoyevsky, except he says he doesn't wanna be seen carryin' around a book called *The Idiot*. I showed up with it one day after class, and he says, 'What did you, write your autobiography or something?'"

Sam pressed the nearby students' hands and kissed the girls' flushed cheeks. Jack followed him to the door.

"See ya at the MLA," he called.

He crunched heavily, determinedly off into the night.

Jack returned to the dim, throbbing room. Patches of brown scum floated in the punch, and he watched transfixed as they merged and cracked. Why did they always split at right angles? When he dipped in his cup, they rushed to the sides and abandoned the pattern they were forming.

6

Ellie approached him, holding her red sweater away from her and flapping it to pump air over her body.

"Whew!"

Jack offered her a drink, but she shook her head. She wanted only water. Jack watched the workings of her throat as she downed a glass.

"You looked good out there," he said. "Where'd you learn how to dance like that?"

"With Sam, you mean?"

He wondered how she knew he meant with Sam. "Well—yes."

"*Dirty Dancing.*"

"I saw that!" he cried. "I can't dance like that."

He was responding faster than he could think, something he almost never did.

"Maybe you're not dirty." Her brown eyes smoked.

"And you are?" he asked.

"Well, my name's *La sale.*"

"That filthy, huh?"

Her eyes widened as she laughed, and it pleased him to know she hadn't expected him to be this daring. His excitement mounted as she blushed. Whatever they were playing, he had scored a point.

"You dance a different way with each guy," she said. "With Sam, it's dirty dancing."

By now, Sam would be hurrying over crusted snow and frowning worriedly at blue Christmas lights.

"How would you dance with me?" asked Jack.

"You don't dance," she quipped.

"Sometimes I do."

"Would you dance with me now?" she challenged.

Jack hesitated, breaking their rhythm. "Maybe."

"Okay. Then tell me about your book."

Jack exhaled slowly. For the past three years, he had been working on a secret project, its contours known only to a select few. His first book, on Robert Musil's *The Man without Qualities*, had impressed the academic world with its lucidity. The incisive works that had followed had cut deep. His study of Thomas Mann, now four years old, had won the Brockhaus Prize. Daring in its simplicity, Jack's writing had earned him his job at a top university, his spacious office in its gothic attic, his friends scattered across campuses around the world, his students who fought to work with him, and his quiet, tasteful home with its Steinway piano and walls of books. Everyone was waiting for his next project and wondering why he wouldn't talk about his new book. It was going to be called *Dionysus in Germany*, and Ellie was one of the few who knew.

Jack had told her the first day that she came to ask him about Friedrich Nietzsche. She had been studying André Gide's use of mythology, and when they opened *The Birth of Tragedy*, she noticed what Jack had underlined.

"All collapsing, surging, irony." She smiled. "You're into Dionysus, aren't you?"

The girl was so penetrating. Jack couldn't lie, and all his thoughts had rushed out at once. Reading Mann, he had felt himself falling toward Nietzsche—no, not Nietzsche—toward something more awful than he could name. After thirty years of writing about German literature, he was going to argue that National Socialism wasn't Dionysian. It wasn't drunken chaos, an upheaval of libidinal forces. The Shoah wasn't an orgy. If anything, the Nazi movement was the exact opposite, a drive of murderous order.

The chapter on Mann had been a joy to write. The Nietzsche chapter would be too, hustled along by his upcoming seminar. What fazed him was the chapter on the Nazis, whose administration his mother still praised. He needed more material, and it would be a long time before he was ready to write.

"The Mann chapter's in good shape," he said. "Nietzsche starts as soon as we're back from the MLA."

"That sounds good. What are you going to say?"

Jack smiled at her timidly. "I'll know when I've said it."

"Oooh—oooh—evasion!" she crowed.

"Dionysus would approve, don't you think?" He reached for the red sweater slipping down her moist arm, only to see his hand halt in midair.

"But the Dionysian is the truth," she said.

"The truth that always evades a direct question."

"Oooh—oooh!" Ellie laughed.

With her thumb and forefinger, she hoisted the red fuzz back up onto her shoulder. They circled, parried, and made bets on the scum-bergs in the punch.

Tony approached hesitantly. "Hey, El, you need a ride?"

"What, do I look like I need one?"

"No, but Greg's heading out, and he lives near you. He's the last boat."

The music still pulsed, but the rooms had emptied. In the kitchen, Tony and his housemates were organizing a flotilla to transport the casualties home.

"Where do you live?" Jack asked Ellie.

In his giddiness, he had forgotten their unspoken curfew. With poverty on three sides and a lake on the other, no one walked around alone at night.

"Fifty-Fifth and Blackstone."

"Oh," said Jack. "That's right near me. I can walk you home."

Tony glanced at her questioningly, as though seeking a sign.

"Fine by me," said Ellie.

Ellie went to the bathroom, and Jack sought their coats. On the much-reduced mound floated a red-haired girl, the one who had fallen on the couch earlier. Fascinated, Jack watched her breathe and wondered how a person could drink until she collapsed. Damp tendrils of hair curled over her forehead, and a blood vessel pulsed under the skin of her throat.

Jack spotted his own coat right away, gray, quilted, and expensive. Ellie's gave him more trouble—dark brown, she had said, with a fur collar and cuffs. God, it was right under that sleeping girl! He

9

grabbed the stiff wool and pulled. The girl whimpered and raised a limp hand. He tugged slowly, steadily, until she rolled onto her side and the coat came free. Her exposed thigh was soft and moist, even whiter than her throat. Jack draped a loose coat over her, and she pulled it to her in murky slumber.

How would Ellie react if he helped her into her coat? Some women got so mad when you did that. Others, willing but confused, turned the wrong way so that you had to follow as they spun like a dog preparing to flop down. Jack draped the coat gently over one shoulder, and Ellie met his movements with willing grace. The fuzzy collar trapped her long hair, and she signaled for him to pull it out. The hair was a whisper, a kiss against his hands.

"You guys heading out?" asked Tony. "Be careful out there." To Jack he said respectfully, "I'm so glad you could come."

"It was great," said Jack. "Really. Thanks for inviting us."

Without thinking, he'd slipped into the "we" with which he and Bea detached themselves from social gatherings. He thought about Jerry, and Sam's autobiography. Sam must be home by now, comforting his son.

The cold assaulted Jack with his first breath, stinging his eyes and invading his lungs. White pellets of salt lay on the ice inert, unable to melt their way in. With lowered eyes, Jack sought the bare patches fluctuating around the center of the sidewalk. He wondered how Ellie managed in her heels and took her arm to steady her, only to find that he was a little unsteady himself. To shield her from the cold, he wrapped his arm around her. Except for her nibbling taps and the crunch of his steps, the streets were completely silent. Red and blue lights shone eerily from the stone houses. Out of respect for the sleeping city, Ellie spoke in low tones. Her voice flowed like a melody over the rough continuo of their footsteps.

Ellie was talking about her interviews: Alabama, San Diego, Colorado, Stevens Point. She had a good shot at a job, he realized, and she was excited at what the next months might bring.

At the mention of each campus, Jack responded, "I know someone there."

"You know someone everywhere."

"Not like Sam—he's amazing." To warm her, he rubbed his gloved hand against her arm.

"Sam won't do me any good. He works on eighteenth-century British novels."

"He's been doing this for a long time, though. Stick with him, I'm telling you."

"Oh, I'm sticking with you."

Her strong, slender arm stretched itself around his waist.

The streets passed by in a barely perceptible rhythm: Fifty-First. Fifty-Second. Fifty-Third. The cold air tasted of tar, a bitter gift from the mills in Gary. Fifty-Fourth. Fifty-Fifth. Jack tried to imagine San Diego—parties without coats, night air that smelled of flowers.

"Well, this is it," said Ellie.

They stopped under an art deco awning of chrome and etched glass. In protective silence, it pointed the way into a heavy, U-shaped building.

Ellie asked softly, "Would you like to come in?"

"Sure, for a while," said Jack.

He always liked to visit people's apartments to read the clues their spaces offered about their lives. Ellie jounced her purse once and used the jingle to locate her keys. Her fingers tautened her leather glove as she struggled with the hardened lock. Jack followed her across the lobby past a glittering tree and a row of dolls in red caps. The stairs creaked under his feet as he tried to match her quick rhythm. Ellie pushed open her door, and he was safe in her space. It smelled of balsam from a sprig of branches and of another sweetness he couldn't name.

"What is this place?" he murmured.

Jack felt very big—a big man in a big coat in a small room. "Du nimmst zu viel Platz!" his mother admonished, secretly pleased that her son stood six foot two. Now Jack was taking up too much space in the apartment of a tiny young woman. The air pulsed with the all-penetrating spirit of Ellie, *eindringlicher Geist*. Jack drew in his breath. It was very late, and he was thinking in German.

A pair of twisting floral columns invited him into the room. At the front window, a light-colored desk waited for Ellie to return to work. Jack made a mental note to watch for her whenever he passed on Fifty-Fifth Street below. A blue velvet couch and armchair recalled the elegance of fifty years past and scoffed at the cheap, scarred table before them. The worn brown carpet also insulted the couch, but Ellie had sewn blue flowered curtains to brighten the room.

"Can I get you anything?" she asked.

"Nah, I'm fine. Had too much already."

"Okay, then let me take your coat."

Jack unwrapped himself, and his heavy coat collapsed on the couch.

"C'mere," ordered Ellie. "I want to do something with you."

Jack looked down questioningly and laughed. "What—"

"Down here." Ellie patted the scruffy carpet. "I want to show you something."

Jack yielded, amused, and she arranged him on his back, his arms out to the sides, his ears between her speakers. She snapped off the light and settled with her head next to his, her body pointing the opposite way. In the faint blue glow of her Christmas lights, they lay like two pieces of an Escher puzzle. Jack craned his neck and looked back to watch her hazy breasts rise and fall.

"No," she said. "Close your eyes." She pressed a button on the remote.

In the troubled darkness, the first beats stopped his heart: a descending fourth in the timpani. The drop loosed a joyous, bubbling cascade in the strings, and the rushing water shot him downward. He seized Ellie's hand to keep from falling. The strings joined the flutes in a triumphant procession, a spirited, rippling flow. The music announced joy unexpected, birth out of death, and it ran with a terrible ecstasy. It was the *Christmas Oratorio*. It was Bach.

"Jauchzet, frohlocket!" cried the chorus, turning the music to spoken sounds. "Shout, rejoice!" An inner force surged in him to join the triumphant rush. Jack found himself shaking as Ellie's fingers gripped him. Overhead, he imagined a camera scanning them in the blue light. The thrust on each third beat nudged them, so that under the camera, they began to spin. Slowly they turned, then faster and faster, their bodies radiating like the spokes of a wheel. *If this were a science fiction movie,* he thought, *my mind would move into her body, and hers into mine.*

The river broadened, and the music grew calmer, stirred only by ripples in the flutes. The moves of each voice warmed him like a friend's face—a sudden leap for the tenors, altos smiling in the heart of their range. When the timpani repeated their cry of joy, Jack's pulse yielded to their demand. He sensed Ellie only through her tight grip. He had lost his own strength, and if she let go, he would hurtle off into space.

The chorus stopped. Ellie must have touched the remote again, since when the tenor began telling the Christmas story, his voice came from far away.

Jack opened his eyes. Ellie had drawn herself up on one elbow and was looking down at his inverted face.

"How—how did you know?" he asked.

In a gentle rhythm, she alternated moist kisses with words.

"I just knew. You seemed like a Bach person."

"And— and you?"

"I sing in a choir. This is us, this is me."

"The voice of God." Jack heard his own words as though someone else were speaking them. "This is what God sounds like." His voice sounded more distant than the tenor's.

"Not God," she said. "Life. I've always thought this music sounds like you feel when a child is born. You have a daughter, don't you? Did it feel like this?"

"I—I don't remember," he whispered.

Ellie worked her way down his forehead with soft, caressing sweeps.

"Your eyes are wet," she murmured.

She brushed her lips across his lids, and he trembled. He reached for her and caught only air. Ellie was still inverted, existing only as a voice in his ear.

"What is it? Don't cry, Jack."

"My father—" he gasped. "My father—"

Her lips played over the ridge of his ear, and his arousal surged like water in a sinking ship.

"Ellie—"

"Shh ..."

She had reached his mouth, and he opened to her determined sympathy.

"I—I'm married," he breathed. "I—"

"I know."

He wondered what she was made of, that Bea's existence meant nothing to her. *Bea, existence, to Bea or not to Bea,* he thought crazily.

Ellie mingled her daring kisses with words. "Think of this as a vacation, that's all. I don't want anything from you."

She ran her lips over his neck, and her hair swept his face. The alto began her liquid aria, "Bereite dich, Zion." Under the tickling fuzz of Ellie's sweater, her breast felt warm and alive against his cheek. He reached up over his head and pulled her down and around on top of him.

"I want you," he whispered.

"I know."

His arms squeezed her guiltily.

"Come."

She pulled him to his feet and led him deeper into her space. In her bedroom, an inquisitive brown bear frowned at a quilt glowing peach pink in the soft light. Here, too, she had improvised curtains,

and the pink calico resonated with the Botticelli prints on her walls
to create a warm radiance. Jack pulled the red sweater out of her
skirt and up over her shoulders. Her breasts were a song, the curve
of her hip a familiar chord. The quilt and curtains exactly matched
the purple pink of her nipples, a color he had never seen before. Ellie
stepped forward to embrace him with peace in her eyes. Softly she
folded back the quilt, and he came to her with the ghosts of soothing
harmonies in his head.

An alarm whooped, an angry bird in the night.

"Cathy?" he murmured. "*Wach auf—*"

Three fluorescent digits hung in the darkness: 4 4 7.

"Jack?" said a faint voice. "Jack? It's not Cathy. It's Ellie."

"Ellie?" He jerked. "My God—"

Jack sent his arm where the lamp should have been and
encountered only thick air. His bladder burned, his head ached,
and his mouth felt sticky and dry. Beside him, a warm, slender body
rolled. My God, he had to get home. Outside, the car alarm screamed
the only four measures it knew.

"Oh—did we fall asleep?" murmured Ellie.

A tender impulse broke through his fear, and he touched her
hard, little shoulder.

"I have to go."

Ellie drew herself up so that she was half-sitting and pulled the
quilt over her breasts. In the pulsing blue light of the clock radio, she
looked like a little child. Jack lurched out of bed, located the light,
and searched for his clothes. Ashamed to be seen, he covered himself
quickly. Ellie scrambled up, even lovelier in the jangling brilliance
of unwanted morning than in the rippling waters of the night. She
shivered and reached for a maroon satin robe that made her look like
Sherlock Holmes. Jack laughed as he pulled at his pants.

"What?"

"You look like a Victorian gentleman."

"Are you sure?"

Ellie unfastened her robe and opened it slowly. She stood like a white pollinated stalk in the midst of a red opium poppy. His arousal surged. One jerk at his belt, and the metal found its home in the leather.

"I've got to go."

Ellie closed her robe, and he groped in his pockets to orient himself. Someone seemed to have hit him on the head. He paused at her door while she fumbled with the chain, half-hidden under the bunch of greenery. It came free with a clack.

Ellie looked up at him. "I'm so sorry, Jack."

The teasing challenge had left her eyes and was replaced by a shadowed sadness. Jack pulled her against him, fearing that he might cry again.

"Don't be sorry. It'll be all right."

He made his way out into icy blankness that was neither day nor night. The car alarm still shrieked its outrage to anyone who could hear. He wondered whether it would ever stop and what had provoked its wrath. Probably just vibrations, a jolt from a truck rumbling by in the night.

CHAPTER 2

THERAPY

WHEN JACK'S FEET STRUCK HIS frigid stone steps, he still hadn't thought of a story. The red and blue glass panels framing his doorway greeted him with shocked silence. The truth was so foreign to his ordered existence he couldn't quite believe it himself. Automatically, he looked around for his daughter, Jessie. One morning last summer, he had reached for his *New York Times* and found her crumpled on the stoop. She couldn't say where she had been, because she didn't remember. She only knew that her money was gone and her underpants were in her pocket.

With a barely perceptible click, the door yielded to Jack's key and admitted him to the space he had inhabited for sixteen years. He loved the silence, the rich colors of this place: the black curve of his piano, the mosaic of his books, the glow of polished wood floors against maroon Persian carpets. His living room faced east, and in the window bay, patient plants stood awaiting the light. Seeing a stray leaf on the floor, he stooped to pick it up. He rolled it, cool and rubbery, between his thumb and finger, uncertain what to do with it.

A clang from the kitchen jolted him.

"Bea?" he called softly.

He moved through the darkness with slow, silent steps. In the kitchen, Jessie was lurching through the motions of heating a frozen dinner. Bea maintained a never-ending stack of them as the most practical way to feed people who never knew when they would be home. Whatever drugs Jessie had taken had so mutilated her senses that she failed to notice him as he hovered in the doorway. She seemed aware only of the oven and the aqua box that mocked her efforts to open it.

"Jessie!" he whispered. "Are you all right?"

She had turned the oven to broil but left it gaping open so that its coil hummed with orange rage. The microwave, also wide open, she had apparently abandoned. Jessie threw the dinner—still in its box—onto the oven rack with a disgusted curse, and for the first time, she looked up at him.

Jessie might have been beautiful. Tall and blonde with a long waist and narrow hips, she seemed made to glide rather than walk. The skin-tight black leggings and tiny sweater she wore showed off her total absence of fat. Her spike-heeled boots turned her loveliness to aggression, and the black makeup around her eyes made her look like a ghoul. Jessie didn't answer, just stared unknowingly as the paper box began to scorch.

"Are you all right?" he asked again.

Jessie tried to walk around him and stumbled as a boot flopped outward. Jack caught her but recoiled, disgusted by her smell. He hadn't breathed that stench for so long he hardly believed it had entered his home. But there it was, unmistakable: the reek of smoke, cheap liquor, and vomit, the stink of bodies untended and clothes unwashed. From his daughter's pink lips came the breath of the furies.

Jessie gurgled a curse and raked the air with her nails.

"Jessie!" he gasped. "Please let me help you!"

"Fuck you!" she spat and twisted free.

Jack dove for the dinner and burned his hands on the box. He turned off the oven, closed it, and checked for additional damage. There was none.

"Please," he repeated. "Please let me help."

Jessie surrendered to his supporting arm, and he guided her up the stairs. He hoped that the clacks wouldn't wake Bea. As Jessie's weight shifted crazily, her needle-thin heels missed their mark and skeetered off to the side. Her painfully thin body relaxed against his, and he gritted his teeth against nauseous heaves. How horrible she was, this floppy, incompetent thing. How had he created this wretchedness?

Jack arranged his daughter on her bed and laid her on her side so that if she vomited, she wouldn't choke. He draped a blanket over her and pulled off her boots. In the dim light, twisted, ill-smelling clothes formed dark pocks on her white rug. Her dresser, whose open drawers spewed nylon underthings, was littered with dusty makeup boxes and stiff tissues. On the far wall, Jim Morrison leered down with mocking irony, his arms raised from his bony chest. Satisfied that Jessie was asleep, Jack left his daughter and closed the door. They could talk later, if she remembered anything.

In his own room, Bea slept peacefully, the aqua comforter rising and falling with each breath. Jack undressed as quietly as he could. Like his wife, his bedroom was beautiful. A white carpet floated on a golden floor that matched the solid oak dressers. The well-made rocking chair cradled cushions the same cool blue green as the quilt. Together they had picked them out long ago, knowing instantly what they had wanted.

Bea's black hair marked her territory on the far side of the bed. Jack hung his clothes over the chair, which bobbed with an assenting nod. He raised the quilt softly and climbed in beside her. He caught his breath at a murmur in her throat. But Bea, who never seemed to get enough sleep, dreamed on in the graying light. Jack offered himself to what remained of the night and realized with aching gladness that he was free.

When he awoke, Bea was already gone. Of course, it was Saturday. She must have left the bed soon after he entered it to prepare for the women storming her clinic. As an attending physician in obstetrics and gynecology, Bea could have left the Saturday clinic to someone else. But she insisted on going, because that was when working women needed her. No one could control when the babies came, but smarting drips were deferred until Saturdays. Someone had to be there to soothe the burn. Two, sometimes three nights a week, Bea was on call at the hospital, and Jack respected her for working Saturday mornings.

Dizzily, he hauled himself onto one elbow and squinted at the day. Muted by white curtains, the light didn't reveal the time, and he twisted his head to see the clock radio. 10:13. His mind recalled other blue digits and the room in which they had glowed.

He remembered.

Next to his nose, a black hair rested in the hole that Bea's head had made. He hadn't felt this sick in years, and he pulled himself from the bed as from the clinging embrace of an anemone.

Awkwardly, then with increasing competence, his legs carried him to the bathroom mirror. As a rule, Jack avoided vulgar, shiny surfaces, and his house had few of them. Each morning, though, after the gushing relief of urination, he checked himself in that silver square.

Today he tried to see himself with a woman's eyes. What had drawn Ellie to him? At forty-eight, he had gone soft around the middle, but he had little loose flesh—a spartan diet and daily embraces of exercise equipment saw to that. His heavy German bones and muscles supported his large, graying head. Light gleamed from the scar left by the billy club—one memory, at least, that was visible.

What else did she see? The part that had entered her hung dry and innocent, and his lips curved as stoically as ever. Was there really no trace? Between him and his image, Ellie rushed up, and he, too, rose to life. His blue eyes laughed under his graying brows. There was the memory, not in how he looked but in what he did. The truth was lingering in him for all the world to see.

Jack let himself think of Ellie, so young, so determined, so full of energy. Why had she chosen him, a man who couldn't even dance? He brushed one foot across the cool white tiles, ashamed of his natural heaviness. He felt Ellie's ribs under his hands, her skin against his lips. Yes, she desired him, although why, he couldn't say.

Queasily, Jack poured himself a cup of water. This was crazy. He had to flush the poison from his system, and then he could think this through. With aggressive strokes, he brushed his teeth, even though he hadn't yet eaten. He turned on the shower and listened with relief to its warm, familiar patter. He hid himself under Fruit of the Loom shorts, then pulled on layers of gray cotton and wool. On his way down to the kitchen, he checked Jessie's room. She hadn't been sick, hadn't moved at all, and he shut the door as one closes the oven on a loaf not yet done.

In the kitchen he found more traces of Bea. There weren't many, but her breakfast of whole wheat toast and raspberry jam betrayed itself through brown crumbs and sticky points of red. He wiped them away before putting a poppy seed bagel in to toast. He turned on the radio, preset to a classical station.

The phone rang, and his nervous system flashed.

"Hello?"

"Jackie."

His mother. With her deadpan Dietrich voice, she reduced him to the uncertainty of childhood. He stilled the music and rammed the toaster oven's lever back up.

"Hi, Mom."

He could picture her in her Bronx apartment. His mother lived in rooms of lace doilies and chubby figurines whose curves she dusted daily.

"Jackie. How you doing? They say on TV you got a lot of snow. You got snow?"

He turned his eyes mechanically to the window, which looked out onto their patch of yard.

"No, Mom, no snow, just cold."

The New York traffic pricked his ear, a burst of horns and a truck's bang.

"Mrs. Lenz, she got mugged two days ago. They got her purse. She just went to the bank, two hundred dollars!"

"Wow, Mom, that's terrible. Really, you should get out of there."

He knew the game that he had to play. With reasoned arguments, he must convince her to abandon her fortress while she resisted with a will deeper rooted than reason. In her eighties, she still waddled to the store dragging a cart and met her friends for coffee and cake at the diner. To Bea's dismay, she hadn't learned it was inappropriate to call her children with advice on how to improve their lives. In her eyes, it wasn't she who should abandon the neighborhood. A squadron of storm troopers should move in to clean the Puerto Ricans out.

"Scheiß Schwarzen!" she cursed.

"Mom, you can't call them that. It's not right," he protested. "Some are good, and some are bad, just like us."

"How do you know?" she challenged. "How many you know? Big man like you, they don't punch you in the face."

Jack evaded her thrust. "It doesn't matter what color they are. If violent people live there, you should get out."

"Well, maybe Rudi," she sighed.

He brightened to hear their first act concluding and braced himself for the second.

"Rudi, he's doin' real good. He says Peter got a special science prize last week. And strong too, he beat everybody at wrestling."

"That's great, Mom."

She hungered after tales she could carry to his older brother, Rudi, and his perfumed wife, Doreen. Feeling resistant, Jack offered her none. His heart beat against the silence.

"Was macht die kleine Mistkäferin?"

Jack smiled at her endearment for Jessie, "the little dung beetle." It seemed ludicrous now when he thought of her long, angry body.

"Oh, she's okay. She goes out a lot."

"You watch out for that girl, you hear?" she warned. "Who she goin' out with? That girl's spoiled rotten. She does just what she wants."

Outside the window, a sparrow fluffed its feathers against the cold. He ought to put out some seed.

"I never seen nothin' like it. She got no respect for nobody."

"Yeah, I know, Mom, and I always respected you when I was sixteen, same as you respected your parents."

"You damn right I did."

Jack glanced at his bagel and rammed the lever down. The toaster oven glowed to life. A poppy seed fell on the coil, and he watched to see what would happen to it.

"Mom."

"Yeah, Jackie."

"I have to go. I have a lot of papers to grade today."

Between him and Nietzsche stood a levee of student writing, his grad students' thirty-page studies of Thomas Mann and his undergrads' more poignant readings of Goethe.

"Always these papers—why do they write these papers? What do they know? Why don't they just listen to you?"

"It's important, Mom," he defended. "They need to think, develop ideas."

She continued to deny the existence of their ideas while he

repeated his efforts to escape. Despite her scoffing, she would soon be annoying Rudi with tales of his intellectual feats, just as she demoralized him and Bea with reports of Rudi's burly, inventive sons.

"Say hi to Rudi, Mom."

"Yeah, okay. No snow at all, huh?"

Jack glanced out the window, where no new softness had altered the hard ground. "No, no snow."

"Alles Gute, ja?" She hung up with a clunk.

On the coil, the seed had shrunk to a speck that might have dropped from a fly. Jack pulled out the sugar-free plum jam and welcomed Telemann's octaves into the room.

Unlike Ellie's desk, Jack's faced west, away from the street. He liked to watch the birds as he worked, sparrows that hopped and pecked, cardinals that flashed between branches, nuthatches that darted up the trunk of their one good tree. Today his friends were out in force, excited by the seed he had thrown.

Jack had Bea to thank for his sanctuary near the kitchen.

"Why do we need a pantry?" she had asked. "Just look at that window—all that afternoon sun."

Under her direction, workmen had ripped the doors off the cabinets, and the pantry, a relic of the neighborhood's former elegance, had become a larder for his thoughts. His favorite books lined the upper shelves like a set of familiar teeth, and years of collected papers—less sightly but no less weighty—occupied the lower spaces for colanders and tureens.

Under the window, Jack's desk covered the entire back wall. He knew the sun's progress so well he could read its beams as it brightened the hardened snow. Today the rays were advancing more slowly than usual. The shadow line put it at one thirty when a toilet swished. How was he going to get Jessie to that family therapy appointment at four? In a few minutes he would have to face her. Oh well, this paper was pretentious—"The Spiraling Trope," it was called—and he felt ready to eat again. He hoped that Jessie had washed her hands.

With each uneven step, Jack's heart beat faster. He gathered himself to face Jessie as she entered the kitchen. In the soft afternoon light, she was pretty again, despite her disheveled state. She had pulled on a slithery pink bathrobe with feathered cuffs. Probably she had left her dirty black leggings as a fresh blemish on the rug. Jack smiled at her, but she ignored him. She headed straight to the refrigerator and yanked it open so that bottles shivered in the door.

"There's nothing to eat."

The low-pitched challenge was familiar. Jack felt as though he were talking to his mother as she announced the game that they would play.

"Why, there are lots of good things in there," he said. "Bagels … grapefruit … ratatouille to heat up—"

"There's nothing to eat."

Jessie stared disgustedly at the fruits and vegetables. She would eat nothing that took any effort to prepare—no slicing, boiling, or toasting. It outraged her even to seek a dish to heat up something in the microwave. Jessie didn't want to eat; she wanted to be fed, and she stared amusedly as he recited the daily specials like a waiter.

"Can I toast you a bagel? What about some ratatouille? I was going to heat up some for myself. You should eat something before we go to family therapy today."

"Fuck that." Her pink lips twisted with disgust. "Real food. Why don't we ever have any real food around here?"

Jack tried to subvert the game but found that the subversions were already in the script.

"What's real food?"

"I don't know. Food that normal people eat."

She had him there. Not only did he have no notion what other people ate, he had never in his life wanted to be normal. He lifted the ratatouille from the shelf and spooned some cold red mounds into a white ceramic dish.

"How about a bagel?" he asked. "Can I make you a bagel?"

She shrugged her shoulders, and he saw with relief that she had removed the black makeup around her eyes—his eyes. It disturbed him to see how much they looked alike. Maybe Aristotle had been right and he had impregnated Bea with a homunculus, which her nourishing womb had only increased in size.

"What kind you want, Misty?" he ventured.

"Don't call me that!"

Jack froze as she turned on him, his hand suspended in the bag.

"I'm sorry, I—"

"Don't ever call me that!"

"All right, I won't," he murmured. His breath slowly reentered his chest. "That was your grandmother's name for you. We used to call you that when—"

"That old cow," she muttered. "I hate that fat cow."

Her contempt jarred him. Maybe his mother was right about Jessie's lack of respect. He wondered where it had come from—and how respect developed in the first place.

"If it weren't for that fat old cow," he said, "I wouldn't exist. You wouldn't exist."

"Who cares?" she snapped, capturing his eyes. "What's so great about existing anyway?"

Jack seized a poppy seed bagel and sawed it in half. As the battle began, the mist in his head obscured his view of the forces he was trying to muster.

"How can you say that?" he protested.

On the cutting board, the bagel fell into two white, questioning Os.

"Say what?"

"That it's not worth existing." Jack drew a deep breath.

"That's not what I said. I asked what's so great about existing."

Did she want him to tell her? She spared him the effort by pushing on.

"What are you, afraid I'll kill myself?"

"Well—yeah, if you say things like that."

"What, do you care?" She held him with a steady gaze.

"Of course I do."

"The fuck you do." Jessie raised her chin. "Just think of all the great books you could write if I weren't here."

"That's not true. I'm your father. I want you to be here."

She looked at him with a mocking, knowing smile.

"I—I care about you," he floundered. "I don't want you to get hurt."

With her eyes on his, she laughed in a rippling stream.

"God, you are so full of shit."

Determined to reach her, he persisted. "Look, where were you last night?"

"With a friend." Her laughter settled to a smile of secret pleasure.

"Just a friend?"

"Yeah, a friend." The robe rippled as her toe traced an arc over the gray floor.

"You can't tell me? I can't know about your friends?"

"No."

He positioned her bagel in the toaster oven.

"But it's not right," he said, "me not knowing what you do. Why can't I ever meet your friends?"

An unseen image evoked a burble of laughter.

"What do you, want to interview them? You want to ask them if they've read *Faust*? You don't know what friends are. You don't have any fucking friends."

"Look, I'm sick of your using language like this," he attacked. "You're supposed to be bright. Can't you find any better way to express yourself?"

"Fuck you."

Even her curses pulsed with intelligence, but he felt a need to resist. "That's pathetic. That is so unworthy of you."

"So why don't you tell me where *you* were last night."

What perverse justice had left this flower in her memory when drugs usually mowed it flat?

"I—I was at a party—"

"With your *friends*?" Jessie's smile returned, a quivering stretch of her lovely lips. Her eyes showed all the mirth of a radar scope.

"I was with some students—they invited me—"

"So you partied all night with your *students*?"

Her emphasis opened meanings that bloomed and dissolved in kaleidoscopic bursts.

"Why don't you bring some of your *friends* home, Dad, and introduce them to me?"

It was no use. In high school, a classics teacher with a mischievous streak had assigned them roles in *Lysistrata*, a play about a female sex strike. Jack had waited eagerly to learn his part, anticipating character analysis from a teacher he'd loved. He had laughed with the others when a pretty, straitlaced girl was assigned the part of Myrrhine. The name meant myrtle berries, the teacher had explained, slang for female genitalia. When Jack's turn came, the teacher had made him the narrator, and the class had laughed just as loud. Jack was the giver of information, the man born never to play a part.

"Jessie," he said, "your mom wants you to try this family therapy."

"That bitch."

The bagel's rough surface was turning a pleasant golden brown.

"Don't talk that way about your mother." His automatic answer sounded absurd, but he could think of no better response.

"She's a bitch," shot Jessie.

"She's not a bitch. She's a good person. She wants to help you."

"*You're* the one who needs help." How could she find her answers so quickly?

"Okay," he sighed. "So we can all get help together. The appointment is today at four. Mom's going to meet us there."

"What, at the Gargoyle Palace?" Jessie folded her arms, and a bit of pink feather floated downward. "You guys are a fucking conspiracy—college, hospital, Experimental School, and shrinks to mind-fuck anyone who doesn't like it. Why don't you just secede and form your own fucking country?"

Jack exhaled into the familiar harangue.

"There's a whole fucking world out there, and you don't have the guts to look at it, let alone explore it. I see you, hugging the lake like a cockroach hugging the wall, driving down the Tube with your hands sweating. 'Please, God, just get me to the Dan Ryan!'"

Jack smiled. Jessie's argot pleased him, affirming the intelligence he had always presumed she had. Fifty-Fifth Street, "the Tube," conducted sweating white drivers from their island of security along the lake, across Englewood on Garfield Boulevard, to the Dan Ryan Expressway seven miles west. Inbound, it crossed the "Neutral Zone" park, flowed under Ellie's window, and emptied onto Lake Shore Drive.

"Is that where you were last night?" he blurted.

"Maybe."

The bagel was turning a richer brown, but he couldn't judge its color well under the glowing coils.

"But that's dangerous!" he gasped. "You mustn't do that. There are people out there who might hurt you."

"Black people?"

"Yes, black people. Most are decent, and they work hard, but some have no respect for human life."

"What, like you?"

His chest tightened. He knew her litany of accusations: he was a racist; he was a nerd; he knew nothing about people, only books; he perceived nothing; he lived badly; and her mother was a bitch. This was a new one.

"You think I have no respect for human life?"

Jessie glared at him, unfazed. "I don't know. I asked you."

"You suggested it."

"Okay, I'm *suggesting* it. Everything you care about is written on paper." Like a lawyer, she seemed to have prepared her arguments during every waking minute.

Jack chuckled. "Well, sometimes on a computer screen."

Jessie didn't laugh. "There are people out there. Real people."

"Real people who eat real food?"

She smiled at an image only she could see.

"Oh, you wouldn't understand."

"Please tell me," he pleaded. "Please tell me—I don't want anything to happen to you."

"Yeah. Right," she scoffed. "You don't want anything to happen to me."

"Why do you hate me so much?" he cried.

Jessie's bloodshot blue eyes tantalized him with an intelligence he couldn't grasp. He was supposed to know. That was his crime: he didn't know how he had wronged her.

An ugly, angry smell filled the room.

"Oh, shit!"

Jack leaped for the toaster oven. Jessie laughed as he yanked out the plug. The stink of incompetence filled the room and would poison the house all day. Jack struggled with the window, which was sealed against the cold. His mother's voice scolded him. "*Lüf*ten! *Lüf*ten!" The window's slam blasted the birds off the trees, and as he flapped a dish towel to clear the air, he despaired of their ever returning.

Jessie must have slipped out while he was raising the window, since when he gave up *Lüft*-ing, the shower pattered to life. Jack caught the martyred bagel and looked at it sadly. It was black, desiccated, evil smelling, inedible. He dropped it in the trash.

Seeing the toaster oven unanchored, he decided to clean it. He shook it vigorously over the garbage, and it snowed singed crumbs. He wiped the dandruff of dust from the space it had occupied until the white counter forgave his neglect. A puff of icy air called his eyes to the yard, where two sparrows had settled under the feeder. They slid out of focus as a film of water seeped from some hidden source. He blinked to clear it. From the dish of ratatouille, he spooned up the rest of his lunch. What did you do at family therapy?

Jack's eyes circled the room as he settled on the flowered couch. Bea's impact jostled him as she dropped down beside him. The therapist must have arranged this place for its effect, and he scanned himself to see what that might be. On every wall, books advertised knowledge of families, children, and their mental maladies. Among the books stood hand-painted china plates propped by hidden supports. Beside the therapist, a yellow vase offered scentless December blooms. Too many books, too many blossoms. Jack didn't like the room.

The brown-haired therapist smiled wearily and asked them how they were.

"Fine," said Jack and Bea together.

Jessie said nothing. She had settled into a white armchair sprigged with the same blue violets as the couch. Resting one long, thin arm on each side, she sat with her black nylon legs wide apart. *She's enjoying this,* thought Jack.

"Well," began the therapist, "I'd like to start by asking you each a question. Then we can take it from there."

"Sure. Go for it," said Bea.

The therapist brightened at the encouragement. "All right. I want each of you to tell me one thing you like about the others. Since you're here, you must have been feeling lots of pain, but I'm sure that's not all you feel. If you could just tell me one good thing you see in each other—it could be anything at all."

31

Her pale blue eyes focused on Jack. Oh, God. He would have to go first. How idiotic, how simpleminded. But there was a certain logic to it. Across from him, Jessie exhaled with disgust, and the therapist smiled with amusement. Oh, well—maybe some good would come of this. He turned to face Bea, who sat waiting hopefully. Her tense lips revealed her opinion of the question, but some part of her seemed to be opening, eager for a compliment.

"Well …" he began. "I love the way my wife is so organized. I've felt that from the first time I met her. She really has her act together. And I respect her work very much."

Bea smiled, and Jack exhaled, surprised at the effort it had taken to make that short speech. On her throne, Jessie snorted and twitched.

"Do you want to say something, Jessie?" asked the therapist.

Jack tensed, knowing she had made a mistake. Jessie hated being called by her name.

"Her work, her fucking work," she growled. "I could have told you these two would say their fucking work. That's all they think about."

"Why don't you let your father finish?" asked the therapist.

"Yeah, that I'd like to hear," she snarled. "Let's see if he can come up with something he likes about her other than her work."

"He said I was organized," defended Bea, but Jessie just laughed.

"No." The therapist gazed at Jessie. "He was going to say something about you."

Jack's chest expanded once, twice. All three women were looking at him, two expectantly, the third with mocking laughter. Christ, what did he like about her? He forced himself to look at Jessie, twitching on her springy chair.

"I—I think she's very pretty," he said, and realized he had stolen the line from Dickens. Wasn't that what Pip said when Miss Havisham interrogated him about Estella? "I—I like that she's tall and slim and has such a nice figure," he struggled. "I think she looks very nice."

Bea laughed with lifted brows. She seemed to have been expecting something else—but what? Jessie smoldered, and he realized he had blundered. Worse than being called by her name, Jessie hated any reference to her body.

"I don't like fat women," he laughed, and glanced in sudden panic at the therapist.

No, thank God, she wasn't fat. Like his wife and daughter, she was tall and lean, but with thinning gray-brown hair. Despite the shadows under her eyes, she looked younger than him and Bea. Jessie met his eyes and laughed, reading his thoughts. He liked her perceptiveness, he realized, but it was too late. His turn was over. Bea was straightening, concentrating, preparing her phrases as an Olympic diver rehearses her twists.

"I think that Jack's work is wonderful," she asserted. "All those ideas—and he's a great teacher too."

Jessie spluttered with disgust, and the therapist yielded to the inevitable.

"What's wrong with that?" she asked. "Why can't your parents feel good about their work?"

Jessie leaned forward, her face hardening. "They're full of shit. They're both so full of shit," she hurled. "They're two fucking parasites, and they stick up for each other. Ideas—he's never had an idea. He writes books about other people's books. He's a pimp for fucking Goethe and fucking Nietzsche. *They* had ideas. The only idea he's had in his life was to make money pimping them."

"That's a very harsh judgment," said the therapist.

Jack choked on a laugh. She seemed inept, but he admired her composure.

"Don't you think it's important to be a good teacher," she asked, "and spread interesting ideas around?"

"How would she know if he's a good teacher?" Jessie jerked her head at Bea, who winced. "She's never seen him teach. What's he ever taught her? How would she know?"

"Hasn't he ever taught you anything?"

Jessie leaned back and folded her arms. "He's never taught me a fucking thing."

"That's not fair!" burst Bea. "He's taught you everything—you take everything for granted! Everyone at the university says what a good teacher he is!"

"And you believe them?" Jessie laughed. "They're like the fucking Mafia over there. They all stand up for each other. It's the emperor's fucking new clothes in that place."

Bea looked despairingly at the therapist as if to say, *There, you see?*

Red-brown spots formed a jagged constellation on the carpet, and Jack wondered whether they memorialized juice or blood. "Blut ist ein ganz besonderer Saft," murmured Mephisto. "Blood is a very special juice." Bea's elbow nudged his ribs, demanding that he defend his work.

"German literature is interesting," he said. "People want to study it. Thomas Mann is wonderful. The book I'm writing now—"

"You don't *write*," snarled Jessie. "You don't *create* anything. You chop other people's writing into pieces, put them in your own fucked-up order, and call it a book. You don't *work*. I know a guy who has to mop out a whole restaurant at two in the morning, then take out the trash. That's work. You live off of other people, selling them ideas you stole from someone else."

Why didn't the therapist intervene? When was this torture going to stop? He thought of a Marxist student in his Mann seminar whom he had let run on, more out of curiosity than intimidation. The boy's impenetrable dogmatism had fascinated him so much he wanted to hear what he would say next. That must be it—Jessie was just too interesting.

Bea leaned forward, and Jack admired her capacity to fight. "How can you have so little respect?" she demanded. "His books are wonderful. How can you dismiss them without having read them?"

"Oh, I get it." Jessie smiled. "I should think they're good because

I haven't read them—just like those other assholes at the Gargoyle Palace."

The therapist laughed, delighted by the phrase, then turned serious a little too quickly.

"What about your mother's work?" asked Jack, realizing there was no hope of redeeming his. "Helping women have babies, helping women take care of their bodies, that must be worth something."

"She helps women kill their fucking babies," snapped Jessie.

"I hardly ever do abortions," retorted Bea. "But I do them when women need them. There are women who—"

"Nobody *needs* a fucking abortion!" Jessie leaned forward, her body shooting fire. "Women get abortions when they don't *want* their babies."

"They have a right—a legal right—" spluttered Bea. "They have a right to choose when to have their children—"

"What, so they can defer fucking up their lives as long as possible? That's what having a baby means to you. It's like getting cancer."

"That's ridiculous!" seethed her mother. "That's insane. I love babies. I love helping women have babies—"

"Yeah, you love helping *other* women, like you love cutting tumors out of them. You love delivering *other* people's babies so much you barely managed to squeeze out one of your own!"

Jack listened, aghast. The therapist's features floated. She seemed absorbed yet unperturbed as her experimental animals snapped at each other's throats.

"Women have a right to decide when to have children!" shouted Bea. "Your father and I decided when we wanted to have you, and we had you! What's wrong with that?"

"That's a crock of shit," snorted Jessie. "You never wanted to have me. You just wanted to keep helping other women squeeze out their babies because it makes you feel useful. You're just like him. He lives through other people's books, you live through other people's babies, and you both take all the fucking credit."

35

"What do you want?" screamed Bea. "You think because I have you, I have no right to work? You think that women shouldn't have lives?"

Jack had never seen Bea lose her composure like this. Having provoked her mother to uncontrolled rage, Jessie leaned back and smirked.

"I think you're a fucking dyke," she laughed. "I think you hate babies, and you hate being a woman, and you wish I had never been born."

The therapist's thin face tightened as though she had taken on a cargo of pain.

"You're being irrational." Bea was fighting for control. "There's more than one way to be a woman. Some want to stay home, and some want to work. That has nothing to do with whether they're gay or straight. I've been with your father for thirty years. Don't you think if I were gay, we'd have figured it out by now?"

Jessie looked from her to Jack and chortled.

"*Kinder, Küche, Kirche*," he murmured.

"What?" The therapist responded instantly to a sound from her most reluctant animal.

"Sorry—*Kinder, Küche, Kirche*—it's German. *Frauensache*. It's a phrase for what women are supposed to do—children, kitchen, church." He looked at Jessie. "Is that what you want?"

"Oh, you think you're so fucking superior with your radical, liberal bullshit," she snorted. "You think you're so much better than women who cook and clean and take care of their kids and go to church. You're antilife! You're not even alive!"

Her red eyes surprised him. Jesse almost never cried, but she seemed close to tears. She was fighting to make them see something they seemed incapable of seeing.

"You want a mother like my mother?" he asked. "You want one who cleans the house the whole time and never read a book in her life?"

36

"That fucking cow," she scoffed.

"Ah, so you agree on something!" The therapist smiled. "Maybe we should pursue that for a moment. What about that? Have you ever gone to church together?"

Bea blushed, and Jack lowered his eyes to the mashed carpet. Freud's condemnation resounded in his head: "So patently infantile." He couldn't imagine how any intelligent person could believe in God. It would be like believing in the Easter bunny.

"We—we're agnostics," began Bea.

Jessie smiled triumphantly. "She feels sorry for people who believe in God, same as she feels sorry for women who get pregnant. It's something that happens when you're stupid."

Bea exploded. "God, the hypocrisy! You talk about church and cooking and cleaning! When have you ever cooked? You condescend to eat what we cook, and you leave the kitchen a mess! Your room is a pigsty! When have you ever been to church? In church they teach you to respect people!"

"You bitch! You fucking bitch!" screamed Jessie.

"Now wait a—" tried the therapist, but their anger shot through her like x-rays.

"You hypocritical little— You look down on our work, and you live off it!"

"You bitch-dyke, you baby-killing bitch!"

"Stop!" shouted Jack. "Don't talk to your mother like that!"

"Just say it!" shrieked Jessie. "Have the guts to fucking say it! You wish I would die, you wish I had never been born, your lives would be so much better without me!"

Bea's shoulders were shaking, and Jack reached out to comfort her. She glanced desperately at the therapist.

"Look at them!" screamed Jessie. "Just look at them!"

"Okay, now hold on!" The therapist raised her grainy voice. She straightened her shoulders. "Let's take a minute here. You're in this together. You have common interests."

Bea nodded vigorously. Jessie withdrew as she always did before authority, certain that "common interests" meant the imposition of foreign rules.

"It's good to show what you feel," pleaded the therapist. "But think about the next step—how to live with each other once you know it."

"I don't want to live with them," shot Jessie. "You think I want to live with them? They don't want me to live with them either. They just don't have the guts to say it."

"You're our daughter," said Jack softly.

"Unfortunately," she answered with mirthless blue eyes.

The therapist didn't react. "I'm hearing a lot of anger here," she continued. "But you have a lot in common too."

Jessie laughed disgustedly. "Like what?"

"Well, you're all highly intelligent people," she asserted.

"Oh, they *act* intelligent—" Jessie broke in.

"No, you *are* intelligent," corrected the therapist.

Jessie glared.

"And another thing—well, just look at yourselves. You're the mirror image of your father."

Had she intended to provoke Jessie, or was she actually that stupid? It must be an experiment. Jack watched a replica of his face twist with rage as Jessie denied their affinity.

"I'm nothing like him!"

Bea laughed, glad to see someone get the better of her daughter. "It's true. You look just like him."

"I can't help that!" screamed Jessie, crying at last. "Fuck, you think I *want* to look like him?"

"He's a nice-looking man," said the therapist gently. "And you're a beautiful girl. You should feel good about that."

"Yes, beautiful," echoed Bea.

Jessie cursed her wetly.

"Look," pronounced the therapist, taking advantage of Jessie's incapacity, "I think you need to focus on your life together. What do you do together? How about planning something you can do together, the three of you?"

Jessie laughed as Jack and Bea sat back, bewildered. Together? Jack couldn't remember the last time the three of them had been in the same place at the same time. It promised to be an adventure in horror.

Jessie leaned forward. "Yeah! We could have a party. We could invite all our *friends*."

The therapist nodded tentatively. Did she know that Jessie was making fun of her? She must be a Freudian, looking for the unconscious wish beneath the joke.

"But you've never wanted us to meet your friends," said Bea incredulously.

"Yeah, well, maybe I want to meet *yours*," said Jessie. "Don't you want your friends to meet me?"

"Maybe you should try it," urged the therapist.

She was serious. Bea nodded slowly. God, they were actually going to have to do it. They would have to have this party or be rebuked for rejecting their daughter. Jessie leaned back, seemingly delighted by this new torture they would have to endure for her sake.

"Shall we keep going?" she asked. "She was going to say something she liked about me."

Man, was that ever fucked up. I'm so glad to get out of there. This is going to be more like it, a real dinner with real people. Best thing I ever did in my life was walk across that goddamn park. Follow the Tube, into the world. Every day fucking trig, fucking French, fucking American studies. Experimental School, they call it. They fuck with your mind, and they watch you like lab rats.

When did I first come over here, two, three months ago? It was still warm back then. I'm walking to that fucking school, and I think, like every day, what if I just keep walking, what if I just don't go? I mean, what are they going to do, fucking wimp, fucking bitch? They don't own me. How will they know?

Big park, big green park, nobody in it but me. Divides—

You know the day destroys the night.

Night divides the day.

Break on through to the other side.

Nobody's here. Boy, is this ugly. Looks different from when you're in a car. No decent stores. Where do they buy their stuff? Hey, here come some guys. What do they—

Hey, girl. I say, hey, girl. What you doin' here, you lost?

No, I'm not lost.

So what you doin' here? Don't you know the black guys gonna getcha?

He's cute, that one, making like Dracula, showing me his fangs and his claws.

I can be here if I want.

Ooh, she cool, she one tough white girl. What you doin' here, girl? Why ain't you in school?

Why aren't you? I ask, and they hoot and say, We don't go to no school.

Me neither, I say, not anymore. They screw you over there, they fuck with your mind.

Hey, Tyrell, says the big one, you hear the mouth on her? She say fuck. You think you bad, girl? Didn't your mama teach you nothin'?

She's a stupid bitch, I say, and she didn't teach me anything.

They crowd in close, all around me, making these hooting noises. The big one's hands settle on my chest like two hungry crabs.

Hey, leave go of her tits, says Dracula.

Fuck you, Beej, he says. You call these tits? They two little mosquito bites.

Why you grabbin' 'em, then? asks Beej.

I start to laugh. This is funny.

Yeah, leave her, Hakim, says Tyrell. You fuck with a white girl, they fuck you over, even if she want it bad. She crazy anyway.

I'm not crazy, I say.

Then what you doin' here?

I wanted to see what it's like. I'm sick of fucking apartheid.

Hey, she say fuck again.

Shut up, Hakim, says Beej. You sick of apartheid? You sick of apartheid, an' you ain't even been on this side.

Beej has this wheezy laugh that's really cute, like Mr. Ed with asthma.

She shittin' you, Beej, says Tyrell. They all the same. She shittin' you.

I'm not the same, I say, and Tyrell says, The fuck you ain't. You think you cool now, talkin' to the black guys, then you go home to your Melrose friends.

Fuck you, Tyrell, says Beej. She ain't no Melrose bitch.

She look like one, says Tyrell.

What's your name, girl?

Misty.

Misty, that cool, I like that. You wanna come party with us, Misty?

Yeah, I say.

Oh, shit, Beej, we don't need no white girl.

Shut up, Hakim, says Beej. She ain't so white.

The fuck she ain't, says Hakim, and he and Tyrell, they start acting white. It's, like, the funniest thing I've ever seen. Suddenly they stand different, really stiff and straight, and they walk like robots and check their wrists.

Excuse me, says Tyrell, do you have the time? The black men stole my watch, and I haven't had time to buy a new one.

Why certainly, says Hakim, it's ten after five. Should we have the grilled salmon or the chicken breast tonight?

That's great, I say, that's really great. You sound exactly like my father.

Beej is into it now. Quick, lock the door, Peter, we're coming to the ghetto!

What's a ghetto, Daddy?

That's where the black men live. They don't like nice houses. They like to live in shit so they can suck up all that welfare money.

They hoot again. Ooh-ooh, the black men gonna get us! They run around screaming and waving their hands.

Hey, look at that one, look at that one! He think we gonna get him. He shittin' in his pants!

Beej points to a guy driving by in a blue Honda who swerves away when he sees us. They run at him, yelling and twisting their faces.

I'm laughing so hard I almost pee in my pants. Hey, hey, look, I say. Here come two women now! Them I can do, two fucked-up white bitches: Oh, Linda! Oh, God, it's a—a *street gang*! Quick, get over in the left-hand lane!

They rush at the white women, who run through a red light to escape.

Hey, call the cops, they breakin' the law! Anybody get their license number?

But, Officer, I say, it's not our *fault*. This gang of boys—they were trying to *molest* us!

You said it, Misty, you said it, girl! Where the white women at?

We stay there for an hour outside the chicken place, laughing at the white folks rushing past.

Hey, Misty, says Beej, you gonna come party with us now?

Yeah, I say. What's Beej?

My aunt Lou call me that. She from Louisiana. It mean somethin' in French.

Hey, Misty, asks Hakim, how much money you got on you?

At last, real food. Three months of shit from these guys, but at least I can get some real food. Baked chicken, corn bread, sweet potatoes, devil's food cake. Spicy red stuff, bitter green stuff, and something that's red *and* green and full of seeds. Now, that's food.

Aunt Lou, says Beej, you been cookin' all day?

Oh, it's good to be cookin', she says. You be cookin', that mean you got food. You have some more chicken, Bijou, you a growin' boy.

Yeah, he growin'—he growin' bigger an' badder, says his sister, Tanesha. Can't you feed him somethin' make him shut up for a while?

You hush, Tanesha, says Aunt Lou, and go take care of that child. He cryin' again. He need his mama.

He always cryin', says Tanesha.

Same as you when you a baby. That what they do. Pretty soon he be big like your brother, and you wish he little and cryin' again. Misty, honey, you want some more chicken?

Yes, please, Aunt Lou, I say. This is really good.

For a skinny girl, you sure can eat, she says. Don't your mama feed you nothin'?

No, I say. There's never any food in our house.

I love Aunt Lou, a great big woman in a soft pink dress. She shakes her head.

Where your mama and daddy today?

Oh, they're working, I say. They're always at work.

On a Saturday?

Yeah, they always work Saturdays.

She shakes her head in a powdery wave.

Where your mama work?

At the hospital, at the clinic.

Your mama a nurse?

She's an obstetrician.

Your mama a doctor? cries Tanesha.

Yeah, a doctor.

What your daddy do?

He teaches at the university.

Your daddy a teacher?

A professor.

You say that like you don't like it none, says Aunt Lou. That's a good thing, to be a teacher.

Well, he doesn't teach much, I say. Mostly he writes books.

Aunt Lou shakes her head again. You sound like you don't love your parents none. You gotta love them, 'cause they love you. They your daddy and mama.

Yeah. How do you tell someone big and pink that your parents wish you were never born? Tanesha, she's glad little Michael was born, even if he cries all the time. She's sixteen, same age as me. Out here, they don't wait till they're forty to have kids—they don't put it off like it's something that hurts.

What funny noises Aunt Lou makes getting up. Sounds like a set of bad brakes.

Aunt Lou, I ask, can I help with the dishes?

Why sure, Misty, you a nice girl.

Shit, this is taking forever. All this grease—disgusting, these plates just slide—

Oh, I'm sorry, Aunt Lou.

Don't worry. You just get the dustpan there. That too bad, my mama give me that plate.

I'm sorry, Aunt Lou.

Well, you didn't mean to drop it. Plate gotta go sometime, just like we all. Misty, what church you go to?

Oh, I've never been to church, I say.

Well, okay, except once, with my stupid bitch grandmother in the Bronx. But I don't tell Aunt Lou that. God, all these greasy blobs, red and green and yellow mixed together. I think I'm gonna—

Never been to church!

Yeah. My parents don't believe in God.

She stares, and her sweet smell congeals.

You sure— They don't believe at all, not even a little? 'Cause some folks, they think they don't believe, but then somethin' happen, and they believe, just they didn't know they do.

I'm really sure. I'm really sure they don't.

You want to come with me and Tanesha tonight? she asks. There's a special service. We all gonna go.

Is Beej going?

I wish. Maybe if you go, he'll go too.

Well, I'd like to go.

I ask Beej if he wants to go to church, but he just laughs.

Man, she got you already. That women's shit, but you go if you want.

He sure is cute.

Misty, says Tanesha, can I talk to you?

Yeah, sure, I say.

You got that diaper money?

Yeah, here, I got it.

I need more this week. He use seven a day, an' I give half to Jolene, 'cause Bobby took her money.

He stole it?

Yeah, he say he got a debt to pay, but I say he shittin' her, he spend it on rock. What debt he gotta pay?

Well, here's twenty, I say. That's all I could get.

Where you gettin' this money? she asks.

It's my allowance.

Oh, yeah, right, she says. A doctor and a teacher.

Beej, says Aunt Lou, you be good to Misty. She a nice girl.

Yeah, says Tanesha, she a nice girl.

CHAPTER 3

THE NEEDLE

HOW STUPID, THOUGHT ELLIE. SHE should have done this two weeks ago, but that kind of planning seemed cold-blooded. Last week she hadn't dared envision sex with Jack, let alone prepare for it. Most things in life happened because she made them happen, but with men things had to happen by themselves. That was her rule, but where had it led her? What had swum into her hidden parts?

She had thought of the phone book as she smiled at the curly gray hairs on her bed. In the floppy yellow book she found two numbers, and she chose the one that looked toll-free. For $49.95, said a metal voice, she could know in seven days; for $59.95, in four; for $79.95, in two. She punched the springy buttons and asked for a test.

"When was the contact?" asked a male voice—like NASA asking when she had met the aliens.

She said what would have been truth if she had called two weeks ago: "Six months."

Girish—so dark, so bold, with a sharp, spicy smell all his own. Girish, warm and firm under her lips, the sudden gasp, the flutter and twitch. She could almost taste the burst of bitterness and hear his grateful moans. When he came into her, she could stand a film between them—taut, wet, stinking membrane. But not in her mouth, not the way she loved it best. Nothing could come between him and her lips.

"You're all right, then," ground the voice. "For a latency of over three months, we guarantee ninety-nine percent accuracy."

The man asked her where she lived, and he listed the local testing sites. She recognized only the one in the Loop, and he gave her the coordinates: 121 North Wabash, eleventh floor, suite 1125, 3:00 p.m., Tuesday, December 9. Ellie recited her credit card number. So much money—and she would have to wait a whole week. Maybe Jack wouldn't want to talk to her until then.

As she approached the testing place, she realized that she had never noticed these mammoth buildings. She had focused on the shops that sold bagels, books, and earrings and had missed the monoliths above. Each one stood like a compact village entered through a daunting, burnished brass gate. Well-dressed people worked here, people who exchanged enormous sums by phone. One of these carved towers concealed the testing center.

Ellie spread her fingers and pushed both palms against a smooth, heavy revolving door. The lobby gleamed, and when she saw the receptionist on his throne, she felt like Dorothy before the Wizard. She headed straight for the elevators and let the floor push her up until a *bing* announced her arrival. Suite 1125 stood before her, and she turned the frosted door's cool silver handle. A tamed rock song pulsed against blank walls. Dark wooden tables flanked a green leather couch lonely for human company. Ellie hovered before the glass window. A white clock marked ten minutes to three. Had she been wrong about the time, the place? On a clipboard inside the glass, she read her name upside down.

"Hello?" she called.

She eased her coat off her shoulders. Jack's fingers brushed her memory.

A black woman in a white lab coat emerged from an inner room. She seemed to be the only one there. The nurse had large purple-brown lips. Her straightened hair curved in soft waves, but her eyes were yellow, and her face drooped. As you got older, your skin must loosen. When would her skin start to do that?

"Sign in, please. Follow me."

The woman walked slowly toward an inner room, and Ellie followed, gripping her coat.

"You can leave your things here," said the nurse, pointing to a black-and-chrome chair.

Ellie worried that her brown wool coat would slide off. A high, padded table had been spread with crackly white paper. Beside it stood a doctor's buffet of silver instruments to pierce her and solutions to clean them.

"Okay, you can get right up here," said the woman. "Roll up your left sleeve."

Ellie clenched her jaw. She had never been able to stand the metal mosquitos that drank her blood. Her mind hated them with such ferocity it sometimes shut itself down in protest. Last time she was tested at a health center, she'd given the nurses the scare of their lives. They'd told her not to look as her rich eggplant blood purred into a plastic tube. Instead she was supposed to watch a poster of a dense, chaotic footrace. In the black-and-white drawing, fat children, stringy men, and sweating grandmas scrambled along together. She stared dutifully as the crowd dissolved into gray flakes and the nurse's voice drifted into remote space. She awoke to find herself bent double, her head inverted, the world screened off behind her hair. The nurses were screaming and running in circles. An older nurse had shamed them to calmness, and they'd given her a tube to sniff. Ammonia had blasted her nose until she found the wits to push it away. How humiliating! To faint like some stupid woman whose corset was too tight. Since then, she had made a habit of warning people.

"You just need a little more willpower, dear," one doctor had said, and she'd longed to kick him across the room.

Why did she always have to faint? It must have been the thought that bothered her. The world dissolved the same way each time, whether she looked or not. She hated the thought of being punctured by a metal straw and having to give up her warm blood. When the Red Cross asked her to donate, she cited the rule that no one under 110 pounds could give blood. That thought alone often kept her from eating. No one could have her juice. It would remain to hum through her private channels, visiting her cells alone.

"Can I do this lying down?" she asked. "I have a problem with fainting sometimes."

"Sure, honey," said the nurse.

Ellie bared her arm and drew a deep breath. The worst moment was coming, the junkie moment. The nurse asked her to make a fist and yanked the rubber tube. With hideous vulnerability, her veins rose to the surface, leaving the needle to take its pick.

"I would make an awful junkie," Ellie laughed. "I would be a total failure. I hate needles."

The woman looked at her with yellowed eyes. "Ooh, that's bad stuff," she said. "When you get into that—it's like breathin', like eatin'. You just gotta have it."

Ashamed, Ellie wondered who she was talking to and what this woman had seen. The nurse pricked her so well that the sickening burn arose only at the very end. She folded her arm over the waiting gauze so that the rest of her blood couldn't chase out after the stolen dram. The walls maintained their clean right angles even when she pulled herself up.

"You okay?" asked the nurse.

A darting bird drew her eyes to the window.

"What a beautiful building!" she cried.

Outside stood a tower of graying lace, its windows aligned in ruffled columns. She was living in a city of wonders, and she had never seen them. Her eyes fed only on the sooty crows that cawed in the maple tree outside her window.

"That's the Erickson Building," said the woman proudly. "That's a fine building."

Ellie gathered her coat, her left arm stiffened by a pulling Band-Aid and a wad of gauze. She was glad her sleeve covered it—otherwise, what would people think she had been doing?

"You be careful now," the nurse said, and disappeared with the vial of purple blood.

Ellie scanned herself for damage. She breathed at the elevator and misted its brass plate of lights. How many times were you supposed to breathe in a minute? Probably she shouldn't think about it. The elevator's walls maintained their rigid angles, and its double row of buttons glowed securely. The street welcomed her with roars that shook the brittle air. She felt like celebrating, and she hurried toward the bright department store across the street.

"You lookin' mighty fine today," said a homeless man. "You got any extra change?"

Under his gray stocking cap, his eyes shone like yellow moons. Was he telling a businesslike lie or just appreciating the scenery? The thought of a lover's desire could bring her pulsing to life, so that she thrilled at the crack of her heels on the pavement and the rush of air into her lungs. When she felt this way, men on the street called out to her, reading her arousal as an answer to their longings.

"Sorry," she muttered as the man opened the door for her.

"Bless you, you have a nice day, you hear?" he called.

Ellie glanced at his blackened, torn sleeve, and suddenly it struck her that the test might not be negative. Was something living in her, using her to jump to new bodies? Would she die, having spent twenty-six years preparing for nothing? What did people live for anyway—to reproduce, like a virus? As she struggled to prove she was better than the virus, her mind mocked her diabolically.

Around her, silver mirrors were creating an illusion of limitless bounty. At the makeup counters, women danced excitedly, showing others where the nectar lay. Ellie found herself moving through a honeycomb of pleasure with sweet surprises in each hexagon. Her eyes climbed the Corinthian columns, then fell and flitted from place to place. Each sign worked like a springboard, sending her flying toward the next: Chanel—Lancôme—Estée Lauder—Clinique—

"May I help you?"

A round-faced blonde woman in a white coat was smiling at her questioningly. Ellie hardly ever wore makeup, and she couldn't think of anything to ask for. She couldn't have afforded these cosmetics anyway, offered by helpful young women under dazzling lights.

"Oh, I'm just looking," she muttered.

The woman continued to smile. She had short golden hair and pink skin, all the same shade. Her face must have been demonstrating what the creams in the green boxes could do.

"Well, be sure to let me know if you need any help," she said.

Usually Ellie left at this point, but the rows of pale green boxes held her transfixed. They stood like capsules, perfectly aligned, waiting to be distributed.

A wave of heat rushed up and broke over her skin. A lava bubble rose, and then another. If only the woman wouldn't look at her like that. She inhaled. How many times did you breathe in a minute? The more air her lungs received, the more they seemed to want. She took off her coat. She wandered off to revive herself with some new stimulus, but nothing shook the fear of what her body might do. An array of belts hung like dead snakes suspended by golden jaws. She ran her finger over a fine brown strip—so smooth, so strong, so sweet smelling. Ellie couldn't feel her lips. No. She wasn't going to let this happen. Among the white leaves and flowers at the tops of the columns, she spotted the first flakes of snow.

No! If only she could stop the heat waves. She had to talk to somebody. Yes, she would find someone to talk to. Where were those boxes? The hive had gone gray and uncertain, barely perceptible through dense flakes. Ellie could no longer feel her face. Funny—how did a face feel when you could feel it?

"Ma'am, are you all right?"

She had found her at last, the pretty pink-and-gold woman. Flakes were scattering her voice.

"I'm sorry—I need—"

Oh, the shame. The counter was tilting—no, the floor—

"I'm sorry—"

The shiny counter continued its upward thrust until it slammed into her jaw.

"God, it was awful. It was so embarrassing."

Ellie looked into Lucy's shocked face. She had known that she would love telling this story as soon as she woke up on the sprigged green carpet.

"They had to call the paramedics! They must have been afraid I was going to sue."

Frenzied photons bounced off the canteen's white walls. It was midafternoon, but under the sizzling lights, it could have been any time of day. Shiny tables absorbed some energy, littered as they were with newspapers and crumbs. The grad students ate, worked, and socialized under these fluorescent lights. Professors penetrated the library in surgical strikes, grabbed their volumes, and rushed back to their offices. But the Inferno in the basement was the students' space. Here they aired hypotheses too wild for seminars and gossip too lethal for the main quad. Red-eyed, in twos and threes, they laughed and picked at their microwaved food. On a lone stool along the far wall, an Asian man who had bought two doughnuts speared one on his fork and looked at it quizzically.

"So then what happened?" asked Lucy. "All these things happen to you. Nothing ever happens to me."

"Believe me, this isn't something you want to happen," said Ellie. "It was so humiliating! You're on your back on a rug, and you feel okay, except that five hundred people are gawking down. The poor woman at the cosmetics counter was hysterical." Ellie regretted pinning that word on the blonde woman whose tears had streaked her makeup.

"Wow." Lucy gripped the white table.

"I was amazed at how fast the paramedics came. I was glad, actually, because this one guy who said he was a doctor was starting to run his hands all over me." Ellie grimaced at the memory of the foreign touch.

"Wow. Did you try and stop him?"

"No. What could I do? For all I knew, he really was a doctor." She frowned at the white tabletop as she tried to purge him from her mind. "So anyway, these guys run in with their walkie-talkies burping. They ask me all kinds of questions, like, am I epileptic, am I diabetic, do I take any medications, and I just keep saying no, no, no, I'm fine, I just fainted, that's all."

"Did they buy it?"

"Nah. They carried me out on a stretcher." Ellie laughed her way between pride and shame.

"Holy shit, El!" Lucy's brown eyes bulged, and her earrings trembled. Dangling strips of gold fluttered, shooting flashes of light. "Did they take you to the hospital?" she asked.

"Yeah. And then I sat there for six hours when I had twenty-nine papers to grade." That had been the worst of it, the command to stay put when work awaited.

"God, what an adventure! That is so incredible!" Lucy shook her head, and her earrings danced.

"It was awful."

Lucy frowned and cocked her head. "But what were you doing downtown in the afternoon? You never go downtown."

"Yeah, and I never will again," Ellie answered quickly.

Luckily, Lucy didn't persist. She stared at Ellie and shook her head. "You have the most amazing life. You've got four interviews—"

"So? You've got one at probably the best English department in the country."

"Shit, you mean *this* isn't the best English department in the country? I'm outa here." Lucy laughed low and deep.

The Asian man glanced over his shoulder and took a bite of his second doughnut.

"So when are your interviews?" asked Lucy.

"Lousy times. Colorado is the first afternoon. Then one each day in the early morning—San Diego is the last day at nine." The sound of "San Diego" sparked a burst of light and color.

"Is that the one you want?"

"I don't know," said Ellie slowly. She didn't want to jinx the process, and she hesitated to presume she would get even one offer.

Lucy persisted. "If you could pick, which one would you—"

"Oh, yeah, right, like I'll be able to pick."

"You might." Lucy leaned back, and her earrings settled.

"Well, I've never really cared that much where I am." Ellie reflected. "I would want the best school, I guess, no matter where it was. What about you? When's Hopkins?"

Lucy stiffened, entering her own interview fantasies. "Pretty good time, I think. One in the afternoon the second day."

"Oh, that's a great time. You'll be recovered but not worn out yet."

"Yeah, I guess so." Lucy's broad pink mouth widened into an ironic smile. "Is Girish going?"

"The word god? You bet." Ellie grinned. "He's got interviews out the wazoo."

"That's unfair, that is so unfair," moaned Lucy. "He just violates

Goethe's whole law of compensation—brilliant, gorgeous, everyone wants him—"

"You forgot his personality," quipped Ellie. How would Girish's arrogance play in an interview? In his musical voice, he might say almost anything.

"Oh, come on," laughed Lucy. "You're madly in love with him."

"He's an asshole." Ellie folded her arms and met Lucy's dark eyes.

"You're still madly in love with him."

"He's like all of them, only more so," said Ellie. "A relationship with a woman is postmodernistically incorrect. You've got to scatter your semes around, free play of signifiers, but make sure nobody's signifier gets stuck on you."

Lucy laughed delightedly. With shy curiosity, the Asian man turned to look.

"Yeah, the guys here are like locusts," said Lucy. "They come out of their carrels every few weeks to mate, but the rest of the time, they don't want to know you exist."

Lucy paused, holding up her hypothesis against the shifting images of her experiences.

"Did you tell Girish how you fainted?" she asked.

"Nah." Ellie scanned the blank tabletop. "I haven't talked to him in a long time. He calls me when he wants to fuck me, but he doesn't want to be seen with me in broad daylight."

"Come on, don't be so hard on yourself. You know he likes you." Lucy's brown eyes swelled with sympathy.

"I'm not really thinking about him right now." Ellie hesitated. "Something's happened."

"Did you guys break up?" asked Lucy, her eyes widening.

Ellie laughed at this phrase so foreign to Girish's ethos.

"No," she said. "There's never been anything to break."

"But you're not together?" Lucy leaned in, suddenly hungry.

"We were nev—"

"Oh, come on, you know what I mean."

Ellie watched the man finish his second doughnut with one last, thoughtful bite.

"It's not Girish," she said.

Lucy squinted. "El, what's happening?"

Something in Ellie tightened and heaved. "It's Jack," she whispered. "Jack Mannheim."

"Jack Mannheim?" Lucy stared past her, trying to see shapes in a mist. "That's right—I saw you talking to him at that party. Did he say something to you? I've heard he's really tactless. Did he tell you your dissertation sucked or something?"

"No." Ellie shook her head slowly.

"Shit, he didn't make a pass at you, did he?" Lucy's eyes brightened as though they had absorbed the energy of her lowered voice.

"No. Well—" Ellie stopped to breathe.

"Holy shit. Holy *shit*, El! Your life—"

No words harmonized with her memories. "I did it," she said. "Something happened. I've just never felt—"

Lucy's thoughts seemed to rush all one way. "My God, did you sleep with him?"

Her words didn't bond with Ellie's memories. They glanced off her images as her words rolled off Girish's thoughts, failing to connect.

"He's different" was all she could think of to say, the ultimate platitude.

Lucy smiled. "My God, what brought this on? Jack Mannheim, that's like screwing George Washington. The poor guy's so serious, so sad. Good body, though, I guess. I just never thought he was, like, in our mating pool. I was amazed he showed up at that party."

"I told him I'd be there," said Ellie.

"You told him y— Shit, El, how long has this been going on?" Lucy's voice rose.

Mapping the history calmed Ellie. "Oh, I sat in on his course this fall," she said, "and we just started talking. It's funny—he really is George Washington, but he has this feeling for Nietzsche, and he knows so much about Mann. It doesn't fit. It's like, there's something else in there, and I want to find it. It's like, he's a safe, and I want to crack him."

Lucy grinned. "You want to get his combination?"

"I want to get in," said Ellie, responding faster than she could think.

"That is so male, El, that is so *male*. I'm starting to feel sorry for this guy."

Lucy brightened as her idée fixe took hold of this new information. For the past six years, she had been writing a dissertation on seduction tactics in eighteenth-century epistolary novels.

"So what seduction techniques did you use?" she asked. "My God, this poor man."

"I don't know. What are my choices?" Ellie slipped into the game.

Lucy flushed with intensity. "Well, first there's your basic threat. Lots of variations. Fuck me, or I'll fire you, impoverish your family, and tell everyone you're a slut."

"Nope," said Ellie. "How could I scare anyone?"

"Oh, you don't know your own power." Lucy smiled. "Girish is scared shitless of you."

"No way," Ellie laughed.

Lucy pointed a blunt finger at Ellie's chest. "If you could convince anyone you were actually going out, his reputation as a freewheeling seme scatterer would be trashed."

"I wouldn't win his affection, though."

"No." Lucy grinned. "But you could use him for sex."

"Okay," said Ellie, "I'll consider it. So what are my other choices?" She wanted to play her full round. It pleased her to see Lucy so vibrant, since misery often shut her down.

"The next one is guilt," she said excitedly. "Very popular. Highly successful. Your basic Valmont type of deal. If you don't fuck me, you're making me suffer."

Ellie gulped photon-filled air.

"The thought—just the thought—"

"No good, eh?" Lucy's eyes radiated warmth. "Okay, well, then there's flattery—that's number three. Tell him everything he's ever wanted to hear until he fucks you out of gratitude. Works well on low self-esteem types."

Ellie's laughter slowed, and Lucy crowed in triumph. She pointed her finger and bounced up and down. A dark-haired woman looked up from her manuscript with an accusing glare.

"Sh—sh! Shut up!" hissed Ellie. "This is serious."

Lucy subdued herself with effort. "So you got him on flattery?"

"No ..." Ellie reflected. "But I think you're getting warmer."

"Okay, there's one more," said Lucy. Ellie sensed it was her favorite. "Awe inspiration. You convince him you have godlike powers and if he fucks you, he can share them. Usually works only for men, on women, your Old Testament type of deal. 'Ye shall be as gods, knowing good and evil'"

Ellie pictured a tree. "The serpent said that."

Lucy nodded. "Yeah, see? Lots of women go for it. It really works. As if intelligence were passed through semen—if the smartest guy fucks you, you'll be smart too."

"Biologically there could be something to that," said Ellie. "Well, transgenerationally. Your kids could be smart."

Lucy shrugged. "Yeah, but you'd be married to the serpent."

"No. Just fucking him." Where was this game going?

Lucy paused, excited and quivering. Ellie felt the shameful sickness of someone who has had too much to eat.

"It wasn't a seduction," she murmured. "I hate myself for thinking of it that way. I hate myself for having this conversation. It just happened. It wasn't a seduction—it wasn't rhetoric. It was beautiful."

She could hear Girish laugh, as he always did when she claimed that anything wasn't language.

"Is he married?" asked Lucy.

"Yeah." From Jack's words "I'm married," she could form no images. His wife was a fact, an abstraction.

"Oh, wow." Lucy frowned. "Kids?"

"I think so." For the first time, Ellie felt a heave of shame. Lucy's voice was opening dimensions of Jack's life that until now had lain flat.

"Wow. So what are you going to do?"

"I don't know." Ellie breathed in and out slowly. "It's up to him. Just see him for a while, I guess, get to know him. I mean, I don't think he's going to leave his wife for me. I wouldn't want him to. I just like being with him. It's like—I want to break into him, because in him, there's something that's me. Part of me is in there, and I need to get at it. It's like he's me, trapped in a safe."

Lucy's smile returned. "Is he you or the safe?"

"Both," answered Ellie, discovering her thoughts as she spoke.

Lucy tilted her head. "The safe is his body?"

"No." Whatever "inside" and "outside" were, they weren't spirit and flesh.

"He does have a great body, El." Lucy smiled.

Shame crowded Ellie's thoughts. "Does he? I've never really been that into bodies."

"Oh, right," scoffed Lucy. "You like Girish for his personality."

"Girish is history," she proclaimed.

"I'll reserve judgment on that until his next mating cycle." Lucy smirked. "Listen, El. If you're sick of guys who screw you at night but don't want to be seen with you in daylight, do you really think a married guy is going to be an improvement?"

Ellie froze as if she'd been slapped. She drew a deep breath, her face searing. "Yeah," she said. "Because I know that if he weren't married, he'd want to be with me. I've got the comfort of the hypothetical."

"That is the saddest thing I ever heard," said Lucy. "How can you be sure it's true? I mean, it's easy for him to say that. He's speaking from a pretty safe position."

Ellie reached for evidence through which her fingers passed. "He never said it. I just know."

"Wow. This could be really bad, El. I mean, what about his wife? Do you think she knows?"

"I don't know," murmured Ellie.

Lucy stiffened. "What do you mean you don't know—hasn't he talked to you?"

"No," she answered.

Lucy's face hardened. "Shit! What if he—God, what if he just hits you with the old 'don't hold on to this' spiel?"

"He wouldn't do that," said Ellie.

"Are you sure? When they freak, they're all the same, young, old, seme scatterers, George Washington ..."

Ellie saw Jack looking up from a book, his blue eyes scanning frozen ground. "I can feel him," she said. "He's trying to decide what to do."

"Did you get the safe open?" Lucy asked.

"No," she said. "But I heard the person inside."

"What did he say—she say?" Lucy's brown eyes shone.

"He said, 'Lemme the fuck outa here.'"

"The key word being 'fuck.' " Lucy smiled knowingly.

Ellie released all the air from her lungs in a long, slow rush.

"Listen, El, I've got to get out of here too," said Lucy. "I've got to go tell Sam about Hopkins. He'll be at Humanitas drooling over the muffins."

"Go for it," said Ellie. "I've got to stay here for a while and check out something for my thesis." Her voice quickened. "This is getting to be so great. Words, water, money, precious bodily fluids, everything circulates in Gide. I found this connection with Nietzsche. That's why I was talking to—you know. Gide claims he had all his ideas before he read Nietzsche, but Nietzsche uses all the same fluids, the same kinds of exchanges. He describes everything in terms of the body."

Lucy nodded, as though trying to respect Ellie's enthusiasm. "Gide is that sickly nineteenth-century French gay guy, right, the one in love with his cousin?"

"Yeah, that's him," Ellie laughed. "But it wasn't circulation he wanted, at least not at first. In *The Immoralist*, life is this huge, gushing, one-way flow—"

Lucy cringed. "Wow, like a bleeding wound?"

"I don't know yet," said Ellie. "I'm still trying to figure it out."

"Well, you'd better figure it out before your interviews. Go check out those fluids. Go get 'em, girl!"

"And you go get Sam." Ellie smiled. "Tell him I dig his dancing, and feed him a muffin for me."

"Yeah." Lucy's chair scraped the white linoleum. "We'll go do some fluids."

Over slurping, hissing espresso machines, fierce gargoyles watched philosophers with engorged heads. The plaster role models gazed down on jostling people spilling their coffee in scalding brown slops. In risky moves, they squeezed between tables too closely spaced for bodies broadened by coats and packs. In the corner, a banished philosopher stood nearly buried under a collapsing pyramid of oatmeal cups.

At three o'clock, the feeble afternoon light glanced off the windows' tiny panes. The ebony wainscoting absorbed the few rays that got through, and books and papers masked the tables' red glow. Nowhere on this campus was there enough light. In the seminar rooms, Jack's students went glassy-eyed from the late-night ambience, and here in the Humanitas café, gargoyles reigned triumphant in their eternal night. Almost every seat was taken by a scholar with a manuscript and maroon cup. Except for Jack and Sam, most sat alone, but the espresso machines roared like an excited crowd.

Sam bit into his low-fat apple muffin with the hunger of a famished wolf.

"You done yet?" he asked with his mouth full.

"Oh, I'm getting there," said Jack. He spread his fingers to drink heat through his cup. "I'm done with the papers from the Goethe class, but I have four to go from the Mann seminar."

"Anything good?"

"Oh, a few." Jack considered. "Some of the undergrads got into *Elective Affinities*."

"Oh, I *love Elective Affinities*!" Sam's deep brown eyes widened and glowed.

"Yeah, this one guy read it in terms of the metamorphosis of plants, intensification, transformation, merging ..."

Sam swallowed the last quarter of his muffin and gazed longingly at the hanging baskets of croissants, turnovers, and scones.

"Oh, did you want something else?" asked Jack.

"Nah. I promised Ruth I'd cut down." Sam patted his round belly with more pride than shame. "I'm not allowed to die of a heart attack till I figure out how to put my kids through college."

Jack smiled. "So that would give you—"

"Ten years. Then I retire to my country estate and start to eat seriously. What are you gonna do when you retire?"

Jack studied the biscotti standing in their glass jars. "I haven't really thought about it—write more books, I guess."

Sam pulled his eyes from the baskets and his mind from his future gourmandise.

"Hey, how'd that party end up?" he asked. "That was a good one—I was sorry I had to go."

"Was Jerry all right?" asked Jack, guilty that he had forgotten.

"Yeah, they're adjustin' his meds again." Sam scowled. "Monday we took him in for a tune-up. They just don't know, that's all, but at least they've got the guts to say it. We took him up to the Mayo last year, and it was the same story, a crapshoot. They just crank up some of his transmitters, turn down some of his transmitters, and try to keep the kid from freakin' out."

Sam withdrew into smoldering thoughts.

"I'm sorry," said Jack.

"Don't worry about it." Sam shrugged. "He's a tough kid. But—"

"Excuse me." A thin girl with short brown hair brushed Sam's arm with trembling fingers. "I'm sorry to interrupt"—she moved her chin slightly toward Jack to acknowledge a privileged conversation between professors—"but I just had to let you know—I've got an interview with Hopkins!"

Instantly Sam lit up. "Lucy, that's fan*tas*tic! See? I *tol*eja somebody was gonna call! I knew you could do it." He looked her in the eye and nodded knowingly. "The best places wait till the end."

"Congratulations," said Jack, trying to place her.

He wondered why she seemed to know him. He was going to ask her what her dissertation was about, but someone nearby who had overheard called her over for details. Sam frisked himself, searching for a piece of paper, and scribbled on a napkin, "Call Patterson—Hopkins—Lucy."

"She didn't have any interviews," he muttered. "Eighth year. I was so worried. Great thesis on the rhetoric of seduction. I sure hope she gets this job."

He stared at his jagged marks and raised his eyes to Jack's.

"So what did you want to talk to me about?"

Jack started at his friend's direct stare. "Oh, not much—actually, it was about that party."

Sam's eyes withdrew into darkness. "What about the party?" he asked slowly.

"Well, that girl—Ellie—"

"You're tellin' me this *here*?" Sam gasped. "C'mon—we gotta get outa here. Come on down to my office."

Sam crushed his napkin and stalked down the hall.

"It's no big deal, really. Take it easy," called Jack.

Sam's thick neck remained locked in a forward position. For the first time in years, Jack's friend seemed really angry at him. The dark wooden door clicked shut, sealing him into the chaos of Sam's space: avalanches of paper waiting to be touched off; books piled, rather than stacked, on every horizontal surface, including much of the floor.

"Oh, Jack," moaned Sam. "What did you do? I should have stayed to take care of you."

"Well, I walked her home," he began. "And she wanted me to come up and see her apartment."

"You never do that." Sam shook his head vehemently. "You never do that. You never go up to see their apartment."

Jack stopped. "What do you mean?" he asked. "Has this happened to you?"

Sam smiled. "Maybe fifteen, twenty times."

"You're kidding." Coldness spread down Jack's arms.

"No, I'm not kidding," answered Sam softly.

"But what do they—"

"What do they see in me?" Sam chuckled. He swept his thick arm downward with a courtier's gesture. "I dunno. Must be they want me for my body."

A knock rattled the wooden door, and Sam grinned at the girl who pushed it open. He glanced at his watch. "Oh, Dianne, your paper, that's right, we were gonna—"

"Oh, it's all right," she said quickly. "Really, if you—"

"No, no," responded Sam. "Somethin' just came up, that's all—you know, professor stuff. If you can just gimme ten minutes—"

The fair girl blushed. "Okay. I'll come back. Really, it's okay—"

"No, no," insisted Sam. "Stay here, but close that door for me, will ya?"

Dianne withdrew, closing the dark door behind her.

"So," he asked Jack, "didja fuck her?"

Heat crept over Jack's scalp like an army of red ants on the move. He tried to answer but couldn't. That was the maddening beauty of Sam—he always did your talking for you.

"Oh, man," moaned Sam, shaking his head. Something seemed to shift in him like a grounded boat in a rising tide. "Was she good?" he asked.

Jack smiled, unsure how to answer.

"Yeah, she would be," Sam sighed. "Hot—tight—great lips—"

Jack couldn't speak. Sam's voice faded as he reveled in unseen images, but he shook them off.

"How could you do that?" he demanded.

"I don't know what happened." Jack swallowed. "She really seemed to want to. She is a grown woman, Sam."

"She's a *girl*." Sam patted his belly. "We're old men. We're married, for Chrissake! We've got kids to think about. She doesn't know what that means."

Jack asked his body a question, but he couldn't hear the answer. It was muffled by a perfect reconstruction of Ellie's hair brushing his face.

"She's so beautiful, Sam. She's all music—"

"You're crazy, Jack. You're outa your fuckin' mind. Listen." Sam stepped forward and reached up to grab his shoulders.

"You gotta stop this *now*, before you really fuck up your life. What you gotta do is, you gotta have a line. You talk to 'em, you share their brilliance, you share their music, you dance with 'em, you touch 'em, flirt with 'em if they want it, and if they're gonna get mugged, you walk 'em home. But you don't go up to their apartments. That's the line. You don't cross that line."

Jack imagined Sam trembling behind a line of French guns. An army of Nazi beauties advanced with sharp steps, marching around the Maginot line that couldn't turn.

"So what do you tell them?" asked Jack. "What do you say when they ask you up?"

Sam smiled sadly. "I tell 'em I'm a tired, fat old man and I need to go home to bed."

Ellie would never buy that, thought Jack. "And if they don't buy it?" he asked.

"Well, then I gotta bring out the big guns."

Another knock shook the door, and Sam yanked it open.

"Aw, geez," he groaned. "Can you gimme five minutes? I swear, no more than five minutes."

He closed the door, and a sheaf of dusty papers slid off a table. Jack bent to retrieve it, but Sam waved him away.

"Leave it. Shit, I got six or seven people out there."

"Oh, I can go," said Jack quickly.

"*No!*"

Jack froze, his hand extended toward the knob.

"Look, does Bea suspect anything?"

"No," said Jack carefully. "She was up late writing cards, and then she had to get up early to go to the clinic. She was asleep when I came in. I think Jessie might suspect something, though."

Sam clapped his hand to his forehead.

"Geez, that's worse! You better start the damage control. How is Jessie anyway?"

His eyes penetrated deeply, defying all subterfuge.

"Oh, she's okay," began Jack. "Same as always. Adolescent rage."

Sam looked at him with sympathy and something else he couldn't define.

"But she's okay?" he asked.

A rap jolted the door, which Sam had failed to close fully.

"No, no, he's with someone," hissed a female voice.

The exchange outside superimposed itself on Sam's next question. "Who's with him?"

"Oh, that tall guy from German, that good-looking guy."

A musical rivulet of giggles flowed.

Jack wondered whether the students could hear him and Sam, considering how closely he could follow their conversation outside. Sam talked on, undaunted.

"You gotta think of Jessie and Bea, but you gotta think of Ellie too. You gotta think of yourself. You had a good time, right?" He faltered as more images possessed him. "You had a great time ... but just leave it at that. Tell her she's wonderful, tell her she's great, tell her you're glad it happened, but you can't do this to your family. Say you're too old for this kind of stuff. Geez, you could be her father!"

If only, thought Jack. *If only my daughter were like Ellie ...*

Sam studied him, anxiously seeking assent.

"Will you do it, Jack? Will you tell her that?"

"I'll try."

"Don't try. Do it."

Sam moved toward the door, beyond which the conversation was growing louder.

"What are the big guns?" asked Jack.

Sam looked at him wryly, and his lids drooped over his Cleopatra eyes. "I tell 'em I'm a tired, fat old man and I have to go home to my wife."

Jack shuddered. Under Sam's ocean of sympathy lay a hard, unknown bed. Jack opened the door to face a cluster of students, who brightened at his departure. In one impulse, they rushed forward.

"Okay," roared Sam. "Okay now, don't start a riot here! Dianne, she was first. Ten minutes, just gimme ten minutes—"

He stopped and frowned and reached into his back pocket.

"Corinne, darlin', couldja run down to Humanitas and get me one of those apple turnover things?"

Jack read through the posters outside the department office. Their words and colors soothed his inner throbbing. A long, glossy picture of a rushing waterfall advertised a summer theory workshop. He leaned in to catch the time of an upcoming cello recital. Saturday—

That step. From far down the hall came a quick, hard beat. He saw Ellie even before she turned the corner, all tautness, vitality. *Eindringlicher Geist.* God, what could he say to her?

When Ellie saw Jack, she stopped like a mule confident it had reached its goal. She was dressed all in blue: indigo blouse, sky-colored leggings, and some kind of violet-sprigged scarf. Her clothes encased her energy like Spiderman's tights. With a questioning smile, she moved toward him, then jerked her head once each way. Her blush excited him. Until now, he had never known the power of his influence.

"Come to my office?" he asked softly.

Ellie nodded. She seemed uneasy, and he wondered if she missed the days when she could visit him worrying only whether he was too busy to see her. Today his professional space seemed to intimidate her as it had the very first time. Like organ pipes, his books stood upright, proud of their places in a fine instrument. Portraits of Mann, Nietzsche, Goethe, and Bach exchanged mistrustful glances across his wooden desk. The room breathed with quiet, musty life, content with itself in the semidarkness. Jack locked the door but didn't turn on the lights. Ellie took a step toward him.

"I'm sorry I haven't called you," he began.

"I know," she said. "You've been thinking."

His hands trembled. "You know my thoughts."

"Some of them," she said. "I love your thoughts." From her low, steady voice, she seemed more confident than he was.

"Ellie—"

"Are you all right, Jack?" she asked.

"I'm having a rough time with this," he said. "I don't know what to do."

"I understand." Her blouse rippled as she nodded slightly.

"I—I need some time. I'd like to spend some time with you, talk with you about this. I'd like to spend some time with you at the MLA."

Ellie beamed, her energy arcing in flashes. "Oh, Jack—that would be—"

"But I need time," he warned. "I'd rather we didn't see each other until then."

"I understand," she said. "Are you okay, Jack? Cathy doesn't suspect anything, does she?"

"*What?*"

He staggered back into a wall of books. "Cathy?"

"Jack!" she gasped. "I'm so sorry! I shouldn't have said anything. I'm so sorry. I won't ever say—"

"Cathy?" he murmured.

"I'm so sorry, Jack!" Her voice wavered as it rose. "I didn't mean any disrespect to your wife! I wouldn't ever say or do anything to hurt her."

"My wife's name is Bea," he whispered. The cold metal shelves froze his back.

Ellie stepped forward and seized his hands. "Please don't hold this against me, Jack! I love to be with you. I just want to be with you any way I can. I don't want to hurt your family."

She raised his fingers to her lips, then backed away, unable to stop her tears.

"You think, Jack. I'll do whatever you want."

She closed the door, but he couldn't move. He stood slumped against the wall of books, his stare dissolving the darkening space around him.

Cathy was the thinnest girl he had ever seen. Everything she wore seemed to flutter in the wind that blew between the gray college buildings. With her penetrating voice, she loved to shriek. When she screamed, the cords stood out on her neck, and he crushed her in frantic efforts to quiet her. When he was deep inside her, his fingers took root in her curls, and living cables squeezed his thighs. She gripped him until he lost all control, and she laughed at the strangled sounds he made. Afterward he stared paralyzed at the pulsing mosaic of her eyes. The blue-green blobs defied all his tracking schemes as they swam beneath his gaze.

Cathy was the only woman with whom he had ever danced. If she loved a song, she would spin around, head back, mouth open, arms raised. In her head, she said, there was a needle, and it told her which way was up. No matter how fast she whirled, Cathy never got dizzy. In his eighteen years, he had never known a woman like her. Cathy respected nothing, wanted to burn everything, and took anything into her body.

Cathy had taught him neuroulette, her favorite party game. In watchful sips they drank purple juice and counted the beats in their waiting heads. Under watchful eyes, some of them would move into a space all their own. One night, Jack had watched the room turn blue, and he had lost six hours—or so they said—slicing the air with the rainbows shooting from his fingers. With his mind newly alive, he painted a masterpiece, and in Cathy's hair he found a world of color. Each damp brown lock became a blinking blue spiral through which he could fall forever.

But Jack hated neuroulette. When Cathy got lucky, she writhed and shrieked and slapped horrors with her whiplash arms. Jack pinned her and begged her to come back, but she screamed as though the air had ignited. The ants, she wailed, the ants were marching down her throat, ants with compound eyes that saw into her soul. A million ants, with eyes of a million cells, each of which could see a million ways.

Jack took Cathy and crushed her as she shrieked, electric flesh against his hands. He carried her home, laid her gently in bed, and trembled alone while she slept. In the night she would wake and beg him to come in, since she couldn't stand the emptiness. When he filled her up, it would be all right. The needle would show her the way up again.

"May I have your number, please?"

"Two-five-seven," answered Ellie. "Two-nine-five. Five-six-three-seven."

"Thanks. And the date of your test and the testing center?"

"Wabash Avenue. Tuesday, December 9."

"All right. And your mother's maiden name."

"Morel."

"Okay, ma'am, I can tell you that your test was normal today. Everything's fine. Your result was normal."

"Thank you so much," Ellie breathed.

Thank God! So she hadn't hurt Jack after all.

CHAPTER 4

MIRRORS

WHERE IN HELL WAS THE bus? Fingers of cold were worming their way into Ellie's clothes, and a nearby voice threatened in angry bursts.

"Bitch clean me out," growled a trembling man. "Didn't leave me nothin' to get to work."

On the bank sign across the street, yellow stars formed the digits 7:08. The information line had said the bus would come at 7:04. What if it didn't show up? At 3:00 p.m. New York time, she had to be in a hotel talking to professors from Colorado. She wondered whether the street's gray filth could invade her suitcase as fast as the cold crept up her skirt.

The angry man kicked the sidewalk and cursed the woman who had left him without a dollar fifty for the bus.

"Bitch think she put somethin' over on me. She playin' with my head, you know what I'm sayin'?"

His neighbor dug in his back pocket and nodded. The skin of his neck bulged in rubbery brown folds. "I hear you, man. I been there. I hear you."

Ellie stepped back, fearing that the first man's rage would spread like a mushroom cloud. She fell into a line of bundled figures waiting like pillars in the icy darkness. She had often noticed the dark, bulky people lined up along this dingy brick wall. Among them she felt very pale and small. When was this bus going to come?

People had said she was crazy to take the Garfield bus. For ten dollars, a university van could shoot her across Englewood to Midway Airport. But she was determined. Every day thousands of people paid a dollar fifty for this trip. Why throw away eight fifty that could buy a book, a dinner, a movie, or two shining barrettes for her hair? She had a right to ride on the Garfield bus. At seven in the morning it would be full of working people. Anyone who would grab her purse would be asleep. The notes for her talk she kept wadded in a nylon pouch squashed against her chest.

One of the bundled women sighed and stepped forward. Comforting twin lights approached. Ellie squeezed the quarters she had dropped into her glove and squinted at the figures rolling across the bus's forehead: 55 Midway, this was the one. The bus stopped with a lurch and a hiss. Ellie waited while the regular riders flashed their cards, then planted a boot on grooved black rubber.

From the moving bus, she barely recognized the desolate streets. She sensed progress only when they entered the blank park. If she were out there now on those ghostly lawns, what would happen to her? What if the driver threw her out? But no one gave her even a glance. The riders had withdrawn into their own calculations, and she could imagine whatever horrors she wished.

When the bus cleared the park's western edge, the day asserted itself. Grimy forms coalesced from the dissolving dark. Signs with cramped letters topped stores to cash checks, eat chicken, or buy liquor. Iron bars hung over their windows like heavy lashes over sleeping eyes. Under a bridge glowed a mural with upraised fists painted in strong, calligraphic strokes.

The bus stopped at almost every corner to invite more people aboard. A woman entered with two small children, and an old man helped her to hoist her stroller. As she struggled to fold it, her little ones crept up to Ellie, a boy in blue and a girl in a Tweety Bird hat. On pink fuzz, yellow birds zoomed every which way, some careening upward, others plummeting down. Ellie smiled, and the children stared at her with intelligent brown eyes.

"Hi," she said.

The boy grinned, spread his fingers on his head, and shook it violently from side to side.

"Tremaine, y'all get over here an' quit botherin' that lady!" called their mother.

Ellie smiled at the wiry young woman to show that Tweety and Tremaine were no trouble. The tiny figures in quilted jackets hovered curiously before her. What if she were answerable for the warmth and safety of these little beings? The next touch of the bus's brakes sent the children careening back toward their mother. A few blocks later she unloaded them and their stroller into the frozen grayness. A stooped, trembling woman entered, and Ellie offered her her seat.

The street broadened into a vast channel between brownstones blackened with graffiti swirls. In the newborn light, the houses looked tired and old, long abused by the lives within them. Here and there a house was missing like a gap in a row of rotting teeth. Some blocks were nearly toothless, their last buildings jutting uncannily from bare gums. On the side streets, battered wooden houses sagged, with black bars protecting their closed eyes. One with bloodred trim around the door stared like an old woman, all the deader for its painted red lips.

The bus crossed a wide street, and high school students streamed in until the walls vibrated with their noise. They chided and pushed, forcing Ellie away from the seat under which she had stashed her bag. In a turbulent wave, they jostled and yelled in words she barely understood. They wore baggy pants, bulky jackets, and bulging packs, and one girl with braids was so fat she could barely walk on her sausage legs. How could people take up so much space and feel no shame in their occupation of it? As bodies pressed Ellie from every side, hot pins pricked her arms and chest.

This was what she had feared. No grown-up would hurt her, but young people were cruel: they tormented for pleasure. She twisted her neck to see her bag, but a padded body blocked her view. What if they got her suitcase? What would she do in New York with no shoes, no underwear, no shampoo? She had worn her gray suit, fearing exactly this, and her talk lay stiff and clammy against her chest. But it would be horror to arrive empty-handed. How could she take a shower or change her clothes?

A putrid, overwhelming stench sickened her.

"Shit, what is that?" yelled a girl with a jaunty, lacquered ponytail. "Yo, Cherry, that you? What you do?"

"Ain' me, girl. You clean up your own self," snapped the fat one.

Accusations flashed. The students located the source, a filthy alcoholic who gurgled and snarled.

"Shit, what he doin' here?" exclaimed Cherry.

Ellie felt solidarity with the teenagers as they cursed the old drunk. She didn't dare laugh, since any sound might draw their wrath on her as quickly as it had befallen the old man. The bus crossed another broad street and emptied as fast as it had filled. The loud, enormous bodies rolled off into the dimness, still hooting at the stink bomb that descended with them. An empty silence took their place. Ellie's brown suitcase lay securely wedged under the blue plastic seat.

She had reached Western Avenue, another frontier. At this border, the neighborhood changed to Latino, and the buildings leveled as if they had been mowed and thatched. Over neat pink houses, the uncertain sky revealed its dubious face. Ellie exhaled and told herself that she could get mugged here as well as anywhere. But the people, like the houses, looked less imposing and took up as little space as she did. They climbed on board in twos and threes, women with short legs, set faces, and shiny black hair.

Ellie's thoughts moved ahead to the afternoon and the sale she would have to make. She would have four tries. In her tight suit, she would offer her ideas to four groups of strangers, and hopefully one would close its jaws on the bait. The Colorado interview would start in seven hours. She spotted the airport control tower, a tiny gray robot, and pulled the cord to request a stop. Her boots crunched the grit of the West Side street. She swung her bag onto her shoulder and bounced it to free her hair from its pull. She had made it. She and her shampoo had come through safely, and at 3:00 p.m. she would be talking about flow, blood, and blockage at a Times Square hotel.

When the green light flickered, Ellie slammed the handle down. They never gave you enough time with these doors. You slid your card and then held your breath, awaiting the answering flash. The door swung inward to reveal a dim, muffled space. Gray light from the street barely penetrated the stiff curtain. Ellie kicked her bag toward the two huge beds, whose brown-and-purple spreads hung as neatly as dogs' ears. A flash of movement startled her, and she found her face in a silver square. For three days, this humming cube of browns and mauves would be hers, from the Bible to the bottles of pale pink lotion.

Somewhere in this honeycomb, Jack was moving in. Above? Below? What were his coordinates? Jack wanted to see her, to touch her. She pushed back the curtain to inspect the street twenty stories down. She couldn't tell what street it was—some narrow, gray side street that nourished the backs of buildings. A long truck was backing into a tight driveway, guided by a gesticulating man.

When the truck filled the narrow passage, she let the curtain fall and unzipped her bag.

Ellie loved to unpack. She opened each drawer, fingered each hanger, and distributed her goods around the room. With a frown, she stroked her wrinkled blue blouse. She had only this one gray suit, which she had put on at six this morning. If someone attacked her with coffee or ketchup, she would have to wear the blue blouse, and it needed smoothing.

With her collection of bottles, she invaded the bathroom, which exploded into dazzling brilliance. They gave you too much of everything here: too much light, too many towels, too much bed. She arranged her bottles artistically and practiced her spiel, the cassette that would play when they asked about her thesis. In just over an hour, people seated on a bed like hers would be grilling her about bodily fluids. She locked her eyes on her reflection and ran the tape:

"I'm following Gide's descriptions of circulation through all his fiction and private writing. I got the idea ten years ago, the first time I read *The Immoralist*. Bachir cuts his thumb and licks the blood and laughs, and Michel thinks this is the quintessence of health—to bleed and laugh about it. I see circulation all through Gide's writing— circulation of money, lost objects, scattered words. I think"—*no, I can't say that*—"I *argue* that his idea of health evolves from gushing, one-way flow in his early works to endless cycling in his later ones."

There, that was pretty good. Sam had warned her to have her thirty-second pitch down and to hold their attention any way she could. Her interviewers might be wistfully eyeing their lunch or trying to watch a basketball game.

A bubble slipped through her middle. It was time to claim her room in an animal way and send something slithering down the toilet. She pushed the bathroom door, and it swung shut as she hustled her skirt up and her pantyhose down. She settled onto the white plastic ring, legs apart. She froze.

Gazing at her was a shocked woman with long brown hair. She

was formal to the waist, in a gray V-neck jacket and red silk blouse, but she had a bizarre, ciliated gash between her legs. Around the puckered purple-pink wound, hairs clustered like iron shavings around a magnet. The opening looked like the mouth of a conch, but with an ugly, bristly beard. Why did they put a mirror on the bathroom door? What was there to see but this? Her body forgot all about what it had wanted to do. *My God,* she thought, *this is me. Raw purple flesh, an open wound. In an hour I'll be talking to people from Colorado, and* this *will be under my skirt.* She was always half-conscious of what lurked in men's pants, but this image had never approached her mind. *I'll just sit here,* she thought. *I'll just sit here awhile.* She followed her watch's fragile golden hand as it advanced in tiny jumps. Her eyes moved from its face to the hairy purple gash, then back to the watch again.

Where could Jack be? Ellie vibrated with excitement as she stalked the endless halls. Each time she turned a corner, her heart pounded, expecting to encounter him. Her heels dug the rich green carpet that muffled the enormous space. The halls hummed with fierce, invisible rays brighter but cooler than daylight. The space extended itself through mirrors, multiplying with an incestuous drive. Immense, surreal, the glowing passages reflected themselves inward.

One by one, she encountered her friends. Each face she recognized settled her insides. But still no Jack. Already one of the precious nights had passed, and he hadn't called her. Jack hadn't said when he would be arriving—hadn't said a word since his office that day. Maybe he had gotten in late. She had left her room early that morning to eat before her Alabama interview.

Jack had missed her talk. At a quarter to twelve she unwadded her text, still safe in its sweaty pouch. She read it to a group of seven listeners on a very strange panel. Before they started, the middle-aged chair introduced her first English professor, a frail man at his fiftieth MLA. The old fellow blushed and beamed, unused to being the center of attention. He wore dark-rimmed glasses and sat with his chin raised, as though trying to see over some obstacle. He listened eagerly to every word and asked each speaker a question, sculpting phrases from his notes.

What, he asked Ellie, had changed Gide's mind, so that he saw life as a circle instead of an arrow? "Life," she said, and the old man's features drooped with disappointment. Trying to qualify her answer, she talked about changes in Gide's sexual orientation, his income, his style. This pleased the spectacled man even less. He gazed at his knobby hands, and the chair invited a new question from a young gay man who ruffled his hair when he spoke.

For weeks Ellie had pictured herself speaking to a mosaic of faces but always directing herself to Jack. His had beamed at the center of a glinting design that shot off flashes of light. It had never occurred to her that he wouldn't come. Now, as the second day waned, she feared she might not find him at all. What if he didn't want to be found? She clenched her teeth and listened to a voice saying he would be like the rest, come inside her, then tell her to disappear.

Ellie followed the current down a blazing hall and sought Jack's movements in the people nearby. The youngest scholars fidgeted miserably in their stiff new clothes. Most of the middle-aged people wore black, the women with clunky necklaces, the men with jaunty ties. The oldest, almost exclusively male, moved slowly in tweed jackets and scuffed brown shoes. Seeing people with straining plastic bags, Ellie decided to go to the book exhibit. As the escalator carried her down, a familiar face rose to meet her.

"Girish!"

Girish smiled at her with the mocking, amused look she always managed to produce. He passed her, gloating in his heavy-lidded way, and she turned and ran upstream. Luckily the escalator behind her was empty, and as she rose, he watched with delight. Sprinting up the down escalator reminded her of that commercial where a woman runs on a treadmill to catch an elusive shopping bag. Ellie reached the top and turned to face him, her chest heaving. Few things in the world had the beauty of Girish's face. His dark brown skin was somehow translucent, deepening to charcoal around the eyes. His black eyes smoldered with intelligence as they asked impertinent questions.

"*You* look nice."

There was something mocking even in his compliments.

"So do you."

Girish's gray suit fitted him perfectly. Its clean curves made one forget that his hairy black head was just a little too big for his body. The escalator washed up person after person, and Ellie stepped toward the railing to let them pass.

"What have *you* been up to, my dear?" asked Girish languorously.

His voice varied between the clipped, high-pitched tones of India and the ironic drawl of the British upper class. Ellie usually evoked the drawl.

"Two down," she said. "Two to go."

"Where?" The dark skin of his lids glistened.

"Colorado yesterday afternoon, Alabama this morning."

"Alabama?" Girish laughed in a delicious rumble, and his eyes met hers with irreverent glee.

"Why, of *co-wuss*, honey chil'. Ain' nowhere *I* wouldn't go. *I'm* sellin' myself to the highest biddah!"

Ellie's voice flowed in a warm, fragrant stream. She reached up to pat his moist cheek.

"Alabama? What did they ask you? My God, what does their French sound like?"

To please him, she created French words denatured by heavy southern vowels. Her voice swelled and stretched, uncanny as Dalí's melting watches. Ellie had always been able to reproduce any sound. She loved to make Girish laugh, the only points she ever scored in their game of irony. He studied her, his dark eyes playing over her blouse and hair.

"Did your talk go well?"

"Oh, I think so," she said. "It was great—there was this old guy who's been to fifty consecutive MLAs! They should give him a medal or something."

Girish chuckled. "Like that old woman at the agricultural fair in *Madame Bovary*."

Ellie's memory replayed the scene in which Rodolphe seduces Emma while, in the background, an auctioneer sells manure.

"*Fumiers!*" she cried devilishly.

Girish took up the challenge and recreated Rodolphe's seduction.

"Oh, my darling—"

Ellie brayed and bleated in his face. "Eee-aaaaw! Baaaaaa!"

"You must see it is fate, my dear. We were meant to be together!"

"Baaaaaa! *Fumiers! Fumiers!*"

Each new face rising from below regarded them with amusement until they collapsed, unable to say another word.

"Where are you going now?" asked Girish, his drawl sharpening to a whine.

"Book exhibit."

Ellie jerked her head toward the escalator's latest fruit, a red-haired woman with two bags hanging like elevator weights from her wiry arms.

"Want to come?"

"I have an interview."

She thought she saw regret under his long black lashes.

"Who with? How many do you have anyway?"

"Eleven," he whined apologetically.

"Get out."

"No, I've really been ... *going at it*." He laughed playfully.

"Any of 'em good enough for you?"

He grinned, loving to be called on his arrogance.

"Oh, per-*haps*."

Ellie wondered what it felt like to be Girish, to be wanted by everyone. Girish worked with a leading postcolonial scholar and was considered his department's brightest student. Everyone wanted him and his project, a cross-cultural study of sadomasochism. It wouldn't be a question of who would take him but of who was going to get him. He was on his way to an interview with Yale.

"*Bonne chance*," she said. "Go subvert 'em. Cleave their signifiers from their signifieds."

"But my *dear*"—Girish stretched his arm around her waist—"how many times must I tell you, the signifier is *always already*—"

She pushed him away and blew a Bronx cheer, and he laughed delightedly.

"You are so ar*ti*culate, my dear. I'm sure you'll get that Alabama job."

"Get out of here."

Still laughing, he withdrew across the green-gold sea and disappeared among the bobbing heads. Ellie descended, feeling soft and heavy. Two levels down she entered a maze of booths selling paper packages of thoughts. Dazzled, she grabbed one after another, drawn by their titles as magpies are to things that glitter. She wanted every one of them. There were books on Paris sewers, nineteenth-century gardens, early modern midwives, and foam. Jack's books lay in front at Harvard and Oxford in rapidly diminishing stacks. A woman passed with his *Reading Mann* under her arm, and Ellie felt a secret thrill.

Here and there she noticed a face that she knew, but she felt too dazed to speak. At the Princeton booth, she spotted Lucy's thin legs underneath a wrinkled black suit. Her friend was standing very still and clutching a book without seeing it.

"Lucy?"

"Oh, God, El!"

Lucy was gripping a book of feminist theory. The sight of Ellie released a wave of grief.

"Oh no."

The Hopkins interview! Beaming sympathy, Ellie met Lucy's red eyes.

"Oh, my God, El. I should just kill myself now. I'm never going to get a job." Without releasing the book, Lucy dabbed her nose with her sleeve.

"C'mon. It couldn't have been that bad," assured Ellie. "People always think it went worse than it did."

"This was really bad, El. It was really bad."

Lucy clutched the book tighter as her tears flowed. Ellie felt her own disappointment rush. Her eyes stung, and her throat tightened. Her ache eclipsed all else as it joined Lucy's in a terrible feedback loop.

"I'll never publish a book like this." Lucy shook the bright, thin paperback. "I'll never get a job. This was my last chance. No one will ever want me."

Ellie forced herself to speak. "Tell me what happened. Maybe it wasn't that bad."

"We-ell, you know how there's the Sheraton and the Sheraton Center. This interview, it was supposed to be at the Sheraton Center. I—I was sure it was at the Sheraton Center."

"Oh, shit," murmured Ellie.

A bald-headed man reached for a book and glanced at them contemptuously. "Excuse me."

Ellie glared.

"And it wasn't?" she asked.

"I—I waited in the lobby," wavered Lucy. "I was there half an hour early. At five of, I went up to the room—it was 4010."

"Yeah?" Ellie stiffened with dread.

"But when I knocked, nobody answered. I thought maybe they weren't ready, and I didn't want to be pushy, so I waited and knocked again. But nothing."

"That's really weird," said Ellie. "What did you do?"

83

"Well, I found this maid. She barely spoke English. She kept trying to tell me something about the room, but I didn't understand." Lucy kept her eyes on the green carpet, a screen for her tormenting images.

"Shit."

"So finally she opened the door, and it was completely dark—no furniture, no people. Just—dark."

Lucy heaved as though the world were dissolving around her. Ellie grabbed the book she had been waving and put it back on the table.

"God, that's horrible."

"I—I just panicked," stammered Lucy. "I knew it had to be in the Sheraton across the street, but it was forty floors down and then forty back up."

"But you went, right?" demanded Ellie.

"Of course I went." Lucy laughed, high and brittle. "The elevator was full of tourists. It must have stopped on every fucking floor. I was pressed against some fat slob's belly the whole way. I think I might have caused accidents when I ran across the street. I saw an elevator just about to leave, and I screamed for them to hold it."

"Well, that's a good break," said Ellie, groping for anything positive.

"It was a fucking *express* elevator to the restaurant on the fifty-sixth floor."

"No way!" Ellie gasped.

Lucy raised her reddened eyes. "I'm telling you, God doesn't want me to get a job. I got out and waited for an elevator back down, but nothing was coming, and it was ten after one."

"Shit."

"So I ran down the stairs—in these heels. Sixteen flights. When I got there, I must have looked like something ran over me. The first five minutes I couldn't even breathe." Lucy paused and swallowed.

"But they must have understood," said Ellie. "I mean, that could happen to anyone. It probably happened to some of the others too."

"I doubt it," scoffed Lucy. "Only I could be this stupid. They acted sympathetic, and they were really nice, but when they choose, they'll choose someone who has her shit together. I'm just fucking incompetent."

Lucy whipped her hand against her face, and people around them gasped. Ellie grabbed Lucy's hand, but the explosion of self-hate had spent itself.

"Don't, Lucy," she begged. "Anyone could have done that. It's the easiest mistake in the world. It's a setup, an accident waiting to happen."

"It was my life," she moaned. "It was my only chance."

"But you still had some time with them," comforted Ellie. "Your work is so interesting. You must have told them—"

"No." Lucy shook her head. "They asked me how I would set up an eighteenth-century class and a feminist theory class, and I couldn't even *think*. I don't know what I said, but it couldn't have made sense. When I'd been there five minutes, the next guy called to say he was ready."

Ellie ground a heel into the carpet. "Oh, fuck. They didn't let him in, did they?"

"No." Lucy drew a ragged breath. "I got my full fifteen minutes to expose my stupidity. I barely talked about my dissertation at all."

"Oh, wow ... Oh, God ..."

"All I ever wanted was to teach this stuff—to write these books—" Lucy sobbed. She gestured toward the oblong stacks beside them. "Is that so much to ask? I mean, it sucks. It's a lousy life. Why won't they let me do it? No one wants it as much as I do."

"You can still do it," said Ellie. "There's the spring list."

Lucy's jaw tightened. "Don't bullshit me. No one ever gets a job from the spring list."

"Next year—" ventured Ellie. She had been afraid to speak the words.

"There's not going to be a next year!" cried Lucy. "This is my last year of funding. Next year I work for five bucks an hour and live in my parents' basement."

Barely able to see through her tears, Ellie looked for the Chicago booth. She had seen it just a minute ago but had lost it in the labyrinth. Sam had promised he would be there for anyone who might need him. He would be holding court next to piles of his new book, *Roués and Cads: The Eighteenth-Century Libertine*. Sam would make Lucy stop hitting herself—Ellie didn't know what else to say.

"C'mon."

Lucy yielded to her determined pull. There. Thank God. Around the corner she glimpsed Sam's black hair through a crowd three or four deep. Too weary to wait, she rammed it like an icebreaker, dragging Lucy in in her wake.

"Beautiful girls!" he cried. "Here are my beau—"

Sam stopped as he saw their faces. People around him dropped back, sensing a crisis.

"Aw, no," he murmured. "C'mon. It can't be that bad."

He extended one strong arm to each and pulled them against his ample belly. When Ellie felt his warmth, she realized how cold she had been. She melted as his hand played over her hair. His soft fingers circled the small of her back, and she grew pleasantly, then violently aroused.

"Beautiful girls," he murmured and kissed the tops of their heads. "C'mon, it's not that bad."

All too soon, he released Ellie, as though sensing with his unfailing touch which body needed greater comfort. He closed his arms around Lucy, and she shook uncontrollably, unable to raise her face from his wet shirt.

"C'mon, darlin'." He rubbed his hands over her heaving back. "You wanna go up to the suite? C'mon. We'll go up to the suite and talk about it. It's gonna be okay."

Like Ellie, Sam seemed to have caught Lucy's misery. His dark eyes swelled, and he looked ready to cry.

"You guys, I gotta go," he said to the onlookers. "Gimme—" He looked uncertainly at Lucy. "Gimme—aw, shit, I dunno. I'll be back later on."

He shot Ellie a glance she couldn't quite read—a look of despair, sadness, and angry disappointment. It lasted an instant, and then he existed only for Lucy, rubbing life into her with his heavy hands. "C'mon, darlin'. It's gonna be okay. You want somethin' to eat? I'll getcha anything you want. You know how beautiful you look today? You're gorgeous. You clean up nice."

He broke away, and all eyes followed as he led Lucy from the maze. Ellie snuffed her grief back into her swollen head and fought to regain her dignity. The onlookers dispersed, laughing and shaking their heads. It could have been them, they were muttering. Whatever it was, it could have been them.

Ellie glanced at her wrist. It was five o'clock, and she had had enough. Fuck waiting. She was going to find Jack, and if he didn't want to see her, he would have to tell her to her fucking face. Where could he be? She looked through the program, and aggression brought lucidity. Why hadn't she thought of this before? Just go where he would be, that was the trick. But there was nothing happening at five o'clock. No, wait—the UC Irvine German Department Cash Bar. Jack knew everyone in the country who studied German, and they would all be in that room. It was happening right here, just two floors over her head. Grimly, she strode toward the escalator.

Compared to the brilliant lobbies and passages, the ballrooms were caverns. Their glinting chandeliers offered more decoration than light. In these rooms one accepted one's drink on faith and told the crackers from the cookies by the texture. Were the spaces just naturally dark, or had they lowered the lights on purpose? It must be that at five, work ended and play began, play that was best left unseen.

Desperately, Ellie scanned the figures and tried to read the reflections of light. People stood in bunches of four or five, clutching their drinks and eyeing the nearby groups. Like Ellie, they sought the faces they wanted even as they smiled at those before them. As she had suspected, many were tall Germans, and if Jack was there, she couldn't see him. Like an explorer from another dimension, she slipped through the black space between groups.

There! Jack! The sight of him set off an explosion. How straight he stood, how beautiful he looked in his dark blue jacket and tie! What light there was seemed drawn to his face and played off his high forehead and gray curls. He was listening earnestly to an older man and didn't notice her until she stirred the air.

"Ellie!"

She smiled, unsure what to call him.

"Benno!" he said to the older man. "This is my student, Ellie LaSalle."

She shriveled. Benno extended his hand, and she took it, hating the touch wasn't Jack's.

"Always glad to meet one of Jack's students!" He beamed.

Jack didn't touch her, and he looked every way but hers.

"How did those interviews go?" he asked.

"Very well, I think." She matched his formality, her anger spinning a web between them. "Alabama kept me an extra quarter hour. My talk went pretty well too."

Jack nodded with respectful interest. "Great! I'm so glad. I knew you'd—"

"Hey, Jack, how's Bea?" interrupted Benno, who was apparently hard of hearing. "She still have that Saturday-morning clinic?"

Ellie's mind roared. What was she, a doctor? My God, a doctor!

"Oh, she's fine," said Jack quickly. "Still going at it. She says they really need that clinic—hardly any residents work there. I admire her for it."

"She's a great woman—a great woman," growled Benno.

A burly man extended his arm between Ellie and Jack.

"Seid ihr bereit? Wir holen ein Taxi jetzt. Die anderen treffen uns da."

"Ja, Dieter, Moment noch." Jack turned confusedly to Ellie. "I—I'm going to dinner with some people. I'm sorry, they're all German—we'll be speaking— I'll—"

He broke off, unable to say that he would call her later.

"Jack!"

Several paces away, a group of impatient men motioned for him to come.

"Oh, no—" she stammered. "It's okay. I understand. Please, go ahead. I'm going to bed early. I have another interview in the morning."

His eyes met hers for an instant, clear as two pale blue gems.

"Nice to meet you, young lady!" cried Benno, pressing her hand.

He seemed to appreciate her new suit and slender legs more than Jack did.

"Jack, *komm!*" called the others.

His hand settled on her shoulder. Through the padded gray wool, she sensed a slight squeeze. She felt something that might have been a tremor, but the pressure dissolved before she could judge.

"Good luck tomorrow," he said.

He strode away on long legs to join his waiting colleagues. Ellie trembled. From her mind, a stream of obscenities flowed, a river of toxic filth. She was glad for the darkness. Tears rolled into her mouth, and she drank them, hot and salty. *Fuck him,* she thought. *Fuck him.* At the gift shop, she bought two power bars and an orange and carried them back to her room for dinner.

Oh! Jangling! A bell! The—

"H'lo?"

"Hey, El. Did I wake you up? It's only nine thirty."

"Oh—I—" Air rushed in the gray space that wasn't home. Light danced around the curtain's edge, but it might be coming from electric lamps.

"That's right, I forgot. Your interview." The voice was Lucy's, warm and steady. "I'm sorry. I just wanted to say I'm sorry about before. I'm feeling a lot better now."

Ellie rolled and reached for a pillow. "Did Sam—"

"Yeah, he was great," said Lucy. "You're such a genius. You know what he said? He said he'd get me funding next year if he had to *fuck* someone to do it. He'd sell his body to get me money."

Ellie laughed, hot and dry under the crisp white sheet.

"Can you picture that?" asked Lucy.

"Oh, I think there'd be takers."

Ellie cupped her breast and squeezed the handful of flesh.

Lucy giggled. "Then he made me eat this huge chocolate decadence tart, and he ate one too. I'm not supposed to tell his wife."

"He do anything else you're not supposed to tell his wife about?" asked Ellie.

"Nah. I would have, though. I'm madly in love with him."

"Yeah, I know."

Ellie breathed into the silence.

"El?" whispered Lucy. "You seen Jack?"

"Yeah."

"He—" The question wouldn't cohere.

Ellie grimaced. "You know. He's being a professor."

"Fucking prick, I figured he'd blow you off." Lucy blew out some air.

"No, he's just—thinking," defended Ellie.

"For a professor he thinks pretty goddamn slowly."

"Yeah," she murmured.

"Stick with Girish, El. Better a young prick than an old one." Lucy's voice brightened the black room.

"I'll think about it," Ellie sighed.

In the darkness, Girish floated, admiring her with a mocking smile.

The next evening, Ellie dismantled her reflection piece by piece. First the jacket came away to reveal glowing red sleeves—then the gray skirt, exposing compact thighs. Next the blouse, baring the jaunty silhouette of a black bra. When she peeled the hose away, her flesh relaxed. She undid the bra and massaged her tortured breasts, trying to erase the red line the underwire had cut.

Ellie jumped. Who could be calling, Lucy again? But Lucy was going to the English party Sam had organized in the suite. Lucy had begged her to come, but Ellie preferred her own bed. She felt demoralized and was worried about the San Diego interview the next morning. The more she thought about it, the more certain she was that she wanted that job. She strode to the nightstand and picked up the phone.

"H'lo?"

"Ellie."

Her heart paused, then doubled its pace.

"Jack!"

"I'm so sorry, Ellie." His voice flowed free, as though it had escaped a confining case.

"It's all right," she murmured.

"No, it's not all right." He paused. "I've been wrong to avoid you like this. I feel awful about last night."

"It's all right." She could only repeat the phrase as she kneaded her hardening breasts. "You—you had to think."

"Yeah, I've been thinking." His weary tone suggested weeks of pondering that had led to no conclusion.

"What have you been thinking?" she asked.

"Well—you must see how it is for me. I'm married. I have a sixteen-year-old daughter."

An unknown vise was crushing her, so that she could barely breathe. "Your wife is a doctor?"

"An ob-gyn."

Ellie drank the rasp of his breath.

"Is that why you're calling me?" she asked. "To tell me you don't want to see me anymore?"

"No!" he gasped, so quickly it startled her. "No—no—it's that—I feel—I have no right."

"You don't want me?"

"Of course I want you. I want to touch you. Oh, Ellie, I've wanted you so much."

She raised her free arm in a dancer's arc.

"I'd like that," she whispered. "Would you come to me now?"

He didn't answer, and she feared she had startled him.

"You'd—you'd have to come here," he murmured. "Someone might call."

His wife. Unlike Jack, she was unaccountable. If she disappeared, no one would miss her. How awful always to be tracked, like a prisoner on parole.

"Where are you?" she asked.

"You're sure about this?" He hesitated. "Are you sure you want to do this?"

"Yeah. I want to be with you." She drew a deep breath.

"Okay, then, I'm in 2516."

She smiled, happy to have learned his coordinates, but she felt a sudden twinge.

"Jack? There's something I should tell you first. It's—it's easier on the phone."

Her insides tensed as she imagined the effect of this sentence.

"Tell me."

His voice sounded steady, but fear was grinding beneath it.

"I got myself tested," she said. "I got myself tested, and I'm okay. I—I'm clean."

Jack didn't respond, and she feared the very mention of a test had changed his mind.

"Oh, diseases!" he laughed. "Wow. Thanks. That's—that's good to know. I hadn't thought about that."

"I just wanted you to know," she said softly. She felt ashamed and didn't know why.

Jack fell silent again, and she followed her fleeting pulse.

"I—I've only been with Bea," he said. His tight voice betrayed his embarrassment.

"That's good," she said quickly. "I mean—no—I don't know what I mean."

"Ellie." His voice was loving, pleading.

"Yeah?" she whispered.

"Please come to me now. We can talk about this here. In 2516."

Ellie smiled tearfully. "You're just five floors over my head. I'll be right up."

She rebuilt her reflection piece by piece so that she and Jack could undo it again.

Like a skater, Jack's finger spiraled around the moles on Ellie's thighs. Six of them lay in aligned pairs, and with an imaginary thread, he looped them together. What lovely flesh she had—firm, strong, resilient. She had exhausted him, gripped him until he ached, and now he floated, his desire to touch her reduced to this silly urge to doodle on her thighs. Jack rolled down and kissed the spots slowly, and she gave an appreciative moan.

"Ellie."

Jack played with her breasts, tracing a spiral that began at the circumference and coiled inward. Her nipple hardened to a gumdrop, and he kissed it.

"Ellie."

"Mmm?"

"This is going to be hard. With other people—it'll always be like tonight. I won't be able to—to—" Half-heartedly, he sought a word.

"Won't be able to do what?"

She ran her finger over his neck and kissed the oval she had traced.

Jack felt his consciousness dissolve. With startling accuracy, she had found his sensitive spots, as though she had a map of his nerve net in advance.

He struggled to speak. "I won't be able to—appreciate you properly. To acknowledge you."

"I know."

She outlined his nipple and kissed it three times.

"I just want to be with you any way I can."

Jack touched her soft cheek. "You'd do that for me? You'd do that, even—"

She stroked his thighs and smiled at his fur.

"I just want to be with you," she said. "If it has to be a secret, then let it be a secret. It'll be a good secret."

Jack pulled her against him, tears stinging his eyes. "I don't deserve this," he murmured.

"Shsh …" She ran her fingers down the ridge of his spine, then circled them over his lower back. Jack shivered and closed his eyes. He lay in delicious surrender while she licked between his fingers.

The piercing trill shocked him. The phone. So late? Without thinking, he reached over Ellie to pick it up.

"Hey, Jack."

Ellie wriggled free.

"How are you? What time is it?" he asked.

"I'm sorry," answered Bea. "I thought you'd still be up. How's the conference?"

"Oh, the usual. Remember old Benno from Wayne State?"

He reached for Ellie's thigh and gave it a reassuring rub.

"Yeah, Benno, how's he?" Bea's alto voice flowed like water onto exposed wires. Jack squirmed.

"Oh, he's holding up. He wanted to be sure I sent his greetings."

Ellie drew her legs against her chest and rested her chin on her knees.

"He doesn't still have a crush on me, does he?" For reasons he couldn't fathom, Bea's low laugh calmed him.

"Oh, I think he may have gotten over it."

Jack could see his wife's ironic grin, her fine features, her wavy black hair.

"You know all those Christmas cards I wrote, the night you went to that party?" asked Bea.

"Yeah," he answered.

"Well, I screwed them up," she laughed. "I don't know where my mind was, but at least one of them got into the wrong envelope. Doreen just called to say that she and Rudi got Nancy and Jeff's."

He could picture Doreen opening the envelope, smirking at her sister-in-law's mistake.

"Oh, God," he said. "Well, maybe it's just those two."

"But I can't be sure that Nancy and Jeff got Rudi and Doreen's. If there's one, it could be all of them. I once knew a guy who applied for eighty residencies, and when he was sealing the last envelope, it didn't match the letter." Jack tried to imagine the permutations. To calculate all the possible combinations, there must be a formula.

"What did he do?" he asked.

"Opened up all eighty. Had to type eighty new envelopes."

Jack wiggled his chilled toes. "That's strange. You never do things like that."

He could sense Bea's shrug. "Well, there's a first time for everything. Must be getting old. Entropy taking over. It's amazing how much energy you have to expend just to make everything go to the right place."

Ellie unfolded, stalked to the bathroom, and closed the door.

"Is Jessie all right?" he asked. "What's she been up to?"

"Not good, Jack." Bea lowered her voice, though she must have been alone. "That's what I wanted to talk to you about."

"Oh, God. Has she—"

"Her grades came today," said Bea. "She's out, Jack. They're suspending her next quarter."

He stiffened. "Have you talked to her about it?"

"No." Bea's voice gained momentum. "She was gone when I got here, and she hasn't come back. She failed everything."

"Everything?"

"Even gym," she laughed. "You can fail gym."

"You can fail gym?" He glanced at the bathroom door, under which a fine bar of light was glowing.

"Sure, if you don't go," said Bea. "She hasn't been going."

"But what does she—where does she—" Jack tried to imagine what someone would do all day if she didn't go to school. He couldn't. "What does she do with herself?" he asked.

"I don't know," Bea sighed. "But we're going to have to find out. It's my fault. I've had all these extra hours at the clinic, and I've been putting this off. I just couldn't believe—I mean, when you were sixteen, did it ever occur to you just not to go to school?"

Jack reflected. "No, I liked school."

As always, Bea's thoughts merged with his. "Yeah, me too. It's hard to fathom. Look, when you get home, we'll confront her together. I want to keep on with this family therapy."

"Sure, let's do that," he said. "How's— Where's— Do you know where she is tonight?"

"No. I tried to ask her last night, 'cause she was still here when I got in." Her voice wavered, and he sensed a half-formed laugh. "I think she gets up and leaves right before I get home so she won't have to talk to me, but yesterday she was late."

"What did she say?" he asked.

"She said, 'Fuck off, bitch.'"

He chuckled. "And they say we should try to communicate."

"Oh, yeah." Bea's voice came low and flat.

"Well, look," said Jack, "I get home tomorrow afternoon. My flight gets in at four thirty."

"Oh, that's no good," she said quickly. "I'm on call then."

"I know, but I was going to use the car service."

"Okay, that's good." Bea's tone hardened as she began to plan.

"Can I make you dinner?" he asked.

"Sure, that'd be great." She paused. "Oh, wait—there's no food in the house. I have to go to the store."

"I'll go, then," he assured her. From the bathroom, he could hear no sounds.

"You'll be tired, though," said Bea.

"No, it's a two-hour flight. Anything special we need?"

Suddenly, Bea seemed to be in a hurry. Maybe her pager was throbbing. "No, not really. Thanks, Jack."

"No problem," he told her. "We can talk tomorrow night."

"Okay. Night, Jack."

With a clunk, the receiver fell into place. Ellie emerged from the bathroom. Her nakedness startled him, her tiny breasts, the brown hair spilling over her shoulders. He thought she must be cold, and he pulled the brown-and-purple spread aside to invite her into bed. She crept in sadly and curled herself up so that her head rested on his thigh.

"I'm sorry," he murmured. "I'm so sorry. She hardly ever calls me at conferences."

"No, I knew—I just felt bad—" Her voice wavered. The rims of her lovely brown eyes were red. "I—I didn't think I should be listening, but I didn't have anywhere to go. I sat on the toilet and stuck my fingers in my ears, but I could still hear you."

"Oh, Ellie, no—"

Sure enough, red toilet tracks had defiled her thighs. Half-heartedly, he tried to massage them away.

"I'm just sorry for you," he murmured.

"Don't be sorry," she said. "I'm with you now."

She rolled. Her soft, moist lips were only an inch away, and her breath stirred him in warm puffs. Jack shivered as she brought her lips against him in light, easy touches. He dissolved slowly into warm, liquid pleasure, his fingers raking the damp meadow of her hair.

❧

"Shit! Oh, God, oh shit!"

A voice. A woman, angry. What—

"Ellie?"

She was on her feet, wild and strong in the electric light.

"What—" He pawed at the exposed sheet.

"It's twenty after eight, Jack!" she cried. "I have to be at this interview in forty minutes."

"Did we—" He glanced confusedly at the clock.

"Yeah, we've done it again."

What a wonder she was, laughing in her fear.

"Can you take a shower here?" he asked.

"No, it's too late for that. I'd never get my hair dry."

He squinted at the chaotic loops. A terrible, beautiful thing, to have long hair. He wondered whether in forty minutes she could undo the snarls he'd made.

"Where's the interview?" he asked.

"Here, thank God—1749."

Expertly, she fastened her black bra.

"Good year," he muttered.

Ellie fought her twisted hose. He watched sleepily, admiring her spirit.

"Good year?" she snapped. "What—"

"Goethe's birth." He smiled. "It'll bring you luck."

"If you say so."

She had enough on for the sprint to her room.

"How do I look?" she asked.

"Beautiful. I love wild women."

He couldn't remember having felt this good. He relished the comedy of her escape. Furtively, she peered into the hall as he flattened himself behind the door.

"Good luck, Ellie."

He leaned forward to kiss her, but she was dashing for the stairs.

CHAPTER 5

TO BE NOTHING

"WHO'S CATHY?" ELLIE KEPT ASKING.

Jack sensed that she feared hurting him, but still she brought it up. He hadn't told her, and he couldn't defer it much longer. He could feel Ellie's disappointment at his refusal to reveal himself.

Now that she had conjured Cathy, his old girlfriend materialized everywhere. She emerged from the steam in the shower and the suds in the kitchen sink. Demonically, she haunted his office when he was trying to rest his mind. Fifteen minutes before his first Nietzsche seminar, she appeared in a gauzy skirt and a quivering purple blouse.

"Cathy?" He felt warmth as he nudged her that cold spring day in the park.

"Yeah?"

"Give me some of that."

Jack sucked at the joint and felt the hot, sweet smoke creep into his head. He pulled her closer, and she sighed, as though happy to have him between her and the Central Park rocks. The radio she had brought jabbed the air with tinny spikes. Jack worked his nose deep into her springy curls and smelled accumulating *Dreck*. His mother would hate Cathy with feminine violence. "Schrecklich! So ein chaotisches Mädchen!" Once, he had found a bug crawling in her hair, and she had laughed with delight.

"Cathy."

"Yeah, what?" she growled.

"What's Mr. Mojo Risin'?"

Jack slid his hands under her top to feel her chest expand.

"It's whatever you want it to mean." Cathy arched her back. "It's there for the sound. It means whatever it sounds like."

"So it doesn't mean anything?" he asked.

"Ask Morrison," she laughed. "He probably threw it in one night when he was stoned out of his mind."

"C'mon." Jack pulled out his hands and rubbed them. "It's got to mean something, even if he didn't want it to. I thought maybe horizon—it sounds like horizon. Or another name for him—it sounds like Morrison." He closed his eyes and rearranged a spread of black *m*'s, *o*'s, and *r*'s.

"Mo-rizon? More-risin'?"

Her thin hand caught him, shy, eager, and enormous.

"Oh …" The black letters dissolved.

"You're so pathetic," she scoffed. "I bet he's laughing at you right now, trying to figure out what that word means. You know, 90 percent of everything we say is there just for the sound."

Cathy took another deep drag on the joint and held it away as he tried to grab it.

"Most of what we say is there just for the sound?"

"Yeah." Her confidence amazed him. Where did her ideas come from?

"But what about communication?" he asked. "Don't we use language to communicate?"

"Nah."

Cathy laughed lazily, and he knew she was on. When Cathy was on, she laughed at everything.

"It's more like a decoy," she said. "It distracts the person so you can send the message you want to send and he can let it through."

Cathy handed him the joint, and he sucked it thoughtfully. The glowing wisp was disappearing so fast it was about to sear his fingers. He would have to roll another one. He pushed Cathy forward to free himself, and she whimpered. In the dirty sandwich bag, the weed looked just like her frizzy brown hair. He pulled a portion loose, crushed it between his fingers, and rolled a tube of it in a white square.

"Mmm ..." Cathy looked on admiringly. "You roll the best joints. You're totally pathetic, but you roll the best joints. I knew it the minute I saw you."

He paused, fingering the tight paper. "But I didn't know how until you showed me."

"I knew anyway," she said. "That's what I mean, the message. I see this big guy sitting in Western Civ, this guy who talks too much about anybody German and not at all about anyone else. I knew what you were really saying was that you rolled great joints."

"How come you get to decide what I was saying?" He smiled. "That means I should get to decide what you were saying."

Cathy bathed him in a heavy-lidded, mocking gaze. He couldn't think of what she'd been trying to say, since he couldn't remember what she'd said, all those days when she'd talked to him after class. He could only recall her laughing at him, as she was doing now.

"See?" she giggled. "You're hopeless."

"So what was your message?" he asked.

Her blue-green eyes pulsed. "That I wanted to turn you on and fuck the living shit out of you."

"Jesus!"

"What's the matter?" She smiled. "Did I say something your mother wouldn't like?"

Scheiße. How did she always know when he was thinking about his mother?

"I can tell when you're thinking about her because you breathe different," Cathy replied directly to his thoughts. "She doesn't like women who say 'fuck'? What did she, have you by immaculate conception or something?"

"I don't want to think about it," he laughed. "This is a woman who weighs two hundred pounds, collects fat china figures, and makes you fluff the couch cushions when you get up so they don't look sat on."

He sat down gingerly, and the gray rock chilled his back. Cathy settled between his spread legs and sucked the fresh joint. He didn't ask for a hit, since he wanted to reserve his hands for the wonders under her purple blouse.

Cathy's smoke dissolved in the wind. "Sounds like a real bitch."

"No, that's too easy." He struggled. "She's been through a lot— There are reasons—"

Cathy drifted, humming to herself.

"She sits on life," he said. "She sits on life, and she squashes it."

Cathy's ribs shook with silly laughter, and he wished she hadn't gotten high so fast. He worked his hands upward and squeezed her nipples, hard as raisins between his thumbs and fingers.

"What about your dad?"

Cathy surprised him as always. Every talk with her was neuroulette.

"I told you," said Jack. "He died when I was thirteen."

"But what about before he died? I mean, what was he *like*?"

Jack wondered about Cathy's theory, talking just for the sound. It seemed hilarious. The idea of his father was funny too. He must be high, less on the smoke than on her thoughts. Nestled comfortably between his legs, Cathy shook out her curls.

"Tell me about your father," she demanded.

"He—loved music," he began. "He taught at PS 513."

"Music?"

"Yeah." Jack tried to breathe against the force of her body. "He loved it, but he hated teaching. He wanted to play in an orchestra. Or write. He used to compose music."

"So why didn't he do that?" she asked.

"He had us. You can't support a family writing music." With his palms in the dirt, Jack tried to shift his cold back. Cathy seemed content as she was.

"Didn't your guy have twenty kids?" she persisted.

"That was the eighteenth century. You could do that then. Rich guys supported him. Today you teach high school in the Bronx."

Jack thought about Bach, his guy. One night, Cathy had given him some white powder, and he had snuffed it up, eager to pass any test. It had been his idea to break into a practice room—an excuse to grab her tiny waist and boost her through the open window. Once they were in, he sat at the piano, confident as a pilot in his cockpit. He played fugues and toccatas as fast as he could while she spun and shrieked in the dark. He made music in a giddy race since his godlike fingers knew where the notes would be. That night he took her, crushed her, filled her, and awakened with his face wrapped in her hair.

"So what happened to him?" she asked.

"I told you—" Jack struggled to breathe.

"What did he *die* of?"

He took the dwindling joint and shifted her so that she pressed the place where he was one big pulse.

"Heart attack," he said. "It was horrible. I was in school—they had to call me out of class."

"Yeah, you said."

Cathy didn't seem satisfied, but Jack could think of nothing else to say. He ran his hands over her ribs, her back, and her sides, as though seeking an entry he hadn't found. She giggled.

"A heart attack is funny?"

"No." She quivered. "You're tickling me. Hey, c'mon, roll me another joint!"

Jack squirmed to free himself. Cathy seemed to weigh nothing, but she was grinding him into the frigid rock. As he pulled apart the mossy drug, his glance caught her watching dreamily. He lit the new joint with the dying stub of the old one.

"Can't we slow down a little?" he asked. "Can't we just *be* for a while?"

Cathy flopped onto her back so that her curls were squashed into the dirt. She sucked the joint and moved her hand in loops like a woman sewing. With the glowing point between her finger and thumb, she saluted the sky. Jack lay down beside her.

"Cathy," he said, "tell me about your family."

"What is this, revenge?"

"Yeah." He smiled at the fading sky.

He played with her leg and slid his hand under her skirt. Cathy laughed at him again.

"You're so predictable. You want sex, and you want symmetry. Your turn, my turn."

He gave up on her family but persisted with her leg.

"What's wrong with symmetry?" he asked.

Cathy scowled. "It's a downer, it's boring, it's a lie."

"So lie a little," he urged.

"I always lie." She smiled.

"Not always."

Jack guided her cool fingers up and down against him, hoping that she would pity him. He felt like a glowing steel rod shooting sparks.

"Okay, okay," she giggled. "I've told you, they're fucked up. I hate their guts, and they hate mine."

"But how can they— I mean, they must care about you. They're paying for college."

Jack knew only that Cathy's parents were rich and lived

somewhere on Long Island. There was a brother, a good boy who had gone to medical school. Cathy shook with laughter, and he ran his hands over her, seeking the "off" switch so that she would talk to him.

"That's a good one," she gasped. "They think they're paying for two things: to brainwash me in their establishment concentration camp and to keep me the fuck away from them."

Jack smiled. "Well, one out of two ain't bad. But why do you hate them so much? What did they do to you?"

"It's more what they *are*," she said slowly. "They're antilife. They want to kill everything."

"Yeah," he said. "I know what you mean."

He took the joint, drew it to his lips, and breathed its magic. He was spiraling into a vortex, like a bug in a half-clogged drain.

"Cathy, why me?" he asked slowly. "I mean, what are you doing with me? Why do you want me here? Aren't you afraid I'll kill your life too?"

Cathy giggled, and Jack laughed miserably as he tried to smooth the quivers from her body.

"You roll great joints." She grinned. "And you're a great fuck. You fuck me really well."

His heart thumped with excitement.

"But you might find someone who fucked you better."

"Maybe." She sat forward to rearrange herself. "I fuck who I want, when I want."

Jack pulled her hand back toward the tip of his volcano.

"No ..." She withdrew her hand. "You have great potential, though."

"Potential for what?"

"I don't know. I'm not sure." She smiled. "I haven't decided. But you're not a killer. You can pass for an establishment prick, but you have potential ... I love your stupid questions."

Happy with the compliment, Jack lowered his mouth to hers

and kissed her until her wiry arms pushed him back. She wanted more smoke, and he let her have it. He gazed hungrily into her half-closed eyes, where blues, greens, and browns swelled and spun in a viscous sea.

"Cathy. What color are your eyes?"

"No color." She blinked.

"How can they be no color?" he asked. "What color do you think they are?"

"I don't think they *are* any color. Why do you always have to label things? Color isn't something things *are*—it's something they *do*."

"Goethe," he murmured. "Goethe, *Zur Farbenlehre*. He thought Newton was wrong—color wasn't in light; it was in things."

"Cool." Cathy smiled. "I like your guys. You pick good guys. That's another reason I like you—you turn me on to your guys."

"My guys?"

"Yeah, Bach, Nietzsche, Goethe—your guys. You're a pusher, Jack." Cathy lowered her lids. "I think that's your thing. That's what you're going to do in life, go around pushing your guys."

A cold band tightened across his middle, dividing the warm silliness in his head from the force below. He kissed her again, more roughly this time, and pressed down on her with his full weight. Cathy squirmed.

"What?" he asked gutturally.

"Wait a minute."

Cathy broke free and bounded toward her purse, a great, big, black, shapeless thing. She pulled out an indigo beaded pouch, and before he could stop her, she raised her chin, closed her eyes, tossed a pill in her mouth, and swallowed hard.

"Oh, shit, Cath. What was that? What did you just take?"

She mocked him with sparkling eyes.

"Oh, fuck. What did you just take, Cath?"

He grabbed her shoulders as if to shake it out of her, but she laughed demonically.

"You promised we were going to take it easy today. *Scheiße, verdammt noch mal!*"

Cathy shuddered in delighted spasms. She loved nothing better than reducing him to German.

"Just some low-grade acid some guy gave me. Wanted to see what it's like to fuck on acid."

"What makes you think you're going to get fucked?" he asked.

"Lucky guess," she teased.

"Shit. I won't do it." Jack shook his head. "I should just go. I should just go and leave you here."

"No, you won't. You're going to fuck me now." Her voice lowered to a barely perceptible flame.

"I won't do it." He fought. "It turns me off, babysitting for you."

"Fuck me, Jack."

Anger washed at his arousal. "Don't you even want to wait for it to take effect?"

"Once you get going, you'll fuck me all day."

She walked toward him slowly, doing something with her body that made her purple top tremble and her cotton skirt sway. She stopped just in front of him and reached up to touch his hair with her fingertips. They traveled softly over his ears, his lips, his throat, his middle, and down and around behind him.

"Fuck me, Jack." Her command was the faintest breath.

He seized her and spun her while she clung to him, laughing ecstatically. They fell together, and he clambered on top of her and kissed her greedily. He dug his fingers into her curls and jabbed with trapped, impotent thrusts. Cathy laughed as she freed him, laughed to see him lose all sense, and taunted him with filthy whispers. His first push into her was almost a lunge, and he rammed harder as she shook with endless laughter. If only he could push those ripples away, until she was still and smooth again.

ॐ

Jack scanned the eighteen faces before him and wondered for the thousandth time why the seminar room was so dark. The rich wood wainscoting seemed to have crept up the walls like an insidious vine. Sculpted leaves jutted out from the woodwork and threatened to snag passersby. The windows, carved in a keyhole pattern, admitted mainly sound: sirens approaching the nearby hospital and shrieks of unknown fun on the quad. Today one of these keyholes revealed troubled streams washing the tiles of a nearby roof. On the walls, brass rubbings of flat, emaciated knights faced portraits of round men in black robes. At the far end, a portable green blackboard languished next to a fireplace framed by sooty stone scrolls. On the white ceiling, a fleur-de-lis trellis held a jungle of blossoms and leaves. Lions and goats peered out of this thicket suspended over the scholars' heads. Jack wished he were a student again so that his eyes could travel over it.

They had fought for seats in his Nietzsche seminar like countries vying to enter NATO. Eighteen, he said, no more than eighteen—you can't have a discussion with more than eighteen. The six from German he'd had to take, but for the other twelve slots, he'd held interviews. For days, students from English, French, comparative literature, philosophy, even Japanese and art history had boasted of what they could bring to the class. If only Ellie could have been there. But he had crossed a line, and he had to watch out. Knowing her body as well as he did, he couldn't face her across a seminar table.

Deprived of the voice he wanted most, he had chosen the others almost at random. Above all he had sought interesting people, but what aroused his interest, he couldn't say. He took two Japanese students and one from art history, a tall black girl with a lively intelligence. He rejected the redheaded girl from the party. She seemed bright enough, but she failed to stir him. She was more intriguing asleep than awake.

The only one he took immediately was the Indian boy with deep brown skin and a musical voice. He had come to Jack's office late in the process and said, with astonishing arrogance, that he would probably have to miss several classes because of campus interviews, but he would like to sit in when he could. What was his name—Goulash? Jack knew him instantly and, surprised at his own combativeness, told him he was welcome to sit in—when he could. Nietzsche, he sensed, would approve.

So here they sat on a black January afternoon, waiting to see what Jack was made of. Primed with caffeine, they were craving a challenge. Behind their eyes lurked a critical intelligence coiled to strike, waiting to assert itself at other people's expense. Had he picked the most aggressive, or was this trait ingrained in the whole pool? Goulash really was quite beautiful. Looking at his black hair, round lips, and shadowed eyes, Jack wondered how Ellie could want a faded man like himself.

He began professionally, automatically, walking them through the syllabus and saying what he expected. They frowned and jotted notes, maybe already planning the papers with which they would impress him. He asked how many of them read German, and only about half raised their hands. Funny, he thought, how people claimed to know Nietzsche without having heard his real voice. Jack kept his face set and told them that he would often read from the original texts. Nietzsche was a poet, a musician, and his meaning came partly from the sound of his words. One of the girls from German seemed to glow, and the tiniest flash of animosity flickered in Goulash's eye.

Okay, said Jack, enough preliminaries. Today they would start with some Nietzsche, one of his earliest stories, maybe his most terrible. They would read it and discuss it in the absence of theory, just them and Nietzsche seeking understanding. The students smiled and glanced at one another. No one spoke, but a murmur seemed to wash the room. To analyze a text in the absence of theory—was he a closet theory-phobe, then, this German? Maybe Jack Mannheim wasn't so hot after all. Jack declined to look at Goulash and eyed a burst of leaves on the ceiling.

Jack read them the passage first in English and then in German:

"There is an ancient story that King Midas hunted in the forest a long time for the wise Silenus, the companion of Dionysus, without capturing him. When Silenus at last fell into his hands, the king asked what was the best and most desirable of all things for man. Fixed and immovable, the demigod said not a word, till at last, urged by the king, he gave a shrill laugh and broke out into these words: 'Oh, wretched, ephemeral race, children of chance and misery, why do you compel me to tell you what it would be most expedient for you not to hear? What is best of all is utterly beyond your reach: not to be born, not to *be*, to be *nothing*. But the second best for you is—to die soon.'"

When he reread the tale in German, Jack tickled them with teasing consonants: "nicht *zu sein*, nichts *zu sein*." His voice flowed into an ocean of silence, unbroken by a rustle or scratch. The students waited, uncertain what he wanted, and laughed nervously at a screech of tires below. Nietzsche had written this story at twenty-seven, he said—just a few years older than they were now. He had written it when he was a hotshot young philology professor—he avoided Goulash's eyes—and everyone in academia had been awaiting his book on the origin of Greek tragedy. This was it—his first book, *The Birth of Tragedy*. It just wasn't quite what they had expected.

The students were writing, and Jack wished that he could see their notes. What would they do with those hen-tracked pages? It was as if they wanted evidence—but evidence of what?

"Why is this story here?" he demanded. "What does it mean? What is Nietzsche doing?"

His words dropped into silent waters. Terrified of exposing a lack of intelligence, his students stared at their pages and remained still. No one wanted to be a target for the others. He would have to wait until in one of them, the urge for glory overcame the fear of stupidity. It was a chemical reaction, always with the same result.

One of the girls from German broke the silence: "I think he's trying to show that the truth is too awful for people to stand."

Jack nodded, trying to reward her. "Certainly. But what is this truth?"

Several boys spoke up impatiently. If such a simpleminded response earned his approval, then anyone could say anything.

"Just what it says!" blurted one. "That it's better not to be than to be."

Goulash conferred with a fat, flushed girl, one of the ones who had identified herself as a German speaker.

"But that's not what Silenus *says*," his voice flowed. "He says it two different ways—not to *be*, to be *nothing*."

Jack's insides heated up.

"Right. What would you say is the difference between those two formulations?"

The black eyes smoldered, and the exquisite lids drooped.

"One is the negation of a positive ontology," he said softly. "The other is the assertion of a negative ontology."

"Hey, c'mon, Girish, no theory!" called a brown-haired girl from English.

Everyone laughed. Girish! So that was his name. Jack wouldn't forget it again.

Girish turned to the girl who had spoken, his eyes glittering in the smoky-gray skin around them.

"That wasn't theory," he asserted. "It was a description."

A wave of noise heaved as the younger students fought to challenge him. Did he believe in objective descriptions? Did he think you could make objective statements about what was *in* a text, in the absence of any theoretical orientation? Girish smiled ironically. There was something hypnotic in those mocking black eyes. He had elicited the challenge he wanted to raise by drawing it upon himself.

"I'm not asking the impossible," said Jack. "I'm not asking you to read without thoughts, without templates. It's just that Nietzsche has been appropriated by so many people—covered with so many layers of interpretations. I want you to look at these words, these words that he chose, and tell me what you think this means. I'm asking you to *read* him."

"He *is* asking the impossible," murmured the brown-haired girl, and there was a burst of muffled laughter.

To Jack's surprise, Girish seemed to like the game, though he subverted it at every chance.

"Well, I can't say I'm uninfluenced by preexisting texts," he began dryly. "But I believe it's significant that he states the truth twice. It suggests that there is no truth—not one that can be told in language. These are approximations; this is a parable, a translation."

"Like an asymptote!" cried the girl from art history. Jack tried to remember what an asymptote was. "It's a function—y'know." She struggled. "A function that keeps getting closer to a line, to a given value, as you move toward infinity, but it can never reach it. Like, the truth is that line, and the function is our representation of it."

The students nodded, concealing their jealousy against this outsider who had scored a goal.

"Exactly," said Girish. "Nietzsche was doing just what they asked, only they didn't know what they were asking. He's describing the origin of tragedy. Tragedy is a defense, a response to a truth that can't be revealed."

They circled, prodded, goaded him as they would a proud bull, and he laughed at their ineffective jabs. In a few weeks he would have a tenure-track job, and they would still be poking each other.

"I'm not sure how different these formulations are," challenged a girl with a whiny voice. "I mean, in German, they're separated only by the most minimal *s* sound. If you say it fast, you can't hear it."

"A German would," asserted one of the German students.

The air of the room erupted in hisses as each student compared the sounds: Nicht *zu sein*. Nichts *zu sein*. There were no actual Germans present, so they turned to Jack as the next best thing.

"It's significant," he said, uncertain as he listened to his own voice. "A German would hear two different things."

One of the Japanese students, a slender girl with shiny black hair, had been staring at him for some time. She must be waiting for an invitation to speak.

"Did you want to say something, Mariko?" he asked.

Her voice emerged in struggling bursts. "Yes. Please. I want to know, Why does the king ask Silenus this? Why ask the companion of Dionysus what is best for man? Why does he think he would know?"

Another murmur of admiration flowed, with jealousy roiling below the surface.

"Ah, now we're gettin' somewhere," said the jovial girl from English.

Jack smiled at Mariko and tried to conceal his shame. In thirty years of reading Nietzsche, he had never thought to ask this question.

"That's right," he said. "He could have asked anyone. Why ask the companion of Dionysus?"

"Yeah, why not just ask Dionysus?" asked one of the quick boys.

"He was probably drunk," quipped another.

Relaxed, inspired, the students offered theories and applauded one another. A companion, a *Begleiter*, what was that anyway? A lover? A groupie? A boy toy? Maybe the companion of Dionysus meant all of humanity. Maybe accosting Silenus meant catching and asking oneself. Jack's mind spiraled off to the hidden chamber where he was writing his book. Why ask the *Begleiter* of Dionysus what was best for humanity? Why would he or Dionysus know? Girish smiled at Jack, then raised his eyes to an inverted goat on the ceiling.

Beej says I'm fucked in the head. I tell him about this family therapy thing, and he says, You a head case, girl, you shittin' me. She get paid a hundred dollars an hour to listen to that?

We try to think who makes a hundred dollars an hour—hookers, lawyers, dealers—

No, he says. Dealers, they make more than that.

Beej is laughing. I love to make him laugh. He wheezes like a horse, and I give him shit about it.

Tell me more, he says.

Shit, this stuff burns. Why can't they make something that'll fuck you up that tastes halfway good? I guess that's the point—it has to hurt to get fucked up. It's like some guy sticking his cock in you—hurts less and less as you go along.

Hey, girl, quit drinkin' all that. Save some for me.

I tell Beej this stupid bitch listens while I tell the parasites to go fuck themselves, and they pay her a hundred bucks an hour. I hear them talking—insurance won't cover it, they have to pay for it themselves. Like I'm their problem, and for a hundred bucks an hour, they're solving me.

They solvin' you? Shit, for ten grand I put a hit on you, I solve you permanently.

I punch his shoulder, but he grabs me, or I miss. I don't know, I'm too fucked up. Beej wrestles me down like I'm made of feathers and says he's sorry for these two white fools.

How they make you anyway? You a mutant or somethin'?

No, I say, they're the mutants. I'm normal, y'know, like when two blind people have a kid who can see.

You normal.

Yeah, compared to them.

Huh.

So I ask him, Where are your parents? What are your parents like, if you feel so sorry for mine?

BJ hauls himself up and rolls a joint. Good, I could use a hit. Tastes better than this shit, like lava that rolled through a garbage dump.

What happened to your mom? I ask. Why are you with Aunt Lou?

Fuck you, Misty, he says.

He drops the weed and with spread fingers rakes crumbled leaves from the sidewalk. The flare of his lighter reveals his set face.

They're shitting in their pants, I say, over this high school thing.

What high school thing? He drops the crumbs in a bag.

Oh, this Experimental School, where they fuck up your mind until you're ready for the Gargoyle Palace, then they fuck it up some more. Then you're ready for some fucking job where you can never think or feel.

You crazy, girl.

Good, he's laughing again.

That school, I say, they kicked me out.

They kick you out? What you do, try to burn the place?

No, I just didn't fucking go.

His wheezing laugh tickles me.

Shit, they good. They tell you if you don't go, you can't go?

Yeah, that's right. So right now, they're running around—

I try to get up. Shit, I'm—

Girl, you better stay close to the ground.

Beej catches me and eases me down so that he's sitting close behind me. He holds the joint in one hand and puts it sometimes to his mouth, sometimes to my mouth. He warms his other hand between my legs.

So they're running around like always, fucking wimp, fucking bitch, what are we gonna *do*, shit, what are we gonna *do*? I tell them, just send me to the neighborhood school, but they say, no, it's got to be a private school. So I ask why, and they start shitting in their pants again, because they can't say the real reason. They're so fucking scared of black people, they think I'll, like, *catch* something from them.

You said it, girl, first thing you say all day make sense. 'Cept more likely we catch somethin' from you.

His crab-like hand claws between my legs.

Fuck you, Beej.

Fuck you too, girl. What you gonna do, you gonna go to school with the black kids?

Right now I'm not going to any school, I say. It's too much fun watching them run around having fits. The bitch says it's against the law, me not going to school. She's afraid somebody'll come after them.

Ooh, they breakin' the law! You got 'em on the two things that scare the shit out of white people—bein' in the hood an' breakin' the law.

His laugh shakes me.

You should hear my grandmother, that fuckin' cow, she calls you all *Schwarzes*.

Schwarzes, what that?

It's German for black. Except she calls the Puerto Ricans that too.

Shit, she mix us up with the Puerto Ricans?

His pushes me up to stretch his legs.

Yeah, she's a fuckin' Nazi. It's all the same to her.

Yeah. Old people like that sometimes.

I try a sip of brown fire. Almost gone. Shit, did I drink all that?

Beej. How come you won't tell me anything about your family?

Cause I don't know nothin'. Ain' nothin' to tell.

He rests his chin on my head and kisses my hair.

C'mon, you must know something. What does Aunt Lou say?

She say they dead.

Oh.

A distant siren pierces the night.

That what she say.

Why, you know different?

I rise and fall with BJ's breath.

Well, Tyrell, he got this friend, he say my mama run off when we real small. He say she run off to LA, she a junkie whore.

You believe him?

Could be. He say she too fine for this place.

The siren dies, leaving only the swish of cars.

You ever try to look for her?

Everybody say she dead. She die in a car crash when I was two and Tanesha was just a baby. Just this one fool, he say she a junkie whore in LA.

He probably doesn't know what he's talking about.

Yeah.

His voice is just breath. I push my back into him and wiggle.

Beej.

What? You gonna ask me if I got a father now?

He tenses like he's about to throw me off.

You got a father?

Shit, I *got* one …

Instead of pushing me off, he closes his arms around me like a seat belt.

So how'd you end up with Aunt Lou? She really your aunt?

She my grandma's sister, my mama's aunt. My grandma, she die of cancer ten years back.

Shit.

Yeah.

I like Aunt Lou.

You say that now, girl. You just don't know her yet.

He jounces me playfully.

Aw, c'mon, she's all right.

Yeah, whatever you say.

Beej turns me until I'm facing him.

You gonna be nice to me now?

He kisses me and runs his warm lips toward my ear.

You got such soft hair, all silky … Misty, you fine, girl, you fine.

Jack worked his nose through Ellie's thick brown hair and maneuvered until his lips met her warm neck. Over the brown blur, his left eye caught the blue pulse of her clock radio, a cruel metronome marking their remaining minutes.

He had reached Ellie over an hour late. His seminar's second meeting on the Apollonian and the Dionysian had so excited the students they had followed him back to his office. They had settled down on his tables and floor, fingered his books, and jabbered about dance, excess, chaos, and death. He'd arrived at Ellie's frustrated and apologetic, but she'd laughed and called them his maenads. She'd thrown her arms around him and dragged him unprotesting to her soft, pink bed.

As always, Ellie seemed to read his thoughts. "When do you have to be back?"

"Oh, around six, I guess. Tonight's my night to make dinner."

He felt her think this was an awful way to live, planning your life around meals. Ellie ate when she was hungry and came home when she wanted new surroundings in which to read. She arched her back so that her lower body pressed him, as though to confirm what she had sensed. He was growing aroused again.

"What's for dinner?" she asked teasingly.

Jack joined the game and announced the menu between biting kisses across her back.

"Mmm—stir-fry chicken—mushrooms—broccoli—"

"Broc-coli," she growled, a good, biting word.

Jack rocked against her. Ellie tried to twist around so that she could face him, but he held her firmly in place.

Suddenly she blurted, "Girish says your class is good."

The rocking stopped. Jack pulled at her shoulder until she faced him. Her eyes were studying ripples in the damp sheet.

"Ellie."

Jack inhaled slowly. The question he wanted to ask lay like the thinnest net cast on an ocean of desire.

"What is there between you and Girish? Am I—interfering with something? I don't want to—"

Ellie sighed. "We're not together, if that's what you mean. For a while I wanted to be, but he didn't want that."

She breathed into the silence.

"He wasn't there today," said Jack.

"I know. He has an interview at Rice." She raised her brown eyes to his.

"I can see why they want him. He's very smart."

"Yeah, he's really bright." She flexed her toes against his foot.

"What about you?" he asked. "When's your campus visit to San Diego?"

"Monday and Tuesday. I fly out on Friday."

He nodded. "That's a good sign that they called you this early. You must be one of three finalists. I'd like to help if I can, get you ready—"

"Oh, you're helping me."

Her eyes shone mischievously, and she gave him an appreciative nudge.

"So—there's nothing between you and Girish?"

He sought signs of deceit.

"Well, we're friends …"

"But you're not—"

"Am I sleeping with him? No."

Ellie pulled herself up onto one arm and caressed him with her free hand.

"I'm sorry," he said. "I didn't mean to ask you that. I just had to know. I have no right—"

Her hands rubbed the heavy muscles of his arms and the curling gray hair of his chest.

"This isn't about rights." Her brown eyes glowed. "It's about wanting. Wanting and rights don't go together. I'm with you now because I want to be and because you want to be with me. If either one of us stops wanting this, we both have to stop. Not because of anyone else. This is between us."

Her strength of will stirred him. *Young logic,* he thought. *That is very young logic, just willing other people away.* In an instant he was on top of her. Lust broke through the network of law, and shame and jealousy bobbed like scraps of seaweed on the heaving surface.

A voice spoke from inside of him—his voice?

"I want you. I want you all for me."

"Yes," she whispered.

Ellie wrapped her arms and legs around him and clung with an animal embrace. Jack lost his fear of hurting her and thrust wildly, digging for pleasure. Ellie gripped him until her widespread fingers gouged his back. Her voice came in gasps with each push. They lay in blackness, clinging together as the force field around them buckled. Ellie grasped him, sweating, straining, eager to give him the pleasure he craved. The field collapsed, and he held her tightly, terrified she would be torn from him in the chaotic flood. He was sobbing, and she raised a hand to his wet hair.

"It's okay, Jack. It's good, Jack. It's going to be all right."

He lay in her arms, unable to speak as she stroked him and rocked him against her. He raised his head to see the clock. 5:27.

"May I take a shower?" he asked.

Ellie nodded and kissed him. She hummed as she fetched him a towel.

Her pitiful, uncertain shower reminded him of the gap between their lives: the young one of poverty and freedom; the waning one of restriction and luxury. Dreamily, he soaped himself and smiled at the froth her gel produced. He was washing himself in a young girl's shower, and he felt like a bear in her boudoir. Laughing gently, he rubbed his chest and shed curly gray hairs on her floor. As he dried himself, he vibrated with pride and pleasure.

Ellie's humming had blossomed into singing. She had dressed herself and made the bed but was struggling to untangle her hair. As she studied her reflection, she swayed unconsciously to twelve-eight time.

"Sehet ihn aus Lieb und Huld …"

A dirge—the saddest melody in the world, the opening of the *St. Matthew Passion*.

Jack glanced at her uneasily. "That's an odd thing to be singing."

Ellie looked up, startled.

"Oh, we're learning it in choir," she said. "For Good Friday. It's so beautiful."

She gave up on her hair and returned to the music, defaulting to an "ah" when she forgot the German words. Jack rubbed himself, fascinated. Rising in a minor arpeggio, the melody warmed her room of Botticellis and bears. Ellie was an alto, entrusted by Bach with this call to mourn human cruelty. Her voice was just right for his music—controlled and precise but not too full. She moved through the descending line like a gymnast on a balance beam, leaping so perfectly to the major sixth that even after this odd interval she landed gracefully on the next note.

Jack dropped his towel to place his hands on the lovely muscles driving the music. He stood behind Ellie and rocked along, sharing the force of her diaphragm and ribs. Her voice trailed off, and she turned to face him. Playfully, she rubbed his wet fur.

"Nobody's going to say anything when you show up with wet hair?"

Jack rolled his eyes toward the window, where icy drops were pecking their way in. The cold snap of December had dissolved into black Chicago rain.

"Forgot my umbrella." He grinned. "Absentminded professor."

Ellie strained upward to kiss him.

"Guess that means you'll have to come back and get it, huh?"

"Guess that means I'll have to come back and get it."

Jack caught her around the waist and squeezed her affectionately.

"Hey," he asked, reaching for his pants, "have you ever been to a bas mitzvah?"

"No, why?" She looked up at him strangely.

"Oh, we're—I'm going to one soon. Sam's daughter. He invited us."

Ellie broke into a broad laugh, as did everyone at the mention of Sam.

"Oh, that'll be good. God, what a concept, a little Sam!"

"Two of them." Jack smiled. "This is Rachel, his daughter. She's turning thirteen."

"Oh, a coming-of-age ritual." Her voice tightened.

While Jack fastened his buckle, she watched like an anthropologist intrigued by the male movements of dressing.

"I'd better go," he said, gazing down tenderly.

"I know." She smiled. "Can I see you before San Diego?"

Their meetings always ended like this as they sought a fresh opening between their universes.

"Let's see," he said. "Tomorrow's no good. Department meeting. Wednesday is family therapy. God—Thursday?"

Ellie shook her head sadly. "Thursday's choir—seven to nine thirty."

"What about before then?" he asked.

"Well, I have to eat."

"I'll help you eat." He smiled lasciviously.

"Well, okay. I've been trying to get my talk finished ... And I have to pack—"

"I'll help you pack."

He pulled her to him and kissed her greedily.

Ellie smiled, almost convinced. "Okay, Thursday. I'll call you if I run out of time."

CHAPTER 6

MITZVAH

THEY CALLED IT A *SHUL*. For Jack, no two concepts could have been more different: a school, a place of learning and discovery; and a church, a place of lies, affectation, and wishful thinking. The synagogue had thick stone walls like a church but it was rounder, more organic, almost as wide as it was long. And so new. The polished wood benches gleamed, and tangy glue betrayed its presence under the bright green carpet.

An unfamiliar prickling drew Jack's hand to his head. The yarmulke. As he entered, Bea had nudged him and pointed to a box of caps, and she'd pinned one to his hair as Jessie looked on, amused. The nerves and muscles of his scalp tingled as though a round insect had landed on his head. But he had to wear it—all the men did. He thanked God he didn't have to wear a prayer shawl as well.

Sam greeted Jack with a full embrace and kissed Bea and Jessie on both cheeks. Only Jessie returned his kisses. Ruth, Sam's curly-haired wife, seemed frazzled, but with her usual good humor, she called orders in an accent stronger than Sam's.

"Tell Jerry to get out here! What's he doin' in there anyway? So good to see ya, Jack."

Rachel, far calmer than her parents, stood beaming in her purple dress and shoes.

"So glad you could come, Mr. Mannheim," she said with poise beyond her thirteen years.

Jessie looked at her with amazed disgust and muttered, "Looks like a purple cow."

Bea glared at her, and Jack choked on a laugh, praying that no one had heard.

There was no denying the resemblance. Short, plump, and dark like her father, Rachel had Sam's full lips and liquid brown eyes. The bright purple of her dress couldn't have been worse chosen, emphasizing her bulges and swells.

"Milka," whispered Jessie, reading Jack's thoughts with demonic accuracy. Milka, the best-selling chocolate in Germany, was sold by the kilo to hungry old ladies. Like them, he had always been fond of the happy purple cows on its wrapper.

But Rachel was lovely. As she kissed the worshippers and accepted their good wishes, she exuded warmth equal to Sam's. Jack's friend stood by, joking noisily, but his boisterousness couldn't mask his pride. Sam looked at his daughter with gratitude and awe, as though wondering how someone so ridiculous could have created such a child. When Jack glanced at Jessie, he felt only fear. In her silky white dress, she glided like a swan, but there was no knowing what she would do. He would never dare organize a ritual around her.

The Loeb family took their places on the polished front pew. Ruth adjusted a barrette in Rachel's hair, and Sam restrained Jerry, whose heels thumped the bench. It would be a regular Shabbat service, Sam had explained. There was no special liturgy for the coming of age. A boy or girl just stood up one day to bless the Torah as an adult and accepted responsibility to live by its laws. From that day forward, he or she was mature, answerable to God and the community. Jack tried to think when he had become an adult, and he knew instantly. There had been no blessings on that day.

A sudden hush spread, and all eyes turned to the front of the synagogue. Covered with blue velvet, the Torah slowly bobbed forward. Jack braced himself against a sickening unease. People on the aisles reached out to touch the scroll, women with their prayer books and men with their shawls. Jack didn't dare look at Jessie, since he felt an awful urge to laugh.

These were adults, intelligent people, but they believed they were absorbing the divine. Was it a metaphor, or was it faith? Whatever it was, he preferred it to Christian cannibalism, the eating and drinking of Christ. Did they actually think that by touching this text, they could draw its wisdom into their minds? He tried to think of a text he could worship this way, but none occurred to him, not Goethe, not even Nietzsche. No single text was sacred in itself, just all of them put together. To Jack's surprise, Jessie leaned out to stroke the blue velvet, her thin features softened by reverence.

A low voice murmured, and Jack's hoarded breath flowed. He recognized the words, and his tension melted. A deep-voiced reader described the escape from Egypt—the pursuit and parting of the Red Sea. Jack had always loved that parting, and Handel's chords from *Israel in Egypt* crashed in his head. Seven readers rose to narrate the escape and bless the text before and after each lesson. The chanting fascinated Jack not just for its style but also for its ingenious shorthand. Running from right to left, the foreign characters contained no vowels but tracked the dips and turns around a main tone. The marks that Jack's brain and fingers turned to music followed the same principle, but they had evolved differently. He studied the mysterious marks and strained to break the code.

Rachel stood. Jack's heart beat for her as though she were his own daughter. He worried about the blunders she might make, but Rachel was fearless. She faced two hundred worshippers with a smile of joy, and her clear, young voice never wavered. As she sang of the parting waters, her round body glowed. How could a thirteen-year-old girl have achieved this dignity? Jack glanced nervously to one side, but Jessie was following her, engrossed. Feeling her father's eyes on her, she looked up defiantly.

"Looks like a friggin' grape."

No, thought Jack, this fat, chanting thirteen-year-old was the most beautiful girl he had ever seen. Sam was gazing at his daughter enraptured, his full lips following her tones. Like Rachel, he seemed to radiate light, and the energy they emitted formed a brilliant, connecting arc. Sam raised his hand to his eye. Ruth passed him a tissue and squeezed his arm.

Rachel began her haftorah passage, a lengthier, more demanding tale:

"Now Deborah, a prophetess, the wife of Lappidoth, was judging Israel at that time. She used to sit under the palm of Deborah between Ramah and Bethel in the hill country of Ephraim; and the people of Israel came up to her for judgment."

Jack pictured a procession of shepherds, masons, and mothers wandering up to be judged by a young girl. How did they know she was a prophet? Why did they respect her words? Despite the pull of the forceful young voice, Jack's mind began to roam. How much time would he have to work today? Three, maybe four hours, before the dinner and the party. No music before sundown, Sam had explained, "and it ain't a party without dancin'." This early in the quarter, Jack had no papers to grade. For a few precious hours, he could think about his book—the Apollonian, the Dionysian, the Nazis, the Shoah. Somewhere inside him he could feel the words. His idea was stirring, still mute, sighing in a barely perceptible murmur.

An appreciative stir drew him back to the ritual. Rachel had finished, and she returned to her parents. Sam's shoulders shook as he covered her with kisses. After several more blessings, the Torah was withdrawn, its exit generating less excitement than its appearance. People thronged around Rachel, Ruth, and Sam, touching and praising them as they had blessed the sacred text. Jerry ran off to whoop with a pack of his friends outside. Even in this maelstrom, Rachel maintained her poise, her brown eyes glowing, her cheeks flushed. Jack longed to escape, but Bea pulled him into the fray.

"You have a lovely daughter, Sam," she said.

Jack held his friend for a bizarre moment as Sam clung to him and sobbed. Sam seemed to be melting, laughing, crying, as he exchanged handshakes and hugs. Ruth rolled her eyes and shook her head as she patted her hysterical husband and composed daughter.

"See ya later!" Sam called to Jack and Bea. "It's gonna be a great party!"

Jack broke from the clinging crowd and emerged into the midday light.

"Where's Jessie?" asked Bea.

They had lost her in the swirl, or more likely, she had lost them. Jack scanned the crowd for her long, white form but could find it nowhere. Damn. She had taken advantage of their goodwill to perform her usual disappearing act.

Jack smiled and shook his head. "She's done it again. Maybe she'll be home. Does she have a key?"

"Yeah, I think so," said Bea, her lips tense. "How does she always manage to do this?"

"I don't know," he sighed. "I'm surprised she wanted to come at all."

"So was I." Bea kicked a crescent of hardened snow. "I think she hates missing things."

"Yeah, that's true. Well, at any rate, she's gone now."

He breathed icy air and squinted across an expanse of white. In the past week, snow had crusted the city, and the park dazzled him in the noonday light. The cold tightened his face, and the brilliant white burned his eyes. Sunlight was such a rarity in February that he was longing to soak it up.

"Shall we do a lap around?" he asked.

Bea hesitated, as though calculating how long it would take. A lap meant a march across this snowy steppe, then over the bridge to the lakefront. They would walk along the icy water, past the castle where the land bulged out. Then they would pass through the tunnel and head back toward home. He and Bea made this circuit in all kinds of weather. They were hardy walkers, and Jack's legs ached for movement after an hour of sitting.

"Oh, I guess so," said Bea. "But I should get to the clinic. Ginelle's filling in for me, and I told her I'd be there around noon."

"Tell her it ran long," he suggested. "She'll never know."

Bea glanced toward the bridge. Under her glasses, her blue eyes sparkled as she considered this minor revolt.

"What color do you think it'll be?" he asked, initiating a game they still played.

In twenty years of walks, Jack had never known the lake to be the same color twice. It varied from green to turquoise to gray, and on some clear mornings, close to purple. Bea fastened the uppermost snap of her collar, and her upturned eyes scanned the sky.

"Oh, today? Blue jay gray, I bet. Blue jay color, with lots of whitecaps."

"That's what I'd say," he answered, disappointed at their perfect accord. "Maybe a little on the purple side."

Bea met his eyes and laughed. "God, purple! That dress!"

Jack seconded her opinion, musing as they set out across the park. His senses were still adjusting. Fighting the wind felt different from struggling to be heard over an indoor crowd. A noisy room stole his voice's resonance, but the wind snatched the words as they left his lips.

"Why do you think they let her wear it?" asked Bea.

"Oh, probably it's her favorite color. After all, it's her day."

He dimly recalled Jessie going through a pink phase, which had been mercifully brief.

"Yeah, I guess you're right," she answered. "Anyway, that was nice."

"It was wonderful."

He drew burning breaths in time to the crunch of snow under his feet.

"She must have worked hard to get ready. All that Hebrew—all that chanting!"

"I think the chanting makes it easier," said Jack. "It's easier to remember a word paired with a tone."

"Yeah, I guess that's right."

Bea had always assented on matters of music, since she trusted his ear. She seemed to love listening but had little talent and had left the piano after a childhood of militantly enforced practicing. Jack's musical sense inspired her admiration as a form of perception that eluded her.

With even steps he trudged in silence, over black paths that sliced the white in random curves. Jack's numb left cheek told him that the reigning wind was blowing from the north. When they reached the lake, this icy current would push them down into the tunnel's mouth.

"Jack." Bea spoke suddenly. "We have to decide what to do about Jessie."

That was Bea, efficiency personified. She couldn't enjoy a fifteen-minute walk without turning it to some purpose. Jack spotted the bridge ahead, inviting them down to the water.

"Well," he said, "the Experimental School will probably take her back in September."

Bea's voice tightened. "But only if she proves herself in the meantime. She's got to go *somewhere*, Jack. Christ, she's sixteen. It's illegal. The state could take her away from us."

"Oh, I think it's legal at sixteen," he said. "I think you can drop out."

Bea turned to scan his face. "But we can't let her do that! She's intelligent!"

"Probably intelligent enough to figure out that she needs to go back to school again, eventually."

Bea stalked silently up the ramp, and Jack followed. The bridge was an odd structure, starting up, then doubling back on itself, leading to an arch that spanned Lake Shore Drive. How could he explain to a medieval man that a bridge had been built to span a road? The highway with its encrusted traffic swished like a river, and he was grateful for the elevated path. Bea had been right, as always. The choppy lake glinted with cerulean, blue jay spots. Mentally, Jack shook himself and turned his thoughts back to her.

"Well, look. She keeps saying she wants to go to public school. Why not let her?"

Bea looked at him, amazed. "I can't believe you're saying this. What's come over you, anyway?"

Jack winced, fearing what he might have revealed. His split life had become so easy it had almost begun to feel natural.

"What do you mean?" he asked.

He skidded and grabbed for the icy rail.

"Oh, I don't know. You just haven't been yourself lately. You don't seem to take anything seriously."

Jack arranged his face in what he hoped was a parody of his serious self. It must have worked, since Bea began to laugh. The north wind scoured bald spots in her closely cropped black hair.

"I know this is serious," he said. "I just think if we approach it too seriously, we won't be able to deal with it. We have to go with her, not against her. We have—" A hobo sentence popped up. "It's like the Borg. Resistance is futile."

"That's it!" she exclaimed. "That's what I mean. You never used to say things like that. The Borg—where are you getting that?"

He remembered the source and recoiled. Christ! It was Ellie. He could see her now, suspended over him, her long brown hair tickling his face. "Resistance is futile ..."

"Oh, I don't know," he said measuredly. "Must have been one of my students. But it makes sense. There are things you can't fight. Maybe we should just let her go to public school and find her own way."

Bea shook her head. "I should have known better than to ask a Nietzschean."

"Or have a child with one," he laughed.

"Oh, she's your daughter, all right," she bantered.

Jack tried to respond, but he couldn't think of a single trait Bea and Jessie had in common. Maybe they looked a little alike around the nose.

Bea stopped dead. "We can't let her go to a public school."

His gloved hand settled on her sleeve.

"Well, what are the alternatives?" he asked. "Catholic school? They'd never take her, and if they did, they'd throw her out in a week. She's intelligent, but she uses her intelligence in different ways than we do."

"A private school ..." she urged.

"They cost twenty thousand a year. And she probably wouldn't get anything out of it, not at this age."

"I can't believe you're defending her like this—just giving in to her!"

Bea was walking again now. She must have sensed the futility of standing like a figurehead in the wind. Jack withdrew his arm so that she could move more easily.

"The public school—" she stammered. "You know what goes on there. They'll beat her up, or worse—they'll give her drugs—"

"I know," he said. "But she has to see that for herself."

"By the time she sees it she might be *dead*, Jack." Bea's contralto voice broke.

They entered the orbit of the round stone castle. Jack tried to comfort her, but she pulled away.

"I went to public school—" He faltered. "I took drugs—"

"Yeah, I know," she sighed.

It was like the music. Responsible from girlhood, Bea had never tried a single illegal drug—not even in college, not even in 1968. Jack had often asked why—as a scientist, wasn't she curious? But Bea told him that she drew the line at experimenting with her own mind. How could you call it science if you were experimenter and subject both? She liked her brain the way it was, and there were some experiments you didn't do. But as with the music, she seemed uneasy, almost jealous of sensations and experiences only he had known.

"Why did you do it?" she asked.

"Oh, I was curious, I guess."

The castle's rough gray stones split the wind.

"I never liked it much. I stopped right after—"

"Yeah, I know," Bea said quickly. "You did it for her."

Jack's feet crunched the ice in steady bites. The north wind froze the back of his head and slowed the movement of his thoughts.

"Jessie will find that too," he said. "She has to try it, and she'll learn that there's not much to it."

"I'm just afraid what'll happen while she's learning all this."

The sarcasm in her voice tightened his belly. Bea was against him today, for reasons he didn't understand.

The path descended toward the mouth of the tunnel. Jack braced himself for the walk between oozing walls painted with menacing figures. Bob Marley leered at Jim Morrison, who was crowned with a halo of spray-painted fire. Even in February, the tunnel reeked of urine, and he thanked God there were no small children to tear his nerves with shrieks. Instead he filled the stinking darkness with his own voice:

"Well, we've still got our family project. This week we've got to pick a date."

"Christ, that party," moaned Bea. Her voice returned in unsettling waves.

Last week the therapist had asked them again, while Jessie had watched with a mocking smile. If they refused, they were uncooperative, but if they proceeded, they were headed for humiliation. A party! Sometimes Jack had invited friends for dinner, but he had never attempted a party. Neither he nor Bea liked big gatherings, and efforts to introduce her medical friends to his literary ones had always failed. The healers and the readers squinted at each other and could barely span their river of differences with a net of conversation. Having so many unknown bodies in his house made Jack nervous. God knew who Jessie would invite.

Jack breathed the crisp, untainted air as they emerged from the tunnel into the crusted park. Beside the black path, snow persisted despite trampling and yellow holes.

"Let's just do it," he said. "Let's pick a date."

"I've heard those words before." She smiled. "Didn't your proposal go something like that?"

"Probably," he laughed. "I recycle phrases a lot. Anyway, that didn't turn out too badly, did it?"

Bea gave him a sideways glance. "Ask me again in twenty years."

Jack assembled a calendar before his eyes. "Let's see. Today's the seventh, right? Should we go for a Friday or a Saturday?"

"A Friday, I'd say," reflected Bea. "Saturday there's too much competition. People have concert tickets."

"Okay." He calculated. "So next Friday—"

"The thirteenth? No way. Besides, it's too soon."

"Yeah, you're right." He sighed. "Well, there's the twentieth."

Bea stopped, raised her eyes to the sky, and repeated, "The twentieth. The twentieth. What do I have to do on the twentieth?"

"I could do it on the twentieth," he said slowly, awaiting her response.

"Yeah, I guess I could too."

She looked into his eyes so suddenly she startled him, and his lips spread in a slow smile.

"I think we have a date. Let's put on a show," he said. "You invite the doctors, and I'll invite the—"

He couldn't think of a word for what he and his colleagues did. "Literary scholars," they called themselves, but it lacked the purposeful ring of "doctor."

"The nerds?" suggested Bea.

"Yeah, that's us, the nerds. Sam's pretty cool, though," he added quickly.

"Let's just hope Sam and Ruth can make it," she laughed.

He and Bea had almost completed their circuit. At the next corner, he would turn north onto their street of brownstones, and Bea would rush on toward the medical center. Already she seemed to have forgotten him, now that the party was imminent.

"I'd say thirty, maybe forty people. We'll need a caterer. God, there's not much time … I'll start telling my crowd today."

"I'll tell Sam tonight," he promised. "Oh—what time will you be back?"

"Hard to say," she answered. "I'll have to meet you there. It's in the synagogue, right?"

"Yeah, they're all set up for parties. Just go in and keep walking toward the back, Sam said, past where we were this morning."

"Okay. I'll see you then."

He reached out to touch her, but she was on her way. Below her indigo jacket, her legs moved energetically. Jack glanced at his watch and saw that they had made good time. It was only twelve thirty, and he would have four hours to write. He hoped that Jessie wouldn't be home.

Jack's front door yielded grudgingly to reveal a room full of green light. The last eastern rays were mingling with the life-giving color of his plants. A serene stillness told him that Jessie must be out. Only electrical hums broke the peace. The piano, afloat in a gay, greenish haze, beckoned him and begged for a tune. He hurried into the kitchen to wash his hands, then played the opening melody of the *St. Matthew Passion*.

Could he— No. He had to work, and Ellie did as well. Both kept the unspoken agreement that weekends were for work, unlike weekday afternoons. Ellie couldn't call him at home, and he never called her from his house. At her desk five blocks away, she would be writing about Gide and running her hand through her flowing hair. She always did that, he'd noticed, when she was thinking intensely.

To clear his head, Jack wandered back to his study. He gazed at the snow, the bare tree, and the birds flitting in the afternoon sun. Did they have enough to eat? Yes, Bea must have fed them this morning. His mind bubbled, and thoughts burst up, bearing no clue of how they had emerged.

The Shoah. The sheer stupidity of killing people like Ruth and Rachel and Sam. The waste disgusted him almost more than the crime—the arrogance of one people to think that they could simply do away with another. In their systematic way, the Germans were atoning, but Jack rarely spoke of the Shoah in class. It was time he dealt with it, but what could he say? For two years he had been listening to people's stories against Nietzsche and Mann as keynotes. Not the survivors' narratives, but those of the aggressors. What fascinated him was their attempts to justify the murders. His mother's logic ran through all of it, a seething desire to clean. At his father's urging, he and she had fled the Reich before its armies could claim him. An uncle in the Bronx had helped them settle, and his father said that fleeing was the best thing he had ever done. Jack's mother had never been so sure.

Now as Jack read Himmler and Goebbels, their familiarity sickened him. The propagandists would look at his body with pleasure and laugh at Rachel in her purple dress. The Nazis used words that had passed his own lips, though never in the same context: *einordnen—aufräumen—Schönheit.* As he swam in their phrases, a red flash roused him. A male cardinal was shifting his head in spasmodic jerks.

Suddenly it struck him. There was nothing Dionysian about the Shoah, because it was pure order, pure form. It had nothing to do with will, intoxication, or mass hysteria. It wasn't Dionysian—it was Apollonian, and this talk about frenzy was a myth. The Shoah was a sheer drive toward order, but order without intelligence or creative purpose. Ultimately, any will to order culminates in destruction.

Jack groped for paper and wrote excitedly without consulting his notes. Maybe it was obvious, maybe it had been said, but seeded by this thought, his whole book crystallized. He felt the sadness of Mann's ironic downfalls and heard the raging cadences of Nietzsche's voice. He cursed the Nazis' mad, Procrustean appropriation of this philosopher-artist. He would write the introduction today, right now, without—

The phone's bell pierced his thoughts. Stabbed in midsentence, he tried to ignore it, but the blade worked its way in. *Verdammt.* Well, he would go see who it was. Probably just some telemarketer. It could be Bea, saying she would be home early, or Jessie in need of a ride. No, Jessie hadn't asked for a ride in years, her disgust at being seen with him having eclipsed her need for transportation. Or maybe—God— His heart matched the meter of Bea's recorded voice.

"Hi. You've reached 773-643-1298. We can't come to the phone right now, but please leave a message, and we'd be glad to get back to you. Bye!"

He breathed through red, palpitating instants.

"Jackie. You there?" A husky alto.

His mother talked through answering machines, not to them, addressing the people they were designed to shield.

"Hi, Mom."

"Ah, so you're there. Where you been? I called you today already three times, but you're never there."

With maddening confidence, she seemed to know that if he had been there, he would have picked up.

"We were at a bas mitzvah, Mom. My friend's daughter, she had her bas mitzvah today."

Inwardly, he smiled as he imagined her response.

"Bas mitzvah. One of those Jewish things?"

"Yeah, Mom, *echt jüdisch*. It was nice. The little girl, she recited in Hebrew about the parting of the Red Sea."

His mother exhaled in a rush. "Oh. So you're not working today?"

"Yeah, Mom, I was. I was just—"

Her voice rolled over his. "Oh, so you got time for the Red Sea but not for your mother?"

"Yeah, Mom, I can talk," he said wearily.

The resurgence of his own accent dismayed him. German flowed with a cyclic rhythm, and with his mother, he found himself speaking German with English words.

"Me and Rudi, we were talkin' about Jessie," she said. "About how she's no good, about how she got thrown out of school."

"What did Rudi say?" he asked, his hand tightening on the receiver.

He wanted to end this conversation as soon as possible.

"Oh, he thinks like me, you gotta take a firm hand. *Streng*, you know? Otherwise she'll think she's the boss and do whatever she wants. She'll end up in jail like her father."

Today she was going further than usual. By mutual consent, she left the past untouched and dealt only in vague prophecies of doom.

"Rudi said all that?" he asked mildly, knowing that she attributed her opinions to various authorities.

"Yeah."

She had always been such a good liar.

"Mom," he protested, "that was thirty years ago. That was a mistake. A lot of people got arrested that day, and none of them did anything."

Her voice rose. "Yeah? And that was another mistake, in seventy-one? You didn't do nothing that time either? They made a lot of mistakes with you."

"That's right, Mom. They made two mistakes."

"Huh," she grunted. "I'm just glad your father wasn't alive to see that. You in that *Dreckloch* ..."

"Yeah, I know, Mom," he rushed. "And it was good of you to bail me out. I turned out okay anyway, and Jessie will too."

"She'll turn out good if you make her turn out good—*sonst klappt das nicht.*"

His mother had never heard of the Borg, but as long as he could remember, her toneless German had conveyed the futility of resistance.

"Where is she today?" she demanded. "You even know where she is? You're writing your book, listening to *Juden*. Probably she's out *mit den Schwarzen*. She's gonna get AIDS—"

"Mom!" he broke in. "She was with us at the bas mitzvah. And black people aren't any more likely to give you AIDS than white people!"

"That's not what I hear."

He cursed her silently and wondered whether Jessie's hatred of her mother came anywhere near his own.

"Anyway," he shot, "*das ist nicht deine Sache!*"

"Yeah?" she answered calmly. "When I bailed you out of jail those two times, *war das auch nicht meine Sache?*"

He could see no way out. "A child, a grandchild, that's two different things."

"Yeah? Well, you take care of your kid, and you won't have to worry about what's *nicht meine Sache.*"

"Okay, Mom, I'll do that," he sighed. "What about you? How you doing?"

Her voice lost its booming quality. "Okay. *Mein Kreislauf, mein Herz*, they're not so good."

"You should go to that doctor again," he said.

"Yeah, okay. Rudi says he's gonna take me."

Much as he resented her championing his older brother, Jack thanked God for Rudi. His mother had visited Chicago once, but she hadn't liked it. The streets were too wide, and there weren't any diners. She preferred her shrinking island in the Bronx, with Rudi to escort her around.

"So," she concluded, "you gonna take care of *die Kleine?*"

"Yeah, I will. She's coming with us to the party tonight." Jack paused and added with schadenfreude, "The bas mitzvah—tonight they celebrate."

He savored her silence, knowing she was weighing who could do more harm to her granddaughter, *die Schwarzen oder die Juden.*

"You're crazy," she pronounced. "No wonder she's nuts. She's just like her father."

He laughed, for the first time enjoying the conversation.

"Who do I take after?" he asked.

His mother wouldn't answer. They had an unspoken agreement never to mention his father. Apparently, one transgression today had been as much as she could take.

"Okay," she proclaimed. "I let you work. You work too much. *Alles Gute, ja?*"

"Okay, Mom."

She hung up with a clunk. Suddenly hungry, Jack made himself a piece of toast and ate it as he wandered through the house. The living room was no longer green and had faded to a wan gray. The Shoah ... order ... He had lost his thoughts. Frustrated, he washed the brown crumbs off his plate. He used so much soap that it took him minutes to clear the bubbling suds from the sink. When they dissolved, he sat at the piano and picked out the sorrowful, writhing melodies of the *St. Matthew Passion.*

Fucking freezing today. Why won't they open the goddamn door? Where is everybody? Oh, here's Beej. What's he doing with Michael? Where's Tanesha? Shit, I forgot the money. It's cold even inside, here. Should I take off my coat or leave it on?

Hey, girl, says Beej. You lookin' fine. Wassup, where the party at?

I was at a bas mitzvah, I say.

Bas mitzvah, one of them Jewish things?

Yeah, I say, it was cool. This girl, she was only thirteen, but she read about slaves escaping from Egypt. She sang it in Hebrew. That's how you become a woman there. You get up and sing in front of everybody.

Yeah, that cool. He nods.

Michael is squirming like a cat when you pick it up the wrong way.

Hey, I say, I think you're holding him wrong. I think he wants to get down.

Here, you take him.

Beej thrusts him at me, and Michael wriggles over my chest.

Where is everybody? I ask. Where's Tanesha? Where's Aunt Lou?

Beej laughs at me trying to hold the baby. I never held a baby before. Shit, it's awful, like holding a bag full of cats. Little feet kicking, little hands grabbing. This is supposed to be a person?

Where is everybody? I ask again.

Beej draws a wheezy breath. He looks so good. Those pricks at the Experimental School, they're jerky and greasy and twitchy and tense with pimples all over their bodies. Beej has a real body that flows like water. He just laughs like a guy with emphysema.

Aunt Lou at a funeral, he says. Tanesha, she with Tyrell. He jerks his chin toward the stairs. She ask me to watch Michael for a while.

You mean—

Yeah. He the daddy.

I look down at the struggling kid. Yeah, I guess he looks a little like Tyrell. I never thought about it before. Oh, good, he stopped thrashing. Guess they kick less if you hold 'em facing you. Shit, what's he doing? He's putting his mouth on—

Beej gasps for breath.

Oh, that good, girl, he think you lunch.

Shit, this isn't funny. How do I make him stop?

You can't make him stop, says Beej. What you doin' in that dress anyway? It fallin' off of you, with them little bee-sting tits of yours.

I push Mikey's straining head away. Oh, no. He didn't like that. He's pausing, like he's gonna erupt—oh, *shit*, he's screaming, like a knife in my ear. Beej grimaces.

How do I make him stop? I plead. What do I do?

You can't make him stop, says Beej. He gonna scream till he done.

Shit. Maybe if I jiggle him around, bounce him up and down for a while … I wonder what Tanesha does. Shit, he's going to scream forever. Beej is right, he's going to scream until he's done.

Uh-oh. They're thumping upstairs. They're yelling, pissed as hell—shit, here they come, banging down the steps, Tanesha in a silky purple bathrobe, Tyrell in just some shorts. Wow, he has a great chest. You can see all the muscles. Does skin just look better when it's brown? It must cover up all the ugly shit, the pimples and little hairs and stuff.

What you doin' to that child? screams Tanesha. Can't I have one hour of peace? Oh, hey, Misty. Give him here.

She picks up Michael with his face against her breast, and he shuts right up. Whew. It's like turning off a car alarm.

Shit, girl, says Tyrell. You could have left him. We can't do nothin' no more.

He need his mama, says Beej.

His mama busy, says Tyrell. You can't watch him for five minutes?

You think you up there five minutes? Beej laughs. You do it in five minutes? Shit, I'm glad I ain't your woman, you in there with a stopwatch.

He shudders and moans, low groans for the guy and whimpers for the girl. In between, he squints at an imaginary watch pinched between his fingers and thumb.

Shut up, Beej, says Tyrell.

Shut up, Beej, says Tanesha. He need changin', that why he cry.

I wonder how she knows. I mean, he wasn't leaking, and he doesn't smell.

Why didn't you change him? she demands.

I don't know how, I say. I didn't know he needed it. I never changed a baby before.

C'mon, girl, I show you, she says. I follow her up the squashed-carpet steps to where she keeps the diapers. The room smells of sour salt, like all the things that come out of people all mixed together.

Here, she says. She pulls down his pants, and I smell the sickly-sweet sludge. Michael has filled his diaper with glistening shit. It's almost green, like toxic chemicals.

Ew, I say. That's disgusting.

Oh, you get used to it. She sighs.

This is weird—some places he's pink, and other places he's brown. His little brown penis is so tiny and fragile it looks unreal.

Now you gotta clean him, she says. Here, you do it.

This is gross. I take the baby wipe and touch him lightly. He smiles.

Oh, you gotta rub harder, she says. You won't never get him clean like that.

I try to wipe off all the shit. He seems to like it, and he gurgles.

Hey, Misty, asks Tanesha, you got any money on you?

I'm sorry, I say, I forgot. We went to a bas mitzvah this morning.

She doesn't say anything, but I know she's mad. She must have needed it.

Okay, he clean, she says.

She holds a diaper ready.

Now you fold it like this— Hold still, Mikey!

He laughs and kicks his pink-soled feet.

An' he done. That all there is to it.

For how long? I ask.

Tanesha smiles bitterly. Two, maybe three hours if you lucky. These diapers, they cost fifteen dollars a box. He go through a big box like this every week.

Downstairs, Beej's wheeze lies on Tyrell's laugh like coconut on a layer cake. Their laughter stops when our feet hit the stairs.

Tyrell, says Tanesha, you got any money?

Shit, girl, he says, you always askin' me for money.

I need it, she says. Misty couldn't bring none today.

What you need my money for? he demands.

I ain't askin' you for me, I askin' for your son! she cries. He need stuff, he need diapers an' shit!

What you do with all that welfare money? he asks. That what they give you that money for.

It ain't enough, she says, bouncing Michael. We need all kinds of things, me an' Beej an' Aunt Lou. He your son. He your responsibility.

The word hits him like a well-aimed kick where he must already have a bruise.

Fuck you, girl! he shouts. Fuck your responsibility. You ain't nothin' but a vampire, suckin' my blood!

Beej punches my arm. C'mon, we gotta get outa here. They at it again.

Michael aims his wail into the rising geyser of noise.

You think you can just make a baby an' run off? He your baby too. You give me money for his food!

No! yells Tyrell. You stupid or somethin'? What part of "no" you not understand?

That's funny, but I don't dare laugh. They might start screaming at me. Beej hands me my coat. I wonder why he doesn't say anything.

I know you got money. She jiggles Michael accusingly. Yesterday your payday. You cash your check.

That's right, *my* check, he says. You think they give me that for nothin'? I work till two in the mornin' moppin' out that place. You know how dirty that floor get in February? Them people, they just throw their whole drink in the trash. They don't care who clean it up! That's *my* money! I work for that money! What you do all day?

I take care of your son! she screams. I clean up shit all day too, just don't nobody pay me for it!

Beej pulls at my arm.

You lyin', says Tyrell. You watch that shit on TV, all them dumbass talk shows. You sound like a talk show now. Responsibility! Fuck responsibility! I wanna do somethin' with my life! You just take an' take an' take an' take, an' you don't give me nothin'. You can't even love me no more, you so busy listenin' to him scream!

Somebody gotta take care of him. Tanesha sobs.

That was mean, that part about not loving him. Beej pushes me toward the door.

Shit, girl, cries Tyrell. I never wanted no baby! Why didn't you get an abortion? You ain't good for nothin' no more. Maybe I find me a lady treat me better, show me some respect, you know what I'm sayin'?

Beej nudges me out. Tanesha screams she wishes she had gotten an abortion if she had known he would treat her like this. I wonder if Michael is old enough to understand.

The cold grabs me like two icy hands around my neck.

Where are we going? I ask Beej.

Hakim's place, he says, see if he got some weed.

That was horrible, I say. How come you didn't say anything?

Beej shrugs his shoulders, then draws them in. Ain't nothin' I can say gonna make it better. When World War III break out, you stick your head up, it gonna get blown off.

But what do you think about it? I ask.

Beej glares into the cold. The wind gropes me under my clothes.

What you wanna know? he asks. You wanna know whose side I'm on? She my sister, he my friend. She never should have had that baby.

I thought she wanted it, I say softly.

Oh, she wanted it, all right, he says. Just don't nobody like to be cleanin' up shit all day. She can't go nowhere, she can't do nothin'.

Like my parents, I say, they didn't want to have me either.

How you know that? he demands. Why you keep sayin' that? They tell you that or somethin'?

No, I say. It's how they look at me. Like they wish I wasn't there.

Maybe you right, he says. That how people look at me. That how they look at everyone here. Like they wish we all just disappear. Only we ain't goin' nowhere.

Yeah, I say. Me either.

The synagogue was deep and cavernous. Dark hallways led into its chaotic heart, connecting irregular rooms. Even in the dim light, the strange angles disturbed Jack—rooms with six or seven walls and no windows. How could a structure contain so much space? Jessie pointed down a corridor to his right, where the low throb of music seemed louder.

They were late. He had waited for Jessie until almost six and had been ready to go when her key scratched the lock. Disheveled and heavy lidded, she had been stultified by something—grass, he supposed, but she moved with an angry restlessness that frightened him more than the drugs. There was a deadliness in her laugh, wildness in her disjointed movements. She stared at him mockingly in her white Marilyn Monroe dress.

"Ready to go?" she asked. "Where's the bitch?"

"Don't call—" he started angrily. "How are you feeling? Are you sure you're up for this?"

"Yeah, let's party," she sneered. "Let's go see this place."

Jack set out uneasily, admiring her balance as she braved the ice in three-inch heels.

"Aren't you afraid of getting frostbite?" he asked.

She leered at him with red-eyed, wordless disgust.

The party engulfed Jack in a wave of color. The buffet had just opened, and the plunderers moved in a ripple of reds, greens, and blues. Ruth, warm and lovely in maroon, laid her hand on someone's arm as she offered advice. Children of all sizes were running, dodging, eating, and fighting. They drank in the spectacle with shining eyes.

Sam broke away from a group.

"Jack!" he cried. "You're here! I was scared you'd keep workin' and forget to come!"

Sam embraced him with heavy arms, and from the easy way he hung on him, Jack knew Sam had had several drinks. His tears of the morning had dried, and he was all revelry, all appetite. He would cry no more that day.

"What's this?" asked Sam, grinning at Jessie. "Jack, your daughter's gorgeous."

He took her hands and looked into her eyes. "Good to see you, but watch out for the guys, you hear? You're every man's dream."

Nightmare, more likely, thought Jack. As Jessie leaned in to kiss Sam, the faintest flicker of alarm flashed in Sam's eye. The circle Sam had left was motioning impatiently, and he returned to them. He left Jessie and Jack with strict orders to eat.

Jack joined the line and searched the crowd for Bea, but she must still be at the hospital. Before him lay a cornucopia that only Sam could have assembled. Enormous roasts of prime rib glowed in the darkness, and oily chickens glistened beside them. Potatoes sat round and solid in silver dishes, brightened by green sprigs of parsley. Heaps of red grapes threatened to fall onto rich brown loaves of braided bread. Jack partook of it gingerly, hating to despoil it, but the elbowing children beside him cut and snatched at everything they could reach.

Jack turned to speak to Jessie, but she was gone. She would have scanned the table, then shrugged and turned away. Food disgusted her, and she rarely ate in anyone's presence. At least she was easy to spot. Tall and elegant in her silky white dress, she shone like a candle in the soft light. It was just a bit too big for her, he thought. That halter neck was made for full breasts, and it hung on her a little oddly. He groaned as she smiled at the bartender, who handed her a drink with an umbrella in it.

Round tables floated like lifeboats in the darkness, and Jack searched for faces he knew. Sam, Ruth, and Rachel were engulfed, so he would have to strike out on his own. He sat down alone and smiled faintly at the crowd. A brown basket of rolls marked the center of each table. Jerry and his friends began a firefight in which the round rolls featured as grenades. Ruth nudged Sam, who jumped to his feet.

"Quit that!" he roared. "Whaddaya think you're doin'? You know better than that!"

Jack felt almost sorry when the battle ceased. The boys seemed to be having so much fun. He had never dared to send food flying, not even when he was young. He had always feared his mother's wrath, but his father's icy disgust was the real deterrent.

Before Jack could sample his food, a woman with dyed hair settled beside him. He listened politely as she spoke of her children and murmured when it seemed a response was due. Jessie had landed at a table with an old man, who leaned forward with fascination. This seemed safer than the bartender, so Jack directed his attention to his roast beef, which was really quite good. As he chewed, the woman whined on and on, moving from elegies of her sons to a divorcée's dirge. She seemed to want something from him, but he didn't know what. He studied the wrinkled brown skin of the uninviting cleft between her breasts.

"Hey, Jack!" Sam nudged his elbow. "Hey, Wanda! You're lookin' good! How you doin'?"

Sam seemed happier than ever, ready to burst. He always looked that way in a suit, bulging out at the neck and waist.

"Wanda," he asked, "is it okay if I talk to Jack a minute? I gotta tell him somethin'. Is that okay? We're still on for that dance later, right?"

"Sure, Sam!" cried the woman, breaking into a smile that Jack hadn't seen in half an hour of conversation.

Sam led Jack a little way off and muttered, "Ruth said to rescue you. She saw that Wanda got you. Ever since her divorce, she's been grabbin' every single guy and makin' like the Ancient Mariner. When you go back, just talk about your wife and kid, and she'll leave you alone soon enough. Where's Bea anyway?"

"Oh, she'll be here. She's still at the hospital." Jack smiled gratefully. He waved at Ruth, who blew him a kiss. Realizing he might not get Sam alone again, he said, "Hey, we're having a party Friday night the twentieth. Can you and Ruth come?"

Sam's face lit up an instant too late to cover his surprise.

"A party, all right!" He grinned and thumped Jack's upper arm. "What's the occasion?"

For some reason, this had never occurred to him. Inspiration caught him as he crafted a reply.

"Carnival!" he exclaimed, looking into Sam's rich brown eyes.

"All right!" roared Sam, seizing his arms. "I always knew you had it in you! Good for you! Must be that Nietzsche seminar."

Still laughing, Jack asked, "You can come, then? I mean, I realize it's short notice ..."

"We'll be there," said Sam definitively.

Some people hovering asked to hear about the Jewish Robinson Crusoe, but Sam waved them away. He stepped in closer to Jack.

"How's your situation—that one you told me about?" he murmured. "I haven't talked to you in a while, plannin' all this—" He waved his arm toward the banquet table, which looked as though it had been beset by piranhas. "That all settled now? You get that straight?"

Jack's stomach clenched. "Well—"

"Aw, shit," said Sam. "You're not still—"

Jack nodded, sorry to be disappointing his friend.

"Aw, shit," repeated Sam. "I should have kept on you. I should have ..."

With astonishment, Jack saw that Sam felt responsible. Like the firefight with the dinner rolls, this transgression had happened on his watch. It had all been due to a lapse of attention on his part.

"It's okay," said Jack. "Really. We know what we're doing. She wants to do this, and no one suspects a thing."

Sam shook his head sorrowfully, and pangs of guilt shook Jack that he had never associated with Ellie's young body. By touching her, he was tearing his friend's ethos as a knife rends a tent's cloth. He hated to mar Sam's happiness, especially tonight.

"Just think about what you're doin'," Sam sighed. "You can stop it before it's too late."

"I'll talk to her," promised Jack. "Ellie, I mean. We'll talk seriously about what's going on."

This cheered Sam, and he slapped Jack's shoulder.

"Hey, you better watch out for Jessie," he warned. "She's had three drinks already—I've been countin'. An' get her off of old Bill Diamond. What's she on anyway?"

Jack laughed and shook his head. Jessie was leaning toward the older man, who looked like he was having a nonstop orgasm. Jessie could find the misfit in every crowd. When it was a woman, she described her monstrous parents to spread the word of her persecution. When it was a man, she made sure that tales of her demonic sexuality traveled even farther than reports of her parents' injustice. When she drank, Jessie lost what few inhibitions she had, and old Bill seemed happy to reap the benefits.

"What would you suggest that I do?" asked Jack mildly.

Sam looked at him, jovial but frustrated, uncomprehending.

"Geez, I dunno. What do you always do when she's bad? Spank her, tell her to go stand in the corner or somethin'."

"Sam!" roared a group along the far wall.

"Oh, I gotta go." He grinned. "They need me to start the dancin'."

Jack smiled and nodded. Inspired by Sam, he headed for Jessie, but his eyes caught Bea's slim form flanked by two men. She and her colleagues, Dave Hertz and Tom Plevin, must have come straight from the hospital. Jack hurried over to say hello.

The music began with a heady, thumping beat. It was a wonderful party. At the banquet table, an enticing array of desserts had appeared: gleaming hills of ripe fruit, pastries that oozed poppy seeds and chocolate, and heaps of nutty, crumbly cookies. Jack had never liked sweets, but he smiled to see Rachel and her girlfriends gorging themselves. Ruth was motioning to Sam to stop eating already and come and help with the music.

Sam obeyed without too much protest, and soon the dancing began. Sam ventured onto the dance floor first, leading Ruth through turns and caressing his favorite parts of her. Others quickly joined them, eager to partake of the rhythm now that they had devoured the feast. Bea went out with Tom Plevin, and Jack watched admiringly. Bea had always liked dancing, and he felt sad that he had never been able to satisfy her that way. The doctors' dark heads stayed close together, and he knew they were shouting about contractions and vaginal warts. To Jack's amazement, Jessie sashayed out with Bill Diamond and began a sloppy Salome dance before him. Jack didn't recognize the music—something about a little bit more.

As the dancers turned, Jack dreamed in silence. What was Ellie doing tonight? Jack himself never danced, not since— But with Ellie, maybe he could. One tall girl looked a little bit like her, her long hair whipping out as she spun. She was overweight, though, he noted with disgust. So instead he watched his family—his wife's sexless gyrations, his daughter's drunken display.

Sam, in his glory, was delighting the women with his attentiveness and audacious hands. Every one of them adored him, from yearning old Wanda to the pudgy young girls. How easily he moved from partner to partner. Rachel, still in purple, passed from relative to relative like a shining amethyst drop.

Jack's own daughter was the most popular. Her partners largely supported her, and enraptured men asked who she was. Jack could hear her shriek with laughter as she fell from man to man. That laugh lurked somewhere in her long white throat and emerged at gatherings like this when she stood to win the most attention. Stop her, Sam had said. Stop her how? How could one person control another?

The noise dissolved, and a soft melody arose, a single sax with faint scratchings of cymbal and drum. The gentle music announced a special dance, and Sam led Rachel out onto the floor. Perfectly matched, the proud, plump father and serene daughter gazed fondly into each other's eyes. They moved with the same slow grace, at ease in each other's arms. As Sam looked at Rachel, he glowed with joy, as though wondering how God could have favored him with such a child. Rachel moved more timidly, but all of her young being exuded the same appreciation. She loved her father, and she returned his adoring gaze as the crowd applauded. They were shouting things— blessings, Jack guessed—that he couldn't understand.

The slow tune faded, thrashed to death by a surging, thumping beat. Sam turned to Ruth, and Rachel to an uncle, and the dancing accelerated to a frantic pace. Several of the women asked Jack to dance, but he smiled and shook his head. He couldn't flail around in front of all these people. He watched Bea twirl with her doctor friends and cast occasional worried glances at Jessie.

Jerry and his friends had begun another battle, this time with grapes. Overwhelmed with food, drink, and music, Sam was too happy to stop them. Jack smiled at the boys, but they ignored him, seeing him only as an obstacle to their well-placed shots.

Near the back of the floor, the motion was changing. A hole had opened, and dancers clustered around it.

"Jack!" called a tense voice.

Jack sprang forward and saw that it was Jessie. She lay there heaving, half-rising and collapsing, helpless with laughter at her inability to stand. Several feet away lay a silver-heeled shoe, uncanny and provocative on the bare floor. At least four doctors had gathered around her, and she laughed harder as they checked her eyes and pulse.

"Jack!" cried Bea, alarmed.

He pushed his way through a marsh of words, jovial, judgmental, disapproving. Rachel was staring, her round face full of pain.

"Nothing broken." Tom Plevin smiled. "But you'd better get her home, Jack."

Jack gritted his teeth and helped Jessie up, hating the touch of her scrawny, incompetent body. They would have to go home now, followed by disapproving eyes. Jessie always ruined everything.

Ellie realized it was dark because her eyes stung and the screen had grown brighter than the room. It had been a good day. She had finished off her section on snares, the guts of the *Immoralist* chapter. Now she would be able to defend in June, and she had good reason to finish. Last night, San Diego had called to offer her their job. Fresh from the meeting, the chair had sounded as breathless and elated as she was. Of course she would take it—the other places had been silent, and that could mean only one thing. Ellie had a home now, a destination, a purpose. After a dizzying spin, she had landed in a place of blue skies, red roofs, and dry, sweet-smelling earth.

If only she could talk to Jack. God, what would he be doing? The call had come during their weekend blackout, and she would have to wait until Monday. Why couldn't she call him? It maddened her to be shut out of his life. As his student, with this kind of news, she might have called without suspicion. But she had to respect his one taboo. She reached out to lower the blinds.

At five o'clock, blue light still glimmered outside, since it had been a clear day. With the window half-blocked, she looked down at the street, her lungs longing for fresh air. She hadn't left her apartment all day and probably wouldn't tomorrow. Her senses rebelled, demanding more than the glowing letters they had been swallowing. Where would Jack be? If she yelled the news, he might even hear it. But no—he was at that bas mitzvah. Sam's daughter, that must be nice. She wished that she could go.

The phone rang, and her hand jerked the nylon cord of the blinds. Jack? The caller ID said "unavailable," but she reached out, eager for any stimulus.

"Hel-*lo*," drawled an ironic voice.

"Girish! I thought you were still out of town."

"Oh, I'm *here*," he said playfully.

"Hey, Girish, I have a job!" she cried.

"Why, that's *wonderful!*" he exclaimed, his irony dissolving. "Where? Where are you going?"

"San Diego!"

"Well, good for you, my dear! You'll need some sunscreen, some rollerblades—"

"Oh, screw you, Girish," she retorted. "No place is good enough for you. Anyway, I was planning to get some purple spandex leggings—for teaching. They rollerblade naked."

"Mm—now, that I'd like to see." He laughed in a low, dirty chuckle.

"Hey, what's happening with you?" she asked. "How many places are you playing with now?"

"Oh, not too many," he sighed. "I had to turn down Rice. They gave me only two weeks to decide. But I think I can do better."

"Oh, yeah? Where do you want to go? What are you holding out for?"

She stroked her fingertips down the closed blinds, which coated them with brown dust.

"Intelligence, my dear. Faculty who read books, students who aren't morons, a city that's not a pit, and a two-one teaching load."

"Try some other planet," she snapped. San Diego had offered her three courses a semester, which until now had seemed reasonable. She resolved not to tell him the details of her future job.

"So," she asked, "who's bidding for you? Who are your suitors?"

Girish laughed, as though admiring her spirit. In his relentless game against American culture, Ellie was his favorite opponent. The fact that she saw some good in it intrigued him despite his disgust.

"Oh, a few places," he drawled, relishing her mounting frustration.

"*Where?*"

"Well, Yale, Davis, Iowa, Irvine—"

"Irvine?" she cried. "You never said anything about Irvine!"

"There are lots of things I've never told you about, my dear."

Ellie could hear him smile—his voice flowed differently when his lips were spread.

"So what's happening with Irvine?" she asked.

"Oh, they've offered me two-two, but I asked for two-one. They're waiting to hear back from the dean."

"That would be amazing," she said. "They read books there, but isn't it in Orange County?"

"I'd drive down to see you, my dear, when I needed some culture."

Their laughter settled to a glow.

"So," he asked, "what are you doing?"

She swallowed. "Writing my thesis. What are you doing?"

"Oh, I was doing the reading for Jack Mannheim's course. It's pretty good. Why didn't you take it? Aren't you interested in Nietzsche?"

Ellie's skin hardened, and she felt cold.

"Oh, I didn't think I'd have time," she said. "With writing and interviews and all."

"But weren't you always talking with him about Nietzsche?" he persisted. "I thought you were interested in his work." He pronounced it so beautifully, "were," "work," with a British ghost of an *r*.

"Oh, he's interesting," she said uneasily. "I just didn't have time." Feeling an urge to spy, she asked, "What do you think of him?"

Girish was known for his character assassinations.

"Oh, he's pretty bright," he began, and she flushed with pride, as though he were assessing her own mind. "But he needs to loosen up," he continued. "I can't believe he's teaching Nietzsche. He's a good reader, but Nietzsche is antithetical to his whole being. It's like George Bush teaching Snoop Doggy Dogg."

Ellie burst out laughing, delighted at Girish's zaniness and Jack's ability to project his stiff persona. He did it too well, if indeed it was something that he "did."

"Lucy said he was like George Washington," she ventured. Her heart beat wildly, more conscious than her mind of the treacherous ground she was testing.

"She's right," he answered. "By the way, how is she? Did Hopkins ever call?"

The story of Lucy's calamity had spread so that even students from other departments knew of her spectacular failure. Sam was scrambling for money so that she could stay on next year, but he wasn't doing well. She had begun looking for adjunct work at nearby colleges.

"No, they haven't called," she said carefully, wondering how much she could say.

"They never would have wanted her," he laughed. "She's neurotic, and her thesis is boring. I can't believe they interviewed her."

"You are *bad*," she accused, but she found herself giggling. "I think her stuff is pretty good. That seduction business is interesting."

"Oh, it's not the *project*," he intoned. "It's what she *does* with it. I've had to read almost all of it for the eighteenth-century workshop. Her mind is just—*clunky*! She writes like a bedazzled bureaucrat with a thesaurus up her ass."

"You are *sick*," spluttered Ellie, and he chortled at her naive indignation.

"No, just truthful," he responded.

Silence settled as she considered how to reply. Why bother? She was betraying Lucy by not mounting a defense, but what could she say that would convince him?

"So," he asked, with an ingratiating whine, "what are you doing tonight?"

"Writing my thesis."

"What, aren't you seeing anybody?" he jabbed. "You haven't called me, so I thought you must be seeing someone."

Shit. Could he know? No, Girish must be playing with her, as always.

"The fact that I haven't called you," she returned, "doesn't imply that I'm seeing someone else."

"Well, my dear," he huffed, "I'd agree that in most cases that logic would be invalid, but in *yours* I'd risk it. I know your appetites."

As Girish gained confidence, his drawl returned. He was an expert debater, and he invoked his powers at the most maddening times.

"You've never seen them," she shot. "You've never aroused them to the fullest. You have no concept of my appetites."

"Is that a challenge?" he asked.

She was loving the game. The flattened regions of her mind had risen to savor the evening air.

"A challenge to do what?" she stalled.

"You know what, my dear."

"What," she asked, "have you suddenly found yourself between interviews with an inexplicable urge to mate?"

"I heard your siren song, my dear. You drew me in."

"That is such a crock of shit," she snorted.

The silence pulsed.

"So," he wheedled, "what about it? Can I come over? We could have dinner."

"Well," she said, "I probably don't have anything that you'd deign to eat."

"Oh, I doubt that, my dear." He smacked his lips.

"You are awful." She laughed softly.

"I know," he whispered. "May I come and see you?"

Ellie glanced at the computer, its screen gone dull in its cybernetic sleep. Shit. That test—fifty bucks. She had been certified negative, and God knows what she would pick up now.

"All right," she said. "You can come."

CHAPTER 7

CARNIVAL

JACK HARDLY DARED TO BREATHE. Each time he did, a hundred and fifty slips of paper trembled and threatened to scatter. For over three hours, he had been arranging them, sorting them into family groups. "Will as water," said one; and another, "Hitler on blood." After two years of reading, his Shoah chapter lay before him, a fragile fleet quivering with each breath.

Jack had written this way as long as he could remember. First he read, underlining any phrase that seemed useful. Then he took notes, pages and pages of bounty. When he thought he was ready, he read through his notes and listed the ideas to be sewn together. The climax came with layout, which he had done this morning. He cut up the list and arranged it in front of him, shuffling slips until they formed a pleasing pattern. Then he copied the outline and labeled his notes—3a for Dionysus, 7c for Aschenbach's body—until they formed a catalogue awaiting synthesis. Writing meant creating a thread that linked all the 7c's.

When people asked Jack about how he wrote, he evaded their questions. He was known for the precision and clarity of his writing, but he sensed that if he revealed his secret, he might lose his power. Once, he had confessed it to Sam and sent him into a laughing fit.

"You mean you—you—" he gasped.

When Sam recovered, he said, "Well, whatever works. Me, I just sit down and go at it."

Jack had never been able to write at a computer. He pitied people who wrote staring at screens, and he feared for his eyes, which until recently had been perfect. Ellie wrote at a computer, and he worried about her brown ones. That job—so far away—

Jack believed in his method, which had worked for him ever since he wrote his A papers thirty years ago. The only drawback was its vulnerability. Two hundred pages of notes, garnered over two years, could be consumed by flames in a minute. This morning's thoughts could be scattered by a sneeze. This time he had outdone himself. From two hundred pages of notes he had distilled five pages of thoughts—a hundred and fifty slips when he cut between the lines. Three hours ago, he had despaired of finding a pattern, but now, at last, his fragments formed a mosaic of dazzling logic.

Since his inspiration a week ago, he had deferred writing the Nietzsche chapter, although his seminar kept Nietzsche alive in his mind. Better to attack the unfamiliar and follow his new thoughts wherever they led. He had felt good enough on Wednesday to call Springer, which had been coveting his book for two years. It was as good as written, he told them; he could deliver it in September. With the thought that order killed, it had cohered like a chorale.

A thump shook the ceiling, and Jack skewed a column as he started. Bea was at the clinic and would be gone all day. Jessie must be getting up. Uneasiness rippled through him, and he reached for a pad to record his outline. Water churned as the toilet flushed. Since last week's horror, Jessie had been good. She seemed to like going to public school, and she had even spoken to him occasionally. In the mornings she was dangerous, but she might ignore him and let him work. Her feet struck the stairs with irregular steps that fell more heavily on one foot. There was a pause as she crossed the living room carpet.

"What are you doing?"

Jessie leaned in the doorway in an ironic pose.

"Hi." He smiled. "How are you feeling? What time did you get in last night?"

"What are you doing?" she repeated, imperturbable in her pink bathrobe with feathered cuffs.

"Oh, I'm laying out my chapter," he said. "For my new book on Dionysus in Germany. I'm planning the chapter on the Shoah today."

The therapist had said to tell Jessie about his work, although he had no hope she would respect it. Jessie swung into the room and approached his fleet with middling curiosity.

"Careful," he said, eyeing her fluffy pink cuffs.

Jessie smiled scornfully.

"This is amazing!" she exclaimed. "How long did it take you to do this?"

"Oh, about three hours." He hesitated. "But I've been working on it for two years."

"Wow! So what are you going to say? What's it all about?"

Wary of subterfuge, he explained his chapter. "I'm trying to show how the Nazis imposed order on everything and tried to make it look like it wasn't order."

As he struggled to express his thoughts, they made more sense than they ever had.

"That's interesting," she said. "Everybody does that. How did they do it?"

"Well … they tried to pass it off as nature. They tried to make it look like they were following some sort of natural impulse or will."

Jessie stepped forward and pushed her cuff up to the elbow. She reached down to finger the slips.

"This is incredible," she breathed. "I can't believe you did this."

"Oh, I liked it."

Jack looked sideways and met her eyes as her fingers played with his trembling rubrics. Her eyes were big and blue, shielded by black lashes like his. Though lined with stinging red, they showed perfect concentration as they drank his categories. *Rausch. Wille.* The Jews. Dirt and Cleanliness. Order as Disorder. Order as Murder.

"This is amazing," she murmured.

Jessie sucked in her breath and blew as hard as she could. The pattern exploded, and slips danced through the air like frenzied flakes of snow.

Jack leaped up and raked the air as his chapter scattered over the desk and floor.

"*Scheiße!*" he gasped.

He wanted to hit her or to get his hands around her slender neck. Jessie just laughed, a mocking chortle. She knew that he could never strike her.

"Why did you do that?" he yelled. "I spent hours working on that!"

Her laughter flowed like a sonata through the close air of his study.

"Get out!" he cried. "Get out of here!"

Jessie flounced through the kitchen and up to the shower. Jack stooped wearily to gather his scattered slips and wondered how he would know if any had escaped him altogether.

When it snows, it's beautiful even here. I love how quiet it gets. The buses float by like ghosts, and when you look up, a million kamikaze flakes fly in your face. I can't wait to tell Beej. I can't believe they're going to have this party. Fucking wimp, fucking bitch—got more guts than I thought. I love how they just pick a day without telling me, like I've got nothing else to do. But it'll be so great, seeing Beej in the shitheads' house.

Hey, Beej, I cry, let's go for a walk in the snow!

You crazy, girl, he says, and brushes the cold off my hair. You gettin' crazier every day.

But it's beautiful out there! You've gotta see it! The park's all soft, like a cloud.

Whatever you takin', girl, you give me some, laughs Tanesha.

My parents do it all the time, I say. They walk in all kinds of weather.

That where you get it from, says Beej. You all fucked in the head.

Please, I say.

I want it so badly, to be out in the middle of that whirling white.

Okay, he says. You crazy, but I ain't got nothin' better to do.

He pulls on a navy-blue hat, and his hair disappears. His head looks like a billiard ball, blue on top and brown on the bottom.

Whatever she got, it catchin', says Tanesha.

Out on the street, the world looks like a movie on a bad TV. People wait for a bus, cars slip by, but it's fuzzy, and there's no sound. I like it this way, real but unreal.

Isn't this cool? I ask, but Beej says, I'm freezin' to death.

He has to like the park.

Hey, Beej! I cry. Hey, Beej, guess what!

Man, you hyper today! What you been doin'?

Oh, nothing. I just like the snow.

I know, he says, and rolls his eyes.

Hey, Beej, you won't believe this, but they're having a party. My stupid parents are having a party, and I'm supposed to invite my friends. I want you to come.

We plunge into the park. People waiting for the bus stare at us like we're nuts, so I scream and charge and smash the snow with my legs. It's like moondust, so light that it's barely there. Beej tackles me, and we thrash in the feather-soft white and throw moondust over each other.

Shit! he yells as I toss snow in his face. It's so light against his brown skin. When he kisses me, his mouth is warm and wet, and the snow on my face is burning cold.

Beej pushes himself up. They havin' a party. You all havin' a party at your house, and you want me to come.

I try to kiss him, but he twists away. Shit. I didn't expect him to be thrilled, but he doesn't have to get mad.

Girl, he says, you crazier than I thought.

Well, maybe, I say. It was the therapist's idea. She said we should all do something together, like have a party and invite our friends. They're gonna invite their doctor and professor friends, these dumbass people who've never seen the real world. They'll hang around talking about their students and their patients, 'cause they've got no lives of their own—

Hey, your name Mannheim, right? he asks.

His eyes clear, like he remembers something.

Yeah, Mannheim.

I hate that name. Why do I have to have the wimp's name? Makes me sound like a frigging Nazi. Can't believe the bitch just took it and dumped her own. I guess all women did that back then. Shit, if I don't dump my name, that means I'll be stuck with the wimp's. What's Beej's? Lamont. Jessie Lamont, that's not bad …

Your mama Beatrice Mannheim? She a doctor at University Hospital?

Yeah.

I don't like this.

She a good doctor, he says. She treat the nurses good. Aunt Lou, she got this friend, Nancy, she a nurse at that place. She say your mama treat the nurses good. Most doctors, they treat them like shit. But your mama, she treat them like real people, you know what I'm sayin'?

Damn, he can't fall for her shit, not Beej!

She's just like that at work, I say. You can't judge people by what they're like at work. They can fool anyone there. They shine this energy that hides who they are.

He squints at me like he doesn't believe me.

Could be, he says. All I know is, she treat the nurses good. That what Nancy say.

We push deeper into the white and kick sprays of snow in the air.

If your family so bad, why you want me to go there? You think I'm gonna have any fun?

I just want you to see them, I say. I want you to see how I live.

Sound like you want them to see *me*. Sound like one of them potlucks Aunt Lou go to. She bring a potato salad. You bringin' me.

Shit. He really is mad.

They told me to bring my friends, I say. You're my friend. You and Tyrell and Tanesha, you're my friends, and I want you to come.

We your friends? he asks.

He kicks up a shower of snow, like that geyser at Yellowstone Park.

Why don't you bring your white friends?

I don't have any white friends, I say. They're fucked in the head. They're like miniature versions of my parents. That fucking Experimental School—all they care about is grades, SAT scores, and what college they'll go to. They don't know anything. They don't care about real life. They're not even alive.

So you gonna go to this party, you gonna bring your real-life potato salad, you gonna throw it in their face?

No, I say, it's not like that!

This park is so big, so blank. It just goes on and on. I can't see where the ground ends and the air begins. Only trees break the white, like veins on some old lady's legs.

Shit, girl, you don't know nothin'. You think I'm gonna go to your neighborhood for this party? You got any idea what'll happen if I even walk outa this park?

Yeah, I say, the Romulans'll get you.

Fuck you, girl. To you it all a big joke. I show my ass over there, them rent-a-cops be on me in a minute, askin', scuse me, son, you got some business around here?

But it's the same for white people, I say. If we come to this side, we get hassled too.

BJ stops dead and looks at me like he's never seen me before.

Man, he says, only a white person could say that.

I'm not white! I cry.

Girl, he says, you the whitest thing west of Martin Luther King Drive. You so white your brains is bleached out.

I start to laugh. I can't help it, and for a minute he laughs with me.

It ain't your fault, he says. You think like that 'cause that how they brung you up. Can't you see? It's one thing if some homie hassle you. Maybe he take your purse. It's a whole 'nother thing if the police after you. How many black people you see walkin' around your neighborhood?

That's ridiculous, I say. There are lots of black people. The co-op has more black people than white.

The snow on my face is starting to burn, and I wet my hand as I brush it free.

The co-op! he laughs. His wheeze is scary when he's mad. The co-op, that like our trading post. How many black people you see two blocks from the co-op? We go there, we buy our shit, we get out. You think we go there for the music they play? They don't build stores like that where n*****s live!

That's sick! I cry. That's disgusting! How can you use that word about yourself?

I say it 'cause you think it! he yells.

I do not! I scream. The white park swallows my voice.

You may not say it, he says. You thinkin', long as there's some redneck fool and he say it, you ain't racist. But you think it.

That's not true! I yell. You are so fucked up! I'm not like them! I came over here!

Yeah, you done us all a big favor.

A hot wave heaves in my chest. When it hits my throat, I'm going to dissolve.

I'm sorry, I sob. It's just a party. Forget it. I wanted you to see my life, how horrible it is.

Fuck you, he says. Ten years from now, you gonna be tellin' some bitch how horrible your life is for a hundred bucks an hour. I gonna be cleanin' the chicken place, or I gonna be in jail, or I gonna be dead. I'm freezin' out here. I'm goin' home.

He whips around, and I start to follow.

Beej! I call, but the snow eats my voice. Beej! I scream.

He whirls around like a dead man in his snow-encrusted hat.

What you want? he demands. I said I goin' home. I goin' home by *myself*. You go where you want to go. You ain't comin' with me.

Beej! I cry. Please, Beej, I'm sorry! Please, Beej, you're my friend!

I ain't your friend, he says. Tyrell, Tanesha, they ain't your friends. You fucked in the head. Just 'cause you hate your life over there don't mean you can come an' get one here.

Beej! I cry. The snow bites my face.

Fuck you, girl, he says. Get your white ass on outa here.

Even in the seminar room, Jack could feel the snow's hush. No sound drifted up from the quad, and only a siren pierced the students' murmurs. In the past six weeks, he had come to know them well. The English and German students eagerly blasted any pigeons he tossed in the air. Donna from art history offered relief from their word games by reasoning visually. Mariko, who had seemed quiet at first, was really quite funny if you listened to her. Jack wished he could strangle whiny-voiced Jacqueline, who sat in her black turtleneck as though the world pained her. Nietzsche himself would have preferred Corinne, the jokester from English who supplied Sam with pastries.

They were a bright group, worthy of the philosopher, but the best and worst of them was Girish. The Indian boy faced him at the far end of the table, and Jack couldn't bear to meet his eye.

Three days ago, Ellie had left her pink bed for the bathroom and pirouetted until she made him laugh. His smile faded slowly—everything moved slowly in that warm, glutted state. As he lay there pulsing, measuring his breaths, he eyed her Botticellis. His favorite with the angels lay off to one side, but when he rolled his eyes toward it, a black spire broke his vision. Lazily he closed one eye, then the other, and located the spire on the sheet.

It was a hair, a thick, curly, black hair unlike any he or Ellie had on their bodies. In the kitchen or living room it might have had business, but not here in the warmth of her bed. Oh, God! He picked it up and twirled it. The jaunty corkscrew hadn't come from a head. He turned it slowly as a scientist studies a specimen, noting the dimensions of its waxy curves.

Ellie emerged, radiant and glowing, and he whisked off the hair with a stroke of his thumb. He couldn't challenge her, not with four months left. The countdown had made a coward of him, and he couldn't poison their remaining time. Every day he found something new he loved about Ellie. He loved her white breasts, like two Chinese pork buns with spicy pink filling at the tips. He adored her small nails, whose curves never reached the soft ends of her fingers. He admired her fine ear, so keen she could locate objects by sound like a bat. And he loved that with her nimble voice, she could imitate any person or animal. Oh, the things that she could do with her lips! But despite all rationality, these joys lost value if he had to share them with someone else.

Of course, he slept with another woman. He had entered Bea last night in a surprise encounter that pleased them both. There were the calm waters of blue lakes, and the churning of uncharted rapids. If he had both, how could he deny both to Ellie? It was the height of hypocrisy, but he raged against her illicit mingling. His passion made him greedy, and the light on Girish's glossy black hair filled him with fury.

Jack dug his nails into his palms. He had dreaded this class, but he had to stay focused. Today they would be reading Nietzsche's "On Truth and Lying in an Extra-Moral Sense," the most frightening thing the philosopher ever wrote. Nietzsche had abandoned this essay that revealed the cracked foundations of Western thought, and Jack wished he could do the same. He couldn't, though, because the English students expected it. This piece was their favorite, the anticipation of their post-structuralist theory. As far as some of them knew, it was the only thing Nietzsche had ever written, the "Hallelujah" chorus of his forbidding oeuvre.

Jack himself had always felt drawn to the argument. He approached it as one does a roller coaster, waiting in line to pay for its terrors. The essay stopped your heart and snatched your breath away. It inched you up and then shot you down into screaming blackness. Eventually you stood and walked away, knowing that "up" and "down" were relative concepts. After reading "Truth and Lying in an Extra-Moral Sense," you thought and spoke, but thinking and speaking were never the same.

Each week two students responded to the reading. Their presentations forced them to reveal themselves, and they unearthed ideas that Jack had missed. The best way to learn how Nietzsche affected them was simply to observe it. For "Truth and Lying," he had set one condition: one of the respondents had to speak German. Girish and the fat girl, Carol, would be presenting, since Girish had befriended her as the term progressed. Trembling with nervousness, she blushed as he brought his shiny, dark head close to hers.

Before class began, Jack reminded them all about the party Friday night. Bea had suggested asking his students, and to avoid awkward choices, Jack had invited the whole seminar. They seemed pleased, and almost all of them were coming. Only Girish would be missing, because of his Yale interview. The boy looked at him now, calm and expectant, and Jack told him and Carol to start.

Girish let Carol go first. She would summarize the argument and explain the German, and then he would respond. Jack hated him for using this homely girl, but he longed to hear Girish's thoughts. Poor Carol stammered, and her voice dipped crazily. Jack's heart went out to her. Girish nodded vigorously and tried to warm her with an encouraging smile.

According to Nietzsche, she began, our thoughts are metaphors of the nerve impulses that cause them. From the original stimulus, we create images; these, we translate to sounds; and from these, we create the concepts of our thoughts. Each new representation is a metaphor of the previous one—an *Übertragung*, Nietzsche called it, the dragging of meaning from one realm to another.

"And this"—she looked up eagerly for Jack's approval—"is the word Freud uses for transference, *Übertragung*, dragging over."

Poor thing. She couldn't seem to fit her breaths between the words. How could anyone get that fat? What did she eat?

Jack did his best for her, smiling broadly. "That's right. That's important to keep in mind."

He met Girish's eye for an instant and saw laughter under his smoky lids. *Bastard,* he thought, and signaled Carol to go on.

Every concept, said Carol, arises only through a *Gleichsetzen des Nicht-Gleichen*. This was hard to translate—a positioning of unlike things as if they were alike. Jack's German in the first class had impressed them, and in both languages, Carol read the climactic passage on transference from metaphor to metaphor:

> What, then, is truth? A mobile army of metaphors, metonymies, and anthropomorphisms; in short, a sum of human relations that have been poetically and rhetorically intensified, transferred, and ornamented, and that, after long use by a people, have come to be

> thought of as fixed, canonical, and binding. Truths
> are illusions, about which one has forgotten that this
> is what they are; they are metaphors that have been
> used up and rendered powerless to move the senses;
> they are coins that have lost their image and are now
> regarded as metal, no longer as coins.

The students murmured with admiration, not for Carol but for the philosopher. She warmed to the positive atmosphere and picked up her pace.

One could have truth, Nietzsche claimed, only if one forgot one's role as a creative subject. People had an unconquered yearning to deceive themselves, and a dream, if dreamed often enough, would be taken for reality.

"Sie wiederholt nur," whispered one of the German students. "She's just repeating what's there."

Girish shriveled him with a laser gaze.

How odd, thought Jack, his defense of this girl whom he respected no more than a gasping Persian cat. He must be protecting an essential tool, as a picador shields his horse.

"You know, of course, he's relying on everything he's attacking." Jacqueline smirked.

"What's his alternative?" snapped Girish.

Jack found that he was enjoying the show in spite of his better instincts.

"The most interesting thing for me," resumed Carol, "is that he associates each transference, each creation of a new metaphor, with female reproduction. He calls the image that represents a thing the concept's mother, and the nerve impulse that corresponds to the image, the concept's grandmother. Usually any creation of thought or language is represented by male sexuality."

"Yeah!" exclaimed Corinne. "Like a chain of begats. You've really got somethin' there!"

Girish gazed at her with steady, musing irony. The girls laughed and nodded, and the boys frowned and tried to think.

Donna stood up and asked, "Is it okay if I draw something on the board? I'm having trouble with this coin metaphor, and I think if I could just see it—"

Jack motioned for her to go ahead, and the class dissolved into confusion as they discovered there was no chalk. No one could remember ever having seen a professor draw on the board. At last Corinne produced a box from her bulky purse, since she had taught a composition class that morning. Donna filled the dark green space with words and arrows:

Stimulus —> Image —> Sound —> Concept

"You know, if the stimulus is the grandmother, and the image is the mother, then there's a problem," said Jacqueline.

"Yeah, that's what's bothering me!" exclaimed Donna. "What's the sound? He doesn't include it in the family. Why should the stimulus be converted to visual information before auditory information anyway?"

How authoritative she looked at the board, the deep brown skin of her forehead wrinkled in a thoughtful frown. Jack watched, amused, as the women took over the class.

"It's the aunt! The sound is the aunt!" cried Mariko, and the others applauded.

"But this coin thing," continued Donna, "I don't get it. He's trying to say we forget our metaphors are metaphors. If they're coins, wouldn't that mean forgetting that they're metal? Coins represent economic value. Where does the value of a coin come from, the metal in it or the image on it?"

They would go after her, Jack knew, a black woman who dared to challenge Nietzsche.

Before they could pounce, Girish cut in. "That's sort of what I wanted to talk about."

The other students immediately fell silent.

"What interests me," he began, "is not his *argument*—that's fairly obvious—but his motivation, his intentions. What does he *want*? What does he want us to *do*?"

"You think you can discuss his intentions without discussing his argument?" shot one of the boys from German.

Girish deflected him with a look of wordless disgust. "I think his *choice* of metaphors is significant," he continued. "Why compare truth to money?"

Donna listened with genuine interest, and Carol looked enraptured. The girls accepted Girish more readily than the boys, who fumed in the force field of his intelligence.

"Truth and money have only the value we give them," said Mariko softly.

"Right." Girish nodded. "As long as truth is recognizable as language, we suspect it. As long as coins are stamped with images, we remember they're just symbols. Once the images have worn away, we believe the coins have value because they're metal, not because we've assigned it to them."

"Go, Girish!" cried Corinne. "May I have your child?"

"Your child will be a metaphor!" said Mariko, and the whole class burst out laughing.

But Girish was just warming up. As he spoke, his logic gained momentum. His voice fell until it was almost a whisper, and the students strained to hear. Nietzsche was using two main metaphors: the economic one and an organic one of trees and vines. Both carried the same implication: for cultural and natural reasons, there could be no truth; no solid, independent external world. There could be only language, and at most our truth was a consensus about how language corresponded to what it referenced.

Jack felt a physical need to challenge him. "Why nature?" he broke in. "I can see why culture precludes absolute truth, but why nature?"

Girish straightened, and his young body seemed to smile. In the coming struggle, Jack feared he was going to play the bull. Could

Girish know? Did Girish know that he knew? The boy looked at him with calm, steady irony, as though he could see every picture in his head.

"Nature precludes truth because of the structure of our nervous systems," he answered. "Hermann von Helmholtz, who measured the velocity of the nerve impulse, called it a 'sign' of the outer stimulus. He designed physiological experiments, but he said that, at most, we could know only 'signs' of the world. He compared these signs to words. The first metaphor in Nietzsche's chain is the most tenuous: the one that links the event in the world to the nervous system's representation of it. That's nature, not culture."

Now, how in hell could he know that? Jack's desire to conquer dominated his intellectual curiosity, and he lowered his horns for a charge. There were two of them, sharp and deadly: his knowledge of German and his knowledge of Nietzsche. Jack had read almost everything the philosopher had ever written.

What word, he asked Girish, did Helmholtz use for "sign"? Girish didn't know.

The German students smiled to themselves, but Jack knew his attack was pitiful. With growing passion, he spoke of Nietzsche's attachment to biological reality, his deep respect for life despite his own decay. Nietzsche *did* believe in truth, but the truth of life: the truth that all things will die and that the stronger animal conquers the weaker. The students wrote furiously, impressed by his eloquent plea. Jack rarely spoke except in questions, and if he cared so much about something, it must be worth writing down. Only Girish remained motionless, watching Jack with heavy-lidded amusement.

"What do you think Nietzsche wants?" he asked softly.

"He wants us to *live*," answered Jack. "He wants us to dismantle truths inimical to life."

He met Girish's stare and dared the brilliant black eyes to challenge him. Girish had to know. Did they talk about him when they were together? The other students dissolved in Jack's peripheral vision as his eyes locked on their target. Girish stared back without speaking, and Jack thought he saw pity mingled with the boy's silent laughter.

∽

A week after Jack played for Cathy, she taught him how to dance. It was early April, cold and wet, but the clashes on campus shot searing sparks. For days now, Jack had attended no classes. In his world of private passion, he knew only Cathy, who introduced him to soft, wet wonders. His ignorance astonished her, but she loved him for the things he didn't know.

Tonight at this party, she would show him dancing. How could he know so much about music and not move to its rhythms? Jack had always felt its currents, but he couldn't display himself in public. Bullshit, said Cathy. If he was alive, he was on display. Anyone who could play and fuck like he did must know how to move. She would get him drunk, then tell him what to do. Tonight was as good a time as any.

Cathy sat Jack on the couch and ordered him to drink, and he slowly filled himself with beer. He had always enjoyed the way beer warmed him. A good beer buzz was sloppy happiness, not so different from the glow after a good meal. Drinking seemed so much more natural than inhaling things or swallowing them whole. What Cathy took was poisonous, but he devoured it all. At this point, he would have swallowed anything she told him to.

Drowsily, Jack watched Cathy leap from group to group. Like a bird, she moved in unpredictable twitches, never settling, always ready to fly. Only in bed after a writhing climax did her gestures flow smoothly. Her drugs slowed them, but her patternless jerks persisted in every setting.

A clink between bottles drew his eyes to the floor, where two freshman girls sat talking with a red-haired guy. One of the women appealed to him, long and dark with brilliant blue eyes. The other annoyed him with her stringy blond hair and whiny voice.

"They're fucking pigs," she was saying. "A bunch of frightened old men who'll do anything to keep their power. They're killing the blacks, they're killing the Vietnamese, and if we let them, they'll kill us too."

The pretty brunette nodded vigorously, but her anger seemed more contained.

"What they're doing in Harlem is imperialism," she said. "It's just like Africa. They act unilaterally, with no respect for human rights. They build this gym, they destroy this park—they see black faces, and they think they don't have to ask permission."

Jack had heard about the gym the university was building in the nearby park. It epitomized their attitude toward the community, the same attitude Kurtz had had toward the natives who brought him his ivory.

"Things are going to change with Pratt running the SDS," assured the red-haired boy. "Melnick just sent the pigs reports they never read. Pratt knows you've got to confront them, force them to act. We're not going to take this 'discipline' shit. When we go back into the library, we won't fuck around."

His boastful tone seemed made to impress the girls.

"When are you going in?" asked Jack abruptly.

They looked up at him through the brown forest of bottles on the coffee table. Both girls smiled, but the red-haired boy tensed.

"Why? Are you going in with us?" he asked.

Straight and broad-shouldered, Jack knew he looked like the enemy. With his short, curly hair, he could have been a conservative spy.

"I'm going in," snapped the blonde. "No fucking pig's going to use my tuition to make weapons."

"Mine either," said the dark one. "We may not accomplish anything, but at least we'll send a signal they can't ignore."

"If you look at the big picture, you'll see we *are* accomplishing something," patronized the redhead. "If the others all follow, the revolution starts now."

He stood up to look for another beer. The blonde wavered after him as though she didn't quite trust her legs. The dark-haired girl rose too, but to Jack's delight, she settled next to him on the couch. She looked so clean. He hoped she couldn't tell how much he had had to drink. In the next room, Cathy was stamping and flailing. Maybe she was speeding, but probably she was just being her diabolical self. She waved and squinted at the serene beauty beside him.

"You know her?" asked the freshman. "She's amazing. She's so wild."

"Yeah," Jack sighed. "A little too well."

The blue-eyed girl smiled, and he felt the force of her intelligence. She was a biology major, she said, and her name was Bea. She had joined Students for a Democratic Society a few months ago. Jack asked her about the demonstration, about which he knew little. Before Cathy, he had studied constantly, honored to be learning in such a place. He had brought along his parents' reverence for scholarship, and he couldn't believe that this glorious academic world lived off oppression. Little by little they were convincing him, though, his volatile lover and this steady beauty with her alto voice.

Bea spoke of the administration's arrogance and their refusal to consult students or community representatives. They let their scientists develop weapons, and they invited the military on campus to recruit. Now they had even invited the makers of napalm. They did all this without asking anyone, and when the students protested, they pretended not to hear. The point now was to make them hear, to force them to speak.

Jack took a swallow and opened his mouth, but Cathy flew at him from across the room. One of her most devilish tricks was to throw herself on him in public. Knowing how shy he was, she loved to arouse him and let him wrestle with his response. She was training him to heed only his instincts. At first it had angered him, but now he accepted it. She jolted the coffee table so that bottles fell with sudsy clinks. Cathy settled on his lap and forced his mouth open with a pungent, alcoholic kiss. The couch shuddered as the body beside him stood up and walked away. She had done it on purpose. She'd done it on purpose, and—

Jack's arousal struck him more violently than Cathy herself. Gripping her sides, he pulled her closer and filled her mouth with his swollen tongue. Cathy wriggled with delight. Dimly, crazily, he heard people hooting at them to go for it right then and there.

Cathy drew back, and he groaned in frustration. He begged her to come home with him, but she laughed in her throat.

"Not until you dance," she whispered.

She ran her tongue around the rim of his ear and bit his earlobe.

"Okay," he surrendered. "Okay, I'll do it."

Cathy unfolded herself and shook out her crinkled skirt. Jack stood, and the room dipped and shuddered. He was flying on instruments, and he longed for solid ground. Cathy led him toward the dancers, her hips swaying as the music grew louder. Someone had put on the Doors' first album. Since their first one a year ago, they had produced a new record, but like everyone else, Jack preferred the first. Without knowing why, he had always loved the Doors. Their harmonies didn't open new realms, but the songs' simplicity made their poetry stronger. His sensitive ears rejected Morrison's voice. *Who ever let this guy sing?* he wondered. But uncomprehending, he could listen for hours to those snarls of a drunken tiger.

The jaunty bass line of "Break on Through" was winding down.

"Play it again!" screamed Cathy. "Put it on again!"

Other voices joined hers, since it was a communal favorite: "Put it back on, man! Other side!"

Cathy leaned into Jack, and he stooped to let her whisper in his ear. He grew unbearably excited as Cathy alternated words with licking kisses.

"The main thing," she hissed, "is just not to care. No one gives a shit what you look like. You have to shut down your brain, let the music run through you. Just do what it says, and you'll be fine."

Jack tried to kiss her, but she pulled away. How long was she going to torment him? Already she was shaking herself loose, and his heartbeat reset itself to match the bass line.

"Break on through to the other side!"

Cathy quivered and twitched and tossed her hair. Dancing wasn't so hard. The bass line spurred him, and the chords commanded his swinging arms. He tried to pull Cathy against him, but she pushed him away. She wanted to dance, and she was going to dance until she was done. Across the room, the dark-haired biologist was spinning with the red-haired boy. Her rhythmic movements weren't sexy, but they had order and grace. "Light My Fire" swirled up in a glittery cloud, and Jack played its baroque opening in the air. The blue-eyed girl smiled at him over her partner's shoulder. If only her face would stop shimmering so that he could read her eyes.

The music took hold, and Jack moved more easily, scheming drunkenly to catch his queen. Both of them, he thought, he could take on the both of them, but he knew he was impressing neither. Cathy made a fickle partner, sidling up to others and shaking her breasts. Jack seized her and spun her, but she wasn't his. She was dancing with the entire room. As the music wound on, she slowly withdrew. Her curling fingers followed the phrases, and her eyes played in the web her hands spun. She raised her open mouth to the ceiling, as though the dark were dripping nectar she could drink. She had started out dancing with everyone, and she now danced with no one, her fingers kneading the night.

Sweaty, frustrated, Jack stumbled to a table and found a beer that was almost full. He drank it down in deep, angry gulps. Was it dancing she wanted? Well, then, fuck it, he would dance. He flung his body every which way, and Cathy shuffled toward him, impressed at last. His ungoverned arms drew a smile from her. Below her damp ringlets, her burning eyes flared.

Cathy danced until her twitches were exhausted tremors, and she was ready to be taken home. In the wet, gray dawn Jack tried to kiss her. He loved dancing, he loved Morrison, he loved music, he said, even though his father had died for it. Cathy laughed, all sleepy, and told him he was drunk.

Satisfied at last, warm and moist beside her, Jack asked, "What if there is no other side?"

"There'd fucking well better be," she muttered. "There's nothing on this one."

By the time the words left her lips, she was asleep.

From the beginning, Ellie had resisted the party. To come to Jack's house, to shake his wife's hand? Walking across his threshold violated all the taboos they had set up. But Jack insisted. Now that she was leaving, he wanted more than ever for her to see how he lived. It would be fun, he urged. She could see his wife, his daughter, and no one would suspect a thing.

The crossover struck Ellie as a violation, the grossest mixing of kosher and tref. How could she face Bea? She was no actress, and one guilty look could loose a landslide. But in such a crowd of people, Jack pleaded, she might not collide with the crucial particle. She could observe, and that was what he wanted—for her to see him as he really was. After tonight, she might not get another chance. Ellie yielded from curiosity more than complaisance. She wanted to see the woman who had slept with Jack for twenty-six years. When it came right down to it, she couldn't refuse the dare.

For days Ellie had thought of little but what she would wear. As she grappled with her writing and the crows leered from their tree, she pictured herself in red, green, and blue. Should she stand out, try to challenge and provoke her, or blend in like the spy that she was? Her green velvet dress tempted her, cool moss that begged to be stroked. But no, what would the others be wearing? She decided on a warm maroon top and black pants. The wine-colored sweater glowed in the darkness, and the loose-legged slacks trembled with each breath. Jack would love the way she looked. He would want her right there in his house. But now, as she shivered at his heavy brown door, she was starting to lose her nerve.

Jumbled voices emerged from behind red and blue glass panels, and she forced herself to ring the bell. Jack answered, and his face warmed when he saw her. He looked beautiful. No one stood the way he did, and the grays and blues he wore brought his eyes to life in a way the colors did for no one else. In his woolen jacket, Jack was guilty perfection, and his smile revived her with its sad tremors.

"I'm so glad you're here," he murmured.

His touch lingered on her hair as he removed her coat. Behind him, a tall, dark-haired woman appeared carrying a tray of vegetables.

"Who's this, Jack?" she asked.

It was her. The woman assessed her with keen blue eyes. She also wore flowing slacks, and her long, slim body had an athletic look that intimidated Ellie. This woman had been with Jack for longer than she had been alive. The woman laughed apologetically and raised the tray to show that she couldn't shake hands. Every move exuded competence. Ellie comforted herself with the tired sags under the woman's eyes, but overall, she liked the look of her. Always, in everything, Jack had good taste.

"Hi, I'm Bea," said the woman.

"I'm Ellie," she answered. "Jack and I studied Nietzsche together last quarter."

"Yeah, he loves Nietzsche," laughed Bea as she looked for the best place to park the vegetables. "I'm glad you could come. Coatroom's upstairs. Have a drink, make yourself at home."

Jack stood back, looking amused at the affinity between his

women. Ellie had passed through security, but the ease of the encounter made it all the more painful. As she climbed the wooden steps, a bubble ran through her. She would have to use the toilet before she could face them again. For the coatroom, they had designated their own bedroom, the place where that woman and Jack woke up each morning. The oak floor and dressers exchanged glowing looks, and the rocker's curve smiled in the soft light. Every day, under this aqua quilt, Jack opened his eyes to see that woman. Ellie's insides burbled. She would have to use his toilet, and the ugly phrase "master bedroom" rang in her head with all its resonance.

Inside the bathroom, a mirror hung on the door, and she liked what it showed. Unlike that woman, she was tiny, and the soft maroon accentuated her breasts and warmed her face. Her thick brown hair swayed as she rocked alone in Jack's private space. This was his mirror. Could it store her image so that he could enjoy it every day? Oh—oh, God. She reached the toilet just in time. She sat there dreaming, cleaning herself and summoning the strength to go down.

As Ellie left Jack's room, she heard a faint noise—a human sound, a quick release of breath. Who else was up here, and what was she doing? The daughter, maybe. Yeah, it must be the daughter. Curiosity drew Ellie farther down the hall. There it was again, a private sound, a sound that no one should hear. People breathed like that on the toilet. They sighed like that in bed or when they were in pain. What was she doing, and why didn't she come down? Disturbed, Ellie vowed to speak to Jack as soon as she could. He had said that Jessie had problems, and she feared she was hearing them now.

The spacious rooms below matched Jack's descriptions, but she was surprised at what he had left out. In the shadows stood his mute black piano, on which he played his innermost thoughts. His books colored an entire wall, and students were exploring them as dogs sniff each other's crotches. Jack hadn't conveyed the luxury of the place: the matching beige sofa and chairs, the glint of framed pictures, the vibrant red and gold of his Persian rug. She thought with chagrin of her scruffy brown carpet. How could he stand to be with her when he lived in a place like this? This was what you got when you combined a doctor's and a full professor's salary: the reassuring elegance of well-made things.

"Hey, Ellie!" called a friendly voice.

It was Corinne, warm and jovial with a glass of red wine.

"Wow, El, you look fan*tas*tic!" she exclaimed. "What are you doing here?"

Ellie froze. She hadn't invented a cover story, and she might be the only student Jack had invited outside of his seminar. Sometimes he didn't have much sense.

"Oh, I know Jack from last quarter," she said. "I did a tutorial with him on Nietzsche."

Corinne nodded and smiled. Ellie held her breath. What would Corinne make of "did" and "him" in the same sentence? She imagined Girish's cynical laughter. Why did he have to lurk in her head, always mocking her words?

"Where's Girish tonight?" asked Corinne. "I was hoping he would come. He gave such a great presentation the other day."

"Yeah, he's an amazing guy," said Ellie. "I think he's at Yale this weekend."

"Wow," breathed Corinne, shaking her head. "When I grow up, I wanna be just like him."

Ellie shared the laughter in Corinne's brown eyes. People's knowledge of her ties to Girish alarmed her, but they deflected attention from ties more dangerous. How did people know anyway? Maybe Lucy had talked. Ellie scanned the room warily, and they traded news about Lucy. Now that she had failed to find a job, they speculated about what she might do.

A small commotion marked Sam's arrival, and they drifted over to greet him and Ruth. He came bearing a bottle of good red wine, and his voice filled the room as he wondered aloud whether it had frozen on the way over. Corinne scooped up pâté from a nearby platter and brought it to his lips.

"Heya, Sam!" she called. "Here, taste!"

"Ah ..." he sighed and embraced her with the bottle still in his hand.

Ellie marveled at the way he fondled her right there in front of his wife.

"Oh, you're a bad influence, Corinne," he moaned. "You're gonna kill me, but I'm gonna die happy."

"Hey, quit that!" shrieked Ruth, and for an instant Ellie feared a scene.

But Ruth was thinking only of Sam's arteries. "He's on a diet!" she cried.

Sam dissolved into apologetic laughter. "Guess I'm gonna have to be good tonight. My guardian angel's here." In a stage whisper he added, "Hey, don't tell her about that chocolate orgasm last week."

Ruth gave him a good-natured whack, and he extended his arms to Bea. Ellie was sure he saw her, but he ignored her and refused to look her way.

Ellie had arrived quite late, and people were crowding the room. She recognized the students, but the older faces were unfamiliar. They must be the doctors. Jack had said the party was a composite: his friends, Jessie's, and Bea's. But where were the younger people? Where were Jack's daughter and her sixteen-year-old friends? Ellie had looked forward to meeting them and seeing what would remain of Jack when, in thirty years, he was gone.

Tall and straight, Jack drifted from group to group, and Ellie followed him with her eyes. With his quiet gravity, he stood out from the others, and she smiled at her secret knowledge of him. Bea paused to ask him a question, and Ellie winced at her touch on his arm. They moved so naturally together. Ellie felt her bond to him in a crushing new context.

The elements weren't mixing well, so Ellie decided to accost a doctor. Donna and Corinne had cornered two young residents, who brightened at Ellie's approach.

"So," Corinne was asking, "how about it, guys, is a nerve impulse a metaphor for a stimulus outside the body?"

Ellie burst out laughing, and the residents' eyes veered toward her lips.

"Where did you get that?" she asked.

"Guess." Corinne sighed knowingly.

"Now, let me get this straight," said a young doctor with a sharp, earnest face. "You're saying this guy told you a nerve impulse represents a stimulus, like, I say your lips are as red as blood, but I just mean they're red?"

"Ew!" cried Donna.

"A metaphor doesn't have 'like' or 'as,' " grunted the resident with stubbly blond hair.

"It still sort of counts," said Corinne encouragingly. "Strictly speaking, you'd have to tell her that her breasts are two fawns feeding among the lilies."

Ellie blushed as four pairs of eyes shifted focus. The first resident bolted his drink in a quick gulp. He was brown haired, dark eyed, with a tense aggression that pleased her.

"Wow ..." he reflected. "I mean, I guess it's like a metaphor, the body translating something into its own language. It's not the same, though."

"You mean, our comparison of a nerve impulse to a metaphor is another metaphor?" Ellie laughed.

"Yeah," he murmured.

Her belly tightened as his eyes met hers.

"Oh, come on, what's the point of this?" asked his round-faced companion. "I mean, what's the alternative? What else can the body do? Let's just accept it and figure out how it works. What good does it do, worrying whether it's a metaphor?"

"It's interesting!" exclaimed Donna. "It shows us how we think!"

She and the heavy resident squared off, and when Corinne disappeared, the dark-haired doctor settled on Ellie. He seemed to reach out from an exhausted haze as he spoke to her of his deliveries and his southern roots. Ellie offered sympathy when she could, but her eyes kept flitting away. They were drawn to Sam's opulent gestures and Jack's and Bea's anxious exchanges.

Within half an hour, Sam had met everyone at the party. Outrageous scraps of dialogue reached Ellie's ears.

"Just let 'em have as many as they want," he shouted. "If they want septuplets, let 'em have septuplets. There's room for all kinds of stuff in there! You can fit stuff in there you wouldn't be*lieve*—"

Shrieks of laughter drowned his enumeration. It was getting late, and in the spirit of carnival, people were drinking in reckless haste.

Ellie told her doctor she had to use the bathroom. Feeling bold, she looked around for Jack. She found him in the kitchen, uncovering two battalions of miniature strawberry tarts.

"Ellie!" he breathed.

From his lustful smile she knew that he, too, had had a lot to drink. He let the plastic covers fall and stepped forward so eagerly that she was afraid he would grab her. He stopped just short of her and laughed at himself.

"Having a good time?" He grinned. "I'm going to tell Bea to put that brown-haired guy on call permanently."

"Oh, he's harmless," she laughed, her insides curling with pleasure.

Jack stepped closer, shaking his head. "You look—"

A nearby burst of laughter stopped him, and he asked Ellie if she would carry a tray of tiny, fluted red pies.

"Yeah, sure," she agreed. "Jack … where's your daughter? Where are her friends?"

"Oh, I'm not sure what happened there." He smiled. "She seemed so excited about the whole thing, and then all of a sudden she wouldn't talk about it. I don't know whether she invited anyone or not."

"That's too bad," said Ellie. "I think I heard her upstairs Maybe you should go up and check on her."

"Oh, she likes her privacy," Jack sighed, his eyes clouding. "She gets so angry when I go up there. Here, take a tray of these. Maybe I'll go up. Bea's been asking for her too."

In the living room, the noise had risen to a convivial roar. Ellie balanced her pastries and watched for threatening elbows. People oohed and aahed as they spotted her cargo.

She froze. In a corner by the stairway stood a tall girl in black, the thinnest girl she had ever seen. Her hair fell in fluffy blond waves, but her skeletal body defied the world in its clinging black clothes. Like a ghost, she bore Jack's features, and Jack's blue eyes stared from her laughing face.

She was bleeding. As she shuffled from group to group, she raised her oozing, red wrists. As she drew closer, red slashes appeared on her cheeks, as though she had survived an initiation rite. She had even carved up her own chest, where dark red drops formed crooked words. In the taut white V between her breasts, scarlet lines said, "I love BJ."

Ellie dropped her tray with a whump, and Corinne and Donna screamed.

"Jack!" yelled a female voice. "Bea! Oh, God! Oh, my God!"

Jack and Bea rushed forward, and the girl smiled a silly, triumphant smile. Doctors enclosed her and blocked Ellie's view. Her mocking laugh hovered flutelike over their anxious questions.

"Take it easy, honey," said one of the tense doctors. "How did this happen?"

The girl shrieked with amusement when one of them asked her what day it was.

Ellie withdrew until the black curve of the piano caught her lower back. That mad, bleeding face was Jack's, taunting them with its terrible laugh. Jack's shoulders sagged as the doctors pushed him back. While the literary guests looked on, the medical ones probed their specimen. Jack and Bea clung together, and the room dissolved in Ellie's tears.

He had harbored this in his house and never told her? Was this what he had wanted her to see? She inched her way along the black curve, away from the gore at the circle's center.

"Oh, shit!" muttered someone as his heel squashed a sticky red tart.

In silent panic she ran up the stairs and hurled coats aside as she sought her purse. She threw on her coat and clattered back down, but Jack took no notice of her. The door opened easily. As the frigid air struck her face, a girl was giggling something about Edgar Allan Poe.

In the icy darkness, Ellie could breathe again. It would be all right; she just had to get home. But the white, red-lined face pursued her, accusing her with its terrible pain. It stared at her with Jack's clear eyes. Had he caused this, and was she guilty too? Kids didn't turn out this way by themselves. In coming to her, had he abandoned his daughter, or had he wanted her because he lived in a house full of pain? Ellie had thought of razor blades a year ago when Girish left her, but she hadn't wanted to give him that satisfaction.

Ellie picked her way over the black ice. Last week's snow lay heavy on the city, sticky as well-settled frosting. She clutched her collar and tried to seal her coat against the cold. She was approaching the arcade under the railroad tracks, and a dark, smooth stretch lay before her. Her shoes clicked eerily, and she speeded their rhythm. Only two blocks to go.

Running footsteps thudded behind her. Oh, great, just what she needed—a bunch of drunks horsing around. She pressed herself against the wall to let them pass, but they halted behind her in a burst of flamenco stomps. A thick, strong arm grabbed her neck, and a fist slammed the side of her head. There were two, maybe three of them. The biggest one held her, and the others punched her with hard, angry fists.

It was happening so slowly, so terribly slowly. What were they yelling?

"Shut up, bitch!"

Ellie couldn't make a sound. Her throat was stuck. She stood stupid, rigid, and frozen, unable to move or scream. She tried to hand them her purse, but she couldn't move her arm. She stared at it, stuck in rigor mortis.

"Shut up, bitch!"

What sounds their fists made as they crashed into her face! She couldn't feel them, but she could hear them, solid, wet crunches. They were never going to stop hitting her. They hated her, and they were going to hit her until she was dead. Ellie crouched on the sidewalk and raised her arms to her face. An arm seized her purse, and the attackers galloped off down the arcade.

She screamed a terrible, strangled shriek.

Into the blue phone she punched 9-1-1.

"Nine-one-one, please state the nature of your emergency," said a distant voice.

"I—I've just been mugged," she sobbed.

"Tell me your location," said the voice. "We'll get someone to you right away."

"Fi-ifty-Fifth Street," she stammered, "Fifty-Fifth near Harper, under the railroad tracks."

Ellie stared at a mural, where enslaved men hung like glowing, suspended slabs of meat.

A police car skidded to a halt, and two black officers jumped out. Their faces beamed angry sympathy.

"Are you all right, honey?" asked the older one. "What happened?"

"You shouldn't walk around so late at night," admonished his heavyset partner.

"Shit, Henry, it ain't her fault," interrupted the gray one. "Is there anyone we can call for you, honey?"

Ellie shook her head wordlessly, her voice choked by tears.

"I'm alone," she said.

CHAPTER 8

GHOSTS

DESPITE THE DRIVING RAIN, SAM suggested that he and Jack walk up to Fifty-Third Street. With the quarter over, they could finally escape the iron lung of the quad. A few fat flakes fell among the stinging drops, and Jack and Sam said little as they fought the scouring wind. They headed for the bagel shop, where their neighborhood met the South Side. On Fifty-Third Street, you could buy anything if you dared mingle with your neighbors to the north. Cowed by the street's insistent life, most scholars avoided it, but Jack loved the hearty food and the thump of music from passing cars. The snarls of traffic at the four-way stops revealed the mad circulation of life.

At 12:30 p.m., Fifty-Third Street was nearly empty. The faculty had fled to parts unknown, and the students were shivering in their apartments. Since the horror of Jack's party, end-of-quarter madness had set in. Grimly, Jack had dug through an avalanche of papers and deferred an encounter with Sam. If they were going to talk about anything that mattered, they would have to get away from the quad. Sam had been right to shun the spots where even the gargoyles had ears. But Sam's blissful smile at the scoop of tuna on his bagel made Jack suspect ulterior motives. Jack ordered vegetarian chili, and Sam got some for himself. They settled down at the wooden table farthest from the door.

Jack leaned over his paper cup of chili and drank its pungent steam. He raised his eyes to find Sam studying him sadly.

"So," asked Sam, "how's she doin'?"

He took an enormous bite of his bagel. Tuna gooshed out and fell onto the waxed paper wrapping with a thwack.

"She's all right," answered Jack quickly. "She's going to be okay. She's a tough girl. They didn't break her nose, and they didn't hurt her, thank God. It could have been so much worse. I feel awful—I can't believe she just ran out like that ..."

His voice trailed off at Sam's amused look. Something was smoldering in his dark eyes.

"I was talkin' about your daughter," he said, and took another bite.

Jack laughed uneasily. He wished that he could start eating too.

"Oh, she's going to be okay," he said. "She's been in the ward about a month now. They say she's doing much better. I see her every day, and so does Bea."

Sam tested his chili and shook his head. "God, I hate that place," he muttered.

With a boy whose brain challenged modern neurology, Sam knew his way around the medical center.

Sam savored his chili sadly. "You've gotta get her out of there."

Jack nodded, ashamed. "I can't believe she did that. Why would she hurt herself that way?"

"Who's BJ?" Sam asked, and bit into his bagel.

Jack reflected while his friend chewed. "I don't know. Some

friend of hers, I guess. She won't tell us anything. It's like she's a high priestess, and she won't reveal her rites."

Sam chuckled and shook his head. "Teenagers. I'm not lookin' forward to it."

"She always wants to humiliate us," spurted Jack. "She's always done things like this, but—but never— She likes to ruin things. She likes to sabotage them and watch us flounder."

He paused as the wind rattled the glass panel between them and the pounding rain. The force of Sam's gaze made him squirm.

"She's—she's like Mephisto," he stammered. "Alles, was entsteht, ist wert, daß es zugrunde geht."

"Huh?"

Normally Sam understood Jack's German, as Jack followed most of his Yiddish. But this line from Goethe got lost in his food.

"Oh, it's *Faust,*" said Jack. "Mephisto's motto: everything that comes into being deserves to be destroyed."

"Whew!" Sam shook his head. "What are you, Rosemary? You tellin' me your kid's the devil?"

"Yeah." Jack smiled. "Something like that."

Sam slowly put down his spoon. A hot stream was bubbling to his surface, like an angry jet he couldn't contain.

"Look," he said, "I like you. I've always liked you. But sometimes I just don't get you. What the fuck goes on in your head? You're actin' like your kid's the weather, like she's somethin' bad that happened to you. She wasn't born this way. Whatever's wrong with her, you're part of it, and you've gotta figure out how to get her back."

Sam glanced around at the empty shop. "You're fuckin' up big time, Jack." His black eyes burned with each word. "You've gotta stop fuckin' your student and start talkin' to your kid."

Jack raked a tomato to limp strings.

"My relationship with Ellie has nothing to do with this," he said tensely. "We've been good parents to Jessie. We've given her every opportunity. She's just—perverse. She's always been this way—against us in everything. It's hell on earth living with her. When I try to talk to her, she spits in my face."

Sam swallowed his chili as though craving its heat.

"Do you listen to her?" he asked. "Seems like she's tryin' to get your attention."

Jack stabbed his tomato disgustedly. "Well, she's got it, all right. Ours and the attention of everyone we know. She planned it—she wanted to humiliate us in front of everyone."

Sam's feelings seemed to be wrestling behind his black brows.

"You've gotta see it from her perspective," he urged. He captured a blob of fallen tuna between his finger and thumb. "The way she sees it, you're holdin' her captive in your castle. If you invite someone in, she's gonna ask 'em for help. She's gonna send 'em a note in a bottle."

"Some bottle," Jack muttered. "Her smoke signals are tear gas. They blow everyone away."

"Good metaphor." Sam chewed enthusiastically. "She wants to smoke you out."

"I can't tell what she wants!" exclaimed Jack, frustrated. "She won't talk to us, and she doesn't want to be associated with us in any way. It's as if she's punishing us for something, but she won't tell us what we did."

"Yeah, that's bad," Sam sighed. "It must go way back, but it's not too late to fix it. *Do* somethin'. Let her know you're not leavin' her alone, no matter what she says. A family's not a democracy, Jack. You've gotta let her know who's in charge."

Jack stirred his chili to redistribute the heat. Its red brown clashed with the turquoise cup, decorated with mauve streaks. He raised his eyes to find Sam looking at him as a faith healer gazes at someone he has commanded to see.

A wave of protest rose as Jack inhaled. "It's not right. She's an independent person with her own free will. I can't control her. I can't make her do things."

Sam breathed in and out as though trying to control himself.

"That's bullshit!" he spluttered, his voice thick with food. "You fell for your own radical shit! I've been there! I fought for human rights, and they gassed and arrested me too. But a family, Jack, that's different. With kids you've gotta tell 'em what to do! Didn't your parents tell *you* what to do?"

Jack pulled at his memory. "No, not really," he mused. "If we ever did anything wrong, they made us feel so guilty that after a while, we didn't want to do it anymore. But Jessie's like Teflon, guilt rolls right off her."

Sam chuckled and shook his head. He crammed the last of his bagel into his mouth. While chewing, he shifted his attention to another front.

"What's goin' on with Ellie anyway?" he demanded. "What were you thinkin', invitin' her to your house like that? When I walked in and saw her standin' there next to Bea, I almost lost it!"

"She noticed that," said Jack cuttingly. "She was pretty upset."

His reproach provoked further indignation.

"She was upset because you were paradin' her around in front of your wife!" exclaimed Sam. "She was so upset she ran out and practically got herself killed!"

He lowered his voice as the door swung open, bringing a blast of icy air. Jack glanced up but saw only some workers from a nearby construction site. Grim and wet, they scowled at the overhead menu. Jack returned his attention to Sam, who seemed to know that Ellie's presence had been Jack's idea.

"She wanted to come," he protested. "She wanted to meet Jessie and Bea."

Sam scraped the sides of his paper cup to retrieve the last drops of chili.

"Can't you see she did it to please you?" he asked. "She would have met Hitler if you'd asked her to."

Jack shuddered, angry and frightened. Sam rarely alluded to anything German, and this jab warned of weapons held in reserve.

"Look," said Jack hotly, "she's a free, intelligent woman. She can do whatever she wants."

"Yeah?" shot Sam. "I hear she's doin' Girish. She free to do that?"

"Where did you hear that?" demanded Jack.

Sam smiled deeply, comfortable with his powers.

"You never reveal your sources," he murmured. "But don't worry, my information's good."

Jack must have looked wretched, for Sam spoke more compassionately.

"Look. You've gotta ask yourself where this is goin'. You gonna divorce Bea, you gonna marry this kid?"

"No!" gasped Jack, and Sam's shoulders relaxed.

"Okay, so you're not completely nuts. That's a start," he said cheerfully.

Sam's face assumed the sad, confused look it got when he discovered there was no more to eat. Jack choked on a laugh and took advantage of the pause to swallow a spoonful of chili.

"So what's the deal, then?" asked Sam. "She's out of here in what, two, three months? You gonna invent conferences on the West Coast? You gonna do her on the phone?"

"Email," corrected Jack, and they laughed uneasily.

"So why not just stop now," urged Sam, "while you still can, before your wife finds out and things get really fucked up?"

"No one's going to find out," insisted Jack.

"Yeah, right," muttered Sam. "That's what Nixon said."

He looked around restlessly, as though searching for something.

"Do you want anything else to eat?" asked Jack innocently.

"Nah, I shouldn't." Sam sighed and patted his rounded belly.

With effort he returned to the subject at hand.

"So are you gonna give her up? What, is the sex that good?"

"It isn't the sex," whispered Jack, tormented.

"Yeah, right." Sam smiled. "And they want me to ride jockey at Belmont."

"No, really." Jack struggled. "It's—it's—the connection. I feel connected to her somehow."

"Are you tryin' to tell me you love her?" asked Sam. "You feel connected to Bea too?"

"Yes, to both of them!" cried Jack. "But it's different with Bea— it's a different kind of bond."

Sam frowned, as though worry were flooding his anger. "This ain't *The King and I*," he said half-humorously. "You get only one wife here. You pays your money, you takes your choice. You done good—you got yourself a good one. Now you gotta make sacrifices to preserve what's valuable."

"What *is* valuable?" asked Jack miserably as the wind shook the glass panel.

In a final surge, Sam lost control.

"I don't get you!" he almost yelled. "I don't get you! I used to like you! I mean, this place is full of pricks who've never seen anything, and you know stuff—you've always been real. You grew up in the Bronx, for Chrissake. What the hell happened to you? What goes on in your head? Don't you care about anything?"

"Truth," said Jack. He answered so quickly that the word passed through a mouthful of chili and emerged as "troof." Jack swallowed, then shot back at Sam, "Why? What do you care about?"

"My kids," said Sam forcefully. "And—and Ruth. Ruth and my kids."

They looked at each other as though mourning something they had lost.

"It's okay," muttered Sam, retreating. "I'm sorry. I was out of line."

"No," said Jack. "It's all right. I know you're trying to help."

They stared at each other until a prickling in Jack's nose made him worry he was going to cry. Sam looked old and weary as he weighed the words he was about to speak.

"I'm gonna tell you somethin'," he began cautiously. "I'm gonna tell you somethin' I probably shouldn't be tellin' you."

Jack straightened, intrigued.

"I told you I've never done anything," he continued. "I told you I've been tempted but I've never been unfaithful to Ruth."

"Yeah," breathed Jack, worried about what he was going to hear.

"Well," said Sam, "I lied."

Jack could think of nothing to say. He stared at Sam's impenetrable smile.

"Oh, I'm a good liar." Sam sighed and shook his head.

"My God," whispered Jack. "When was this? Was it more than once? Was it anyone I know?"

"Oh, it was a long time ago," said Sam. "Nobody you know. A really long time ago. God, it was awful."

"Did Ruth—"

"No." Sam cut him off. "And she never will either. And if you tell anybody"—he gazed at Jack steadily—"I'll kill you."

Jack felt his innards turn cold. Sam smiled straight into him, but his dark eyes showed no mirth. Sam's thick wrists and meaty hands would obey his powerful will. He wasn't kidding. Sam could destroy him, if not by violence, then with his damnable web of connections.

Sam's chair scraped the gritty floor.

"Gimme a minute," he said, and ambled heavily away.

Jack stirred his lukewarm chili and listened to the construction workers. He heard the word "Bulls" a few times and quickly lost interest. Sam hurried back, a large chocolate chip cookie in each hand. He offered one to Jack, but he shook his head. Sam wrapped one large cookie in a napkin and smiled guiltily.

"For later," he explained. "I've got a lot of papers to grade."

Jack wondered how Sam could assuage a death threat with a cookie, but he warmed in spite of his fear. Sam's lips closed softly on the chocolate chip round, and he shut his eyes to savor the pleasure. Jack looked at his friendly bulk and couldn't suppress a smile. A long time ago, he had said, but he was such a good liar. It could have been any of them. It could have been Ellie herself.

"What I just told you," muttered Sam, "I told you to show you I been there."

He closed his eyes again, and an erotic smile confirmed the truth of his confession.

"I'm tellin' you to let you know you can stop, even if you think you can't," Sam insisted. "I did, and you can too. It hurts like hell, but it feels better as soon as it's over."

Jack nodded, unconvinced, and felt Sam give up the struggle. Sam swallowed the last of his cookie.

"I gotta get goin'," he mumbled. "I'm meetin' the dean in half an hour."

"What for?" asked Jack.

Sam shook his head. "Don't ask. You know Ellie's friend Lucy? Well, I still can't get her any teachin' for next year. If she can't teach, she's outa here, and it's not lookin' good. Poor kid. She's smart, and she's writin' good stuff. This administration suffers from chronic financial constipation. They won't pass money for anybody."

Jack laughed, relieved to hear Sam being himself again. Sam rolled into his coat and stuffed the remaining cookie in his pocket.

"It's awful," Sam laughed. "It's all your fault. At your party, Ruth got to Corinne. Now she's organized the girls against me, and they won't give me anything to eat. It's a friggin' conspiracy."

Jack considered telling Sam to hang out with boys, but somehow he couldn't picture it. As they headed back to campus, the wind seemed to have reversed, so that freezing drops bit their faces again. Sam reached into his pocket and unwrapped his second cookie.

"You sure you don't want some?" he asked.

Jack shook his head and tried to steal breaths from the wind.

"Don't tell my wife," muttered Sam, munching. "Hey, I think I'm gonna go see Jessie. That okay with you?"

"Yeah, sure, just don't fuck her," Jack heard himself saying.

Sam choked and slapped him on the back.

"There's hope for you!" he cried. "That was the Bronx talkin'!"

Jack laughed with Sam as he took another bite.

Shit, man, I've got to get out of this place. The people in here are seriously fucked up. Gordon, he talks to angels sometimes, and Kelly, she paws through my stuff. She roots through all the drawers in my room, like some squirrel looking for a lost nut. She goes away when I ask, but then she comes back, digging through all my clothes. She says that she did a whole gram of dust. It's sad—must have shorted out her mind. And Lenora freaks out, starts screaming for no reason, until they wrestle her down and stab her with needles. Most of them are losers with fucked-up lives, or people like me everyone wants to get rid of. Now they've got me where they want me, fucking wimp, fucking bitch. They've locked me up, and they just need for me to die.

The parade's been good, though, I've got to say, everyone streaming in to see me. They all look so guilty and so scared. Bitch shows up two, three times a day. In her puke-green doctor suit, she finally looks like what she is. Where did they get that color anyway? She keeps coming and asking me how I feel, once with blood on her from somebody's baby she killed. Probably she thought I wouldn't see it, just a few burning drops. But I know damn well where it came from. When I ask her about it, she looks down, shocked. Must be so used to blood she doesn't see it. Now that I'm her patient, she can treat me like one. Finally she's got my blood on her. In her green, toxic scrubs she looks like what she is, a heartless, baby-killing dyke.

The wimp is funnier—I'd feel sorry for him if he weren't such a frigging prick. He tries to talk to me like he writes his books, with a hundred cue cards telling him what to say. It's like someone's telling him to talk to me, and since he always obeys orders, he does his best. He keeps asking, can he bring me anything, so I say, yeah, bring me my Morrison poster and my CDs. So he actually brings it, and he says he likes Morrison. The guy is so full of shit, it's sad. The fuck you do, I say. Like, yeah, he likes Morrison, but he says that in college, he listened to him all the time. I test him a little, and he does know some lyrics, but he doesn't really *know* them. I mean, you can teach a parrot to talk, but he doesn't understand what it means.

I tell him Morrison is not in his world, and he asks how I know what his world is. He says he took drugs and protested the war, but it's like he's talking about someone who died. I've known you my whole life, I say. Maybe you went through the motions because someone told you to. But there's no way you *felt* any of that. You're a fucking robot, and you'll always be a robot. Only thing that changes is who's holding the remote. Like those Nazi officers, just obeying orders, but I don't say that, because he looks like he's going to cry. I tell him thanks for the CDs, maybe we can listen to one. I put on the Doors' first album, but he still looks like he's going to cry.

Who's BJ? he keeps asking me. Who's BJ? Can't you tell me who he is?

Just a guy, I say. You wouldn't understand.

After a while he gives up and just sits there, but still he won't go away.

Best time I have is when his fat friend shows up, this funny old professor with sexy eyes. Why has he brought his stupid daughter with him? He looks right at home, but she looks scared. What is he thinking, like, I'll want to *play* with her or something? I mean, she's thirteen, and I'm sixteen.

He unwraps this big chocolate thing and tells me to eat it. His daughter, she looks like she could swallow it whole. I say I'm not hungry, and I save it for the nurses. Nobody's going to fuck with my body, make me into a fat blimp like them. You have to watch out for fat people. Just like gay people try to convince you you're gay, fat people try to make you fat like them.

But this fat guy is so sexy I want to, like, *do* him, and probably I would if his daughter weren't there. He looks into me with these dark, wet eyes, and he kisses me like he's loving each bite. It makes me want to kiss him back, and then I see his kid standing there.

His pep talk is so much better than the wimp's.

What are you doin' to yourself? he asks. This is childish stuff. You gotta grow up. You can't cut yourself. Wanna fuck the establishment? Don't fuck yourself. Stick around. Don't check out now. Wait till you're eighteen, then you can do whatever the fuck you want.

He says it all with this, like, *gleam* in his eye, like he wishes his kid weren't there either.

She just keeps staring, like I'm a fucking freak. I feel sorry for her, so I say I liked her bas mitzvah, and her Hebrew singing was cool.

She smiles at me just like her father and says she can teach me when I get out.

What is it with this place, something in the air? Every frigging kid wants to teach. They're all just a bunch of clones of their frigging professor moms and dads.

The fat guy sends her outside to see some pictures we drew, and then he grabs my wrists.

Look at me, he says. C'mon, Jessie. C'mere. Your arms are healin' nicely. You got such pretty skin. Soon it's gonna be all nice and smooth again.

Stop shakin', he says. I ain't gonna eat you. You're twitchin' like nobody's ever touched you before.

He's right. Nobody has ever touched me the way this guy's holding me now.

He looks into my eyes and demands, Who's BJ?

Just a guy, I say, and he growls, Don't gimme that shit.

I try to pull back, but he grips me hard.

He your boyfriend? he asks, and I nod.

Then I shake my head no. He's not my boyfriend. Not anymore.

Look, he says, his voice low and sexy, if you love this guy BJ, don't do this. We guys are all jerks. We think with our cocks. You cut yourself up, he won't care. Carvin' his name on your chest doesn't tell the rest of us anything, because we don't know who the fuck he is. All it does is ruin this pretty, smooth skin of yours. It's a waste, just a *waste*, you hear?

He kisses me where the scars are healing, and it feels so soft, so pure.

You wanna show someone you love him, he says, you do it by stayin' alive. All kinds of guys are gonna want you, 'cause you're fuckin' *gorgeous*, you hear? Plus you're smart, and you've got real style. Once you're outa here, the guys are gonna be on you, and BJ will bang his head against the wall.

And another thing, he says, as long as I gotcha—

He's enjoying this, pressing his round belly against me. I thought it would be soft, like a dough boy, but this old guy is fat and hard.

I'm tellin' you, he says, that your father loves you.

The fuck he does, I say.

He tenses. He's scary when he's mad, and his hands turn to iron shackles.

There's stuff you don't know, but your father loves you. He's screwed up, but he's doin' his best. Give him a break, will ya?

His hands relax as we laugh at my stupid wimp father. He won't release me till I promise him that tomorrow I'll talk to the wimp.

That's not good enough, he says. You gotta promise me more.

What is this? I ask. If the cops made me confess this way, it would never hold up.

Oh, a smart-ass, he says. A girl after my own heart. He drops my wrists, but he skewers me with his black eyes.

Both of us know, he says, that your father's a nut. But he's a good nut, and he means well. And shit, he's the only one you got, so you might as well make the best of it. Look on the bright side. You coulda had me.

He keeps scanning me like he's reading my thoughts. Screams from the hallway tear the air, and Rachel rushes in crying. Lenora must have had a fit, a bad one from the way this girl's carrying on. When the old guy sees her sobbing, he forgets about me, like I disappeared into thin air. Stupid kid, hasn't she seen anyone freak out before? He wraps his arms around her and says it'll be all right, they're taking care of the girl, and he'll get her away from here.

He turns around just once on his way out. If I hear you been up to any more shit, I'm comin' back, you hear?

Yeah, right, I say. Whatever.

He fondles his clone and leads her out the door.

Yesterday morning, Tanesha shows up. She brings little Michael, who's having a good day. He's so sweet when he's good, laughing and kicking, and we play peekaboo and pinch his toes.

Shit, girl, says Tanesha. You gotta get outa this place. Nancy told Aunt Lou about you, an' she real upset.

She's upset? I ask, and she says, Yeah, she worried. She would have come herself, but she ain't feelin' so good.

That's too bad, I say. What's up with Tyrell?

He don't come round no more, Tanesha says. Beej say he with Lucinda, this slutty whore from West Chicago.

Wow, that really sucks.

You tellin' me, girl. They all some worthless, selfish pigs.

I tell her the one about cocks for brains, and she says, That just how it is.

I look at her with her laughing, squirming baby, and I know what she's going to say.

He with Charisse now. We tell him he a fool, but he wanna be with her.

Who's Charisse? I ask, and she says, Don't ask. She nobody. Big mouth, big ass. She been chasin' him forever, just now the first time he dumb enough to get caught. I don't know wassup with him. Prob'ly she'll make him a baby, so she can tell everybody he her man. Me an' Aunt Lou, we like you better, but he don't listen to us.

I thank her for telling me. I like it when people tell it to me straight. I say, Michael's a great baby. Let's make him treat women right, not like his uncle and dad.

You said it, girl, she murmurs, and we listen to music, one ear apiece. She lets me change Michael—I've gotten good at it now. Then she has to go, since she has job training.

When you gettin' out? she asks, and I say, When they think I'm not crazy anymore.

You in trouble, girl, she laughs, and I say, No shit.

When you learn to act like you ain't crazy, you come round and see us, you hear? You just tell 'em what they wanna hear, but inside you be who you wanna be.

Tanesha is right. I've got to get out of this place. I guess I could do it. Just how do I keep a straight face when I tell these fools what they want to hear?

Ever since Ellie had sung that winding melody, Jack had hungered for the *St. Matthew Passion*. Tonight, three months of rehearsal would culminate in three hours of pulsing music. As Jack sought the best acoustic spot, he avoided seats under suspended lamps. He had never heard of one falling yet, but he couldn't listen with the thought of slamming death waiting overhead.

Somehow the chapel felt different tonight. Its vast gray space offered the cold welcome of a clean, modern cathedral. The church had been named for a wealthy family for whom bigness was a virtue. Maroon-and-gold banners draped the walls, displaying college colors like battle flags. Overhead, gothic arches dissolved into darkness, except where they were painted with peppermint stripes. Byzantine medallions shone like wheels of color and sported gold animals with rounded jaws. The altar dripped a gray, lacy mess of incoherent detail. Over it, a blue glass window hung poised like a five-blade propeller. The only grace lay in the organ, where glowing angels blew wooden trumpets. What was wrong tonight? Was something missing? Jack looked around him, but the chapel's elements answered his gaze as though he were taking roll.

In nearby pews, several friends waved, and people greeted Jack and smiled. The university's music lovers knew each other, and this three-hour concert on a rainy Good Friday had attracted the hardiest crowd. Bea should have been sitting next to him. She had been looking forward to the concert but at the last minute had been paged for a delivery. Protesting feebly, he tried to talk her out of it, but she laughed and shook her head. Mrs. Martin was her patient, and you couldn't control when the babies came. Besides, she was expecting trouble with this one. When she got a moment, she would look in on Jessie.

The orchestra members took their places, and the chorus filed in. Impatiently Jack watched for Ellie. Lately it seemed as though he had been able to see her less and less. Ah, there she was! In her black concert gown, she moved as gracefully as a cat. She had pinned her brown hair up, since she couldn't sing for three hours with silken threads hanging between her eyes and the music. Jack knew people who had fainted during the *St. Matthew Passion*, overcome by the sheer force of the thing. But Ellie was an athlete, an artist—*Verdammt*. A tall girl stood in front of her, blocking his view. Despite Ellie's size, the director had placed her in back, where her pure voice could flow down to guide the others. No—"flow" wasn't the right word. Ellie's clean voice worked more like the lasers that inscribed his silver CDs.

Ah, the A. The orchestra was tuning, and the A greeted Jack with its bright ring. Like his father, Jack could pull an A from thin air, and the brief homage to it at the opening of each concert stilled him like a religious ritual. Religion—if only Sam could hear this, but tonight was the first seder. Sam would be home with his family. Surrounded by people close enough to touch, Jack gazed at the performers, alone.

Starting in the strings, the music twisted to life with a terrible, melodic ache. In the opening chorus, Bach had captured the agony of human life. With their beauty, the notes thrilled Jack's ear, but it hurt to listen, as it hurts to watch someone die. Jack held his breath at the first choral entrance, but the altos slipped in perfectly and matched their turns to the winding dance. Like a grieving body, the music pulled itself forward and begged the listener to share its pain. Come, you daughters, help me mourn. In all the world, his father said, there was nothing like this. Bach had turned sorrow to sound, so that anyone who heard it felt the ache.

From the beginning, Jack's father had known that his younger son shared his ear. When it came to music, he addressed Jack as an equal, traded secrets, asked him his views. His mother and Rudi respected music, but Jack heard it in ways they did not. For Christmas, said his father, Bach had written glorious melodies. Now listen to the *St. Matthew Passion*. What do you hear?

Except in the opening, the piece was propelled by exploding fragments. The broken dialogue conveyed the violence of the words. The Evangelist moved the story forward, but the split choir hacked with sadistic glee. As a chorus, the singers asked listeners to sympathize, to feel guilt and pity and shame. But as characters in the drama, they played the monster: the vicious crowd screaming for blood. Few arias or chorales soothed the mind—Bach offered little comforting melody. Instead, the Evangelist narrated, and the choir cried out in savage shrieks.

What a story! A tale of cruelty, stupidity, and waste. Bach vivified a dialogue among people who, given every chance, called only for death. Jack couldn't help thinking of Nietzsche, who condemned Christianity as a religion of cringing slaves. How despicable, to worship weakness. What could be said of a people who tortured their God and then bowed to his suffering form? So patently infantile, so clearly neurotic, Freud had said. Jack didn't believe in God, but he believed in the cruelty of man.

This was what Bach had set to music: "Seht auf unsre Schuld"— "See our guilt." He had created a melodic plea to mourn people's most hideous tendencies. His music demanded you confront your guilt and face all the terrible things you had done. Jack shuddered in its grip. Feeling as though he had killed God's son himself, he ached for atonement that could never come.

It was almost impossible to see Ellie, but Jack knew she was shaping these sounds. He watched for the softness of her braided brown hair, which shone in fleeting glimpses. One inspiring chorale warmed him a little: "What My God Will, May That Be Done." Its harmony affirmed the horrors as part of a larger whole that would end in resurrection. The surge of life seemed so distant, though, and the cruel torture so much more real. Supposedly resurrection was two days away, but Jack saw only endless, aching night.

When the first part ended with Christ's arrest, hot tears filled Jack's eyes. To evade the glances of his friends, he scanned the overhead galleries. Above clean gray stone, an array of faces floated uncertainly. Jack paused at a middle-aged man, who looked somehow familiar. His graying hair was curly and thick, and he wore a rough, heavy brown jacket. He sat quietly as though still listening and kept his weary eyes closed.

Jack read through the program and thrilled with excitement when he saw Ellie's name. With Bea in the hospital, he might see Ellie tonight. He stared at the words until the letters dissolved as he waited for the music to start again.

The second half cut deeper than the first. As false witnesses denounced Christ, Bach made the listeners feel each word. The crowd hit Jesus and spat in his face. "*Weissage!*" they hooted in a swirl of scorn. "Prophesy to us, Christ! Who struck you?" In these notes, Bach conveyed the cruelty of every blow ever cast. Jack felt the fists hitting Ellie and the hate that had killed six million Jews. Bach had turned it all to sound: people's sick need to strike and their befuddled awakening to the awful results of their blows.

The Evangelist sang of Peter's denial and of Judas's suicide. For the Passover feast, Pilate offered to free a prisoner of the crowd's choice. In a dissonant shriek rehearsed for months, the chorus cried out, "Barrabam!" They wanted the notorious thief and not the degraded Christ. What a shame, Jack thought, that Matthew had left out the most cutting line. He could almost hear the bass in the *St. John Passion*, singing, "What is truth?" Why did John have Pilate ask this, when in Matthew, the Roman accepted Christ's words? Jack suspected John's storyteller instinct. Maybe the line about "truth" had popped up and seemed too good to throw out.

"Let his blood be upon us," sang the choir, "and on our children." From this point on, the Passion streamed with hot, free-flowing blood. The schizophrenic chorus spat at Christ, then sang about his pain. Their dark chorale, "Oh Head, All Scarred and Bleeding," made Jack feel Christ's burning wounds. It was he who spat on the bleeding prophet, he who nailed his hands to the cross.

Jack's pain overflowed in tears. Music often dissolved him, and the swollen feeling reigned unchecked. An old woman nudged him and offered a tissue.

"Powerful, isn't it?" she whispered.

Jack nodded without a word.

The bass sang to God with a tormented plea, "Lord, Make My Heart Pure." To clear his head, Jack gazed at the galleries, and his eyes found the middle-aged man. Why was he— The man opened his eyes and looked directly at Jack. He stopped breathing, and the tissue fell from his hand. It was his father.

Jack squeezed his eyes shut. When he opened them, his father was still fixing him with his sad, ironic gaze. He looked as he had on the day of his death—five years younger than Jack was now. As Jack stared in horror, his father smiled with a look of disappointment and pain. What was his father doing here? What did he want? Jack studied his look of injured sensitivity. His father was trying to tell him something. He pointed down toward the singers, and Jack shifted his eyes to the glowing altar. The choir was singing sorrowfully, and the strings stirred the heavy air. There was nothing to see; the only spectacle was the sound. Confused, Jack raised his eyes to the gallery, but his father was gone.

Jack drew a shaky breath and bent to retrieve his tissue. The old woman handed him another as the chorus began its final dirge. The last movement marked a new beginning—the emergence of consciousness and shame. Having tormented and killed their savior, the people wished him a peaceful rest. They sang of sinking down beside him, of dissolving in their tears. "Ruhe sanfte, sanfte ruh," they sighed. "Rest gently, gently rest." The last note was barely a breath.

The explosion of applause hit Jack like a crude, insulting blow. It contradicted each note of the music, but his own hands clapped too, unable to lie still. The old woman struggled to stand, and Jack helped her to her feet.

"Thank you—you're kind!" she shouted over the applause.

In the gallery hung only a blur of unrecognizable faces.

For the first time, Jack embraced Ellie publicly. He crushed her against him until she could hardly breathe. She tilted her head back, and it looked as though he had been crying.

"It was beautiful," he murmured and cupped her face in his hands.

How strange—Jack didn't seem like himself tonight. Things had been tense since that awful party, but his touch said he wanted her still.

A bent, wrinkled woman pulled at his elbow.

"I knew it!" She smiled. "I knew you must have a daughter singing. My husband said I could always tell these things. Lovely job, dear, beautiful job! You must have inherited his ear."

Before Jack could speak, she moved away, having spotted a young man among the tenors. Jack was staring at Ellie in horror, his fingers frozen on her velvet dress. She wondered at his sudden recklessness—everyone in the chapel could see.

"Jack, are you all right?" she asked. "Who was that? Do you know her?"

"No, she was just sitting next to me." His voice broke. "She gave me a tissue—" He held up a dense, crumpled wad.

Ellie stepped back. She had to get him out of here, but she couldn't break away from the singers, who were calling her from every side. Jack reached up to finger her coiled braids, and a soprano shot her an amused glance.

"*Schön*," he whispered.

Ellie pulled his hand away and shuddered at the sadness in his eyes.

"What's wrong, Jack?" she asked, but he only shook his head.

"Nothing. May I walk you home? No one's going to hit you again if I can help it."

The south wind had warmed the wet night and brought black, bitter tar from the mills. They hurried along Fifty-Eighth Street, past the Experimental School and dark, U-shaped buildings full of sleeping people. Jack seemed to relish the sound of her clicking heels and stopped to crush her with a kiss.

"You're beautiful," he said. "You, your music—I haven't told you enough."

She longed only to escape watching eyes in any of a hundred windows.

"Are you sure you can come in?" she asked.

"For a little while," he said. "Bea's doing a delivery."

His realistic answer reassured her, and she realized how much she had craved his voice. Out of habit, she fastened her four locks while Jack embraced her from behind. He seemed fascinated by her braids and kept kissing them as he helped her remove her coat. He tossed it onto the blue velvet chair and faced her with a look of wonder.

"Do you want anything to eat or drink?" she asked. "Do you want to listen to some music?"

Jack shook his head, content as he was. He cupped his palms over her ears.

"I can hear the sea." She smiled, suddenly feeling her exhaustion. *"Whshsh ... shsh ..."*

"Shsh," he echoed, and stepped in close so that she stood in his shadow. He moved his hands slowly down her neck, then out along her black velvet arms. Ellie spread her wings like a condor, and he rested his fingertips on hers. He ran his fingers back in along her arms, and she shivered with delight.

"You're cold," he murmured. His hands settled on her breasts.

"No—" she gasped.

His fingers found her nipples. Ellie felt herself pulsing, tightening.

"Let me warm you," he whispered.

Jack spread his fingers and caressed her, his hands moving in slow circles. Ellie raised her hands to his face. Her tears surged as she met his eyes.

"Jack!" she breathed.

"Shsh ..."

He led her to the couch and kissed her gently, then drew back, drinking her with his eyes.

"I want to talk to you all night," he murmured. "I want to touch you. All night, I want to touch you and tell you things."

"So tell me." She smiled. She kissed his fingers, softly sucking the tips.

"There's so much—" he struggled. "I don't know where to begin."

Ellie ran her tongue along his finger, toward an unknown nexus at the center of his palm.

"Ohhh ..." he sighed. His eyelids drooped. "You'd better not ... I can't think—I—"

She gave his palm a final kiss and switched off the lamp. The room dissolved into grayness, glimmering with uncertain light from the street.

"Talk to me," she whispered. "Tell me about Jessie. How's Jessie doing?"

"The same." He drew a deep breath. "I still go there every day. She doesn't want to tell me anything."

"What does she say?" asked Ellie.

It was easy to answer a stray voice in the dark.

"Oh, usually to fuck off," he laughed. "But sometimes I learn things. I'm learning about what music she likes and who she knows. I've told her all about me. About the drugs I took, the time they arrested me—"

"Did you tell her about this?" Ellie freed his shoulder. "Did you tell her about when they hit you?"

She kissed his scar, and his thoughts seemed to dissolve. She loved exploring him and had long since mapped his sensitive spots. Of all of them, his marred right shoulder seemed most receptive to her touch. When his smashed nerves had knitted, they had gained sensitivity, so that her soft, wet lips set him writhing. She kissed the scar's jagged baldness in slow, wet touches, giving the tiniest pushes with her tongue.

"No—" moaned Jack. "Please, not—"

"Okay." She retreated. "Sorry."

Ellie settled on top of him, and he pulled pins from her coiled-up hair.

"Did you find out who BJ is?" she asked.

"No," he sighed. "Not even Sam could do that."

"Sam?" she asked, startled.

"Yeah," he murmured. "He went to see her, but she wouldn't tell him anything either. Well—he learned that BJ is some guy who dumped her, but we all sort of knew that."

"That's funny," Ellie giggled. "Sam—"

"Yeah, he's an amazing guy," said Jack. "He really wants to help, but she won't talk to anyone. She's like the Sphinx."

Ellie laughed in the darkness. "God, I hope I never have kids."

"Oh, you will," said Jack. "I mean—I hope you will. You'd be a good mother. I'd like to make more of you." He patted her belly affectionately.

"Would you—would you want to have a baby with me?" she asked.

Jack breathed the gray air in silence.

"Maybe," he said. "I mean, if I were free."

This wasn't what he wanted to talk about. Ellie persisted, hoping that if she pressed from each side, the dome trapping his thoughts would yield. Suddenly she lost herself.

"I—I feel—I'm sorry," she sobbed. "I'm sorry, Jack—I don't ever want to hurt you. I don't want to hurt your wife and Jessie. I—I liked her. She was so—"

"Shsh."

Jack pressed her against him, and her cheek rested on his warm chest. Under his tickling hairs, his skin was slippery and wet.

"Shsh," he said. "I'm the one who's wrong. I'm the one hurting you. I—"

"I don't want to make trouble for you and your wife." Ellie's voice heaved. "I—I wish I could be your second wife. I wish I could be your mistress."

"You're much more than that," he asserted. "You're too good for that. You deserve better. Your own family, someday—"

"But I don't want anyone but you!" Her shrill voice slit the dark.

"You will." He stroked her loosening hair. "You will."

He pulled another bobby pin, and the coiled snakes came free.

"You're going to San Diego. You're going to have a wonderful life."

"I want to be with you," she moaned. "I want to be with you."

"I'll write to you," he comforted. "I'll call you. We'll see each other sometimes."

He stroked her in silence until her heaving body lay quiet under his touch.

"Would you want me to come with you?" he asked. "Do you want me to leave Bea?"

"No," she said sadly. "This is who you are—your family, this place. I can't ask you to do that."

"Because if you wanted me to—" He hesitated.

"No," she said quickly. "I don't want you to do that."

He slipped the elastics off her braids and wiggled his fingers through them. In his breathing, she sensed some relief.

"Ellie," he whispered. "What about Girish? I have to know what you feel for him."

His fingers were working their way through her hair.

"I have been with him sometimes," she confessed. "It's different from what I feel for you. He's so funny. He makes me—" Desperately, she sought words that would tell the truth without hurting him.

"It's all right," he assured her. "I know what he's like."

"I used to want him so badly. He made me wish I were dead. He seemed to want me, but he didn't, really. After he'd slept with me a few times, he said no intelligent man could be interested in a long-term relationship with a woman, and if that was what I wanted, I should look for someone else."

"Wow." Jack recoiled. "What happened? Did he change his mind?"

"No," she laughed. "I don't know. Maybe I did."

"Or his libido is stronger than his ideology."

"Could be," she chuckled.

"Well, who am I to talk?" he laughed. "I can't be very bright. I've been with the same woman for twenty-six years."

"I know," she said solemnly. "That's a wonderful thing. I don't want to ruin that."

"Don't worry, you haven't," he answered.

She flushed to discover the depth of her hypocrisy. She must have wanted a different answer. As always, Jack had responded only to her spoken words.

"You're sure you're all right tonight?" she asked. "It's getting pretty late."

"I don't want to go home," he said. "Let me touch you a little while."

Ellie pulled her black gown over her head and slid out of her slip and bra. Exposed to the air, her flesh contracted, and Jack reached for her excitedly. She smiled down at him, her fingers seeking the warm leather of his belt. Impatiently he pulled her to him and brought his lips to her hardened nipple. As his warm tongue found the tip of her breast, Ellie moaned and arched her back. Free at last, her hair fell in a silky shower across his face.

In the darkness, she felt herself floating, tethered only by murmurs below. She kissed his neck and helped him out of his clothes, then settled onto him, triumphant. Ellie's soul stretched itself as he slipped into her and filled her up. She bounced and clutched him, and he gripped her harder. Filled with sleepy joy, she raised her arms in the air and threw back her head.

"Deeper!" she begged. "Please, deeper!"

Jack gasped his assent, and she leaned all the way forward, then all the way back. She wanted him to reach her innermost core, to break right through to her soul. If he pushed hard enough, he just might find it. She bounced and tried to increase the force of that slamming, penetrating blow. Jack trembled and clutched her convulsively.

"Oh, God—" he cried. "Ellie—"

He came with a shout and lay still beneath her. She kissed his ears and crept over him so that she could feel him breathe.

"Good?" she murmured.

"Mm," he moaned.

He massaged her wet back weakly. His touch said that he wanted to rest, so she listened to the lulls between his heart's thumps. His breathing slowed, and she spun in the darkness.

"Jack?" she whispered.

"Oh!" He started. "Oh, wow, I was almost asleep."

"Jack. You still haven't told me, have you?"

"Told you what?"

He sounded very sleepy. She fought the urge to drift off with him, knowing the dangers it might bring.

"You wanted to talk to me. You wanted to tell me something. I don't think you've told me what it was."

"It's all right," he murmured. "This is good, just like this."

She resisted, determined to free him.

"It was something about the music, wasn't it? When you found me tonight, you looked upset. Was it Jessie? Was it something about Jessie?"

"No," he whispered. "It was my father."

Underneath her belly, his breathing quickened.

"That's right," she said. "Your father loved that music."

"Yes," he answered.

The black silence throbbed.

"So it was something about your father?"

He stroked her naked sides.

"I saw him," he said.

"What?" she gasped.

"I saw him. Sitting up in the gallery. On the left-hand side."

"You saw him?" She shuddered.

"It's okay," he laughed weakly. "It is pretty funny. Maybe I should be in the nuthouse instead of my daughter."

"No, really—you saw him?" asked Ellie. "I mean, what did he do? What did he say?"

"Oh, not much," said Jack. "He pointed toward the altar, near where you were singing."

His voice shuddered, and he began to cry.

"Wha—what is it?" asked Ellie, but he kept on sobbing as though she weren't there. "What is it?"

She grabbed his shoulders. Jack made an effort to speak.

"I—I to-old you how he died."

"Yes, horrible," she said. "A heart attack, when you were thirteen."

"It wa-asn't a heart attack."

Ellie had never seen a man cry, and fear hardened her insides.

"What was it?" she asked.

"He killed himself!" spluttered Jack.

"Oh, God," she breathed.

"He-ee hanged himself. My mother found him. She called us home from school. She was crying so hard—and—and cursing. I never heard her curse like that. *Der Feigling! Und dieser Zettel, dieser verdammte—*"

"Jack!" she cried. "Speak English!"

He settled under her clutching fingers and tried to speak again.

"He-ee left a note. He was always so unhappy. I don't blame him, my mother crushing everything—his music—"

"That note," demanded Ellie. "That note, what did it say?"

"It said, '*Es lohnt sich nicht.*'"

"What is that? What is that?" she begged.

"It's not worth it," he said.

When the police attacked, Jack and Cathy had been in the library for six days. Jack hadn't wanted to go, but once they smashed the glass on the security door, the students rushed into the pierced stronghold in a roiling wave. Jack ran right after them, following the bobs of Cathy's bouncing hair.

They had been living on sandwiches and canned fruit, and he was sick of slimy bologna. Lately he hadn't swallowed much of it, since the conservatives had cut off their food. Jack pictured the blockade of neatly dressed athletes outraged by the slobs disrupting their school. For the most part, the invaders had realized the president's worst nightmares. In the administrative wing of the university's finest building, they had rifled through student files and scattered orange peel. What else could they do, with no garbage cans? They had filled them first thing, so that when the pigs shut off the water and threw tear gas, they could splash away some of the burn. For six days, Jack had eaten sandwiches and pineapple cubes and discussed the future of the world. Nights he slept under a balled-up blanket, his breath absorbed in Cathy's springy curls.

Practical and philosophical, the planning meetings droned on. Jack sat through all of them and drank the self-important words. Even as a freshman, Bea emerged as a central figure, and her red-haired friend Robbie proved more decent than he had seemed. Jack had his doubts about their goals and methods, but their way of thinking fascinated him. What if these rebels were right? They voiced ideas he had never dared think, and then they debated how to act on them. In the middle of the night, they crouched in circles and argued about power.

"We've got them running scared," bragged Robbie. "They never thought we'd have the guts to take the library, and now they don't know what to do."

"At some point they're going to call in the police," said Bea. "If they have to, they'll try to kill us. Eventually, any established structure will try to destroy the elements that refuse to join it."

"But you're talking as though it's alive," protested Jack. "A society's not like that—it doesn't have its own will."

Bea looked at him intensely, and his insides quivered under the force of her blue eyes.

"It's alive in the sense that it's composed of people," she said. "Each one has a survival instinct, and together they compose a body with a survival instinct of its own."

"But that's the metaphor the establishment *wants* you to use!" warned Robbie. "The people who hold power use violence to keep their privileges, and they trick people into thinking they represent the interests of a 'body.' We've got to ditch that reactionary metaphor!"

"Do you really think they'd kill us?" asked Jack.

"Not yet." Bea flexed her strong fingers. "We're middle-class. We're white. For now, they just want to scare us. But I bet they'd blow the black students away if they got the chance."

Jack smiled in the dark, glad that it concealed his anger. Middle-class. Everyone assumed that, from the black students occupying a nearby building to the administrators scared to drag him out by force. Jack came from a neighborhood where hardworking people scoffed at the word "college." They jeered to conceal their bitter knowledge that they would never go there, even if they wanted to. Since his father's death, Jack's family had lived on his mother's earnings as a cleaning lady.

That first year, Jack had ridden the subway between two worlds, each morning and every night. His new friends knew no one who didn't attend college, and his neighborhood friends knew no one who did. Somehow Jack managed to pass in each world, but he felt like an impostor in both. He had stumbled his way through this double life until about a month ago.

Since his musical night with Cathy, he had stopped going home and had slept with her in the dorm. His mother responded with angry disgust, sure this co-ed *Schlampe* would get herself pregnant. Then where would he be, with his scholarship and his academic dreams? Jack tried to reassure her, but he couldn't tell the truth. Cathy didn't bleed like other women, so there was nothing to fear.

To Jack, Cathy's commitment to the movement was hard to understand. Bea and Robbie spoke passionately of wars and the need to shake white men's grip on power. They honestly believed that by occupying the library, they were fighting imperialist violence. Cathy hated Bea and Robbie as much as the pigs, and her presence in the library was hard to explain. She liked to disrupt anything organized, and Jack loved her for it without knowing why. People said that Cathy wasn't committed, but most of them liked her company. Her wicked impulses inspired the students when their rhetoric ran dry.

From the beginning, Cathy had protested against the no-drug rule. She asked how they could justify a free commune where you couldn't explore your own mind. Luckily, sex was allowed in their new society, and the organizers approved of the use to which Cathy and Jack put the president's desk. To Jack's relief, nothing terrible happened when Cathy stopped taking drugs. She remained a fountain of angry energy with nervous twitches and a piercing voice. She crouched trembling beside him as the police smashed the barricades at 2:30 a.m.

Gripping his walkie-talkie, Robbie relayed orders from Strike Central outside. "They've got Atkins! They're going to be here any minute. If you don't want to be arrested, get out now. The window's still clear. If you're staying, get ready for some rough handling. Take off your earrings. Tuck in your hair. Link arms, and don't hit back. Passive resistance, don't start any fights."

Jack looked questioningly at Cathy. He didn't want to be arrested. No matter what they were trying to prove, it couldn't be worth that. Silver stripes of tape were spreading across the windows, a defense against bursts of glass. A long-armed girl smeared herself with Vaseline to protect herself from searing sprays.

"This is going to be bad," muttered Jack. "Are you sure you want to stay?"

"You can go," said Cathy contemptuously. "Look, your girlfriend's bailing."

Bea slung a long leg across the scarred gray sill. For days she had been talking about first aid stations, and from Robbie's reports, she was needed below. Bea shot Jack a look of shame and longing, then dropped out of sight.

"Bitch," muttered Cathy, and bitter laughter swirled.

"No, take it easy," said the sticky-armed girl. "I know her. She's okay."

Robbie followed Bea out the window. "Orders," he muttered sheepishly. "They don't want the leaders arrested. Pratt's going too."

From the hallway came a man's voice thinned by a bullhorn.

"What's he saying? What's he saying?" Hissed questions drowned his words.

A tenor voice called, "It's the fucking vice provost. He says if we leave now, discipline will be minimal."

"Tell him to come in here and discipline me!" shrieked Cathy.

Whoops of applause flew like screams before a cavalry charge.

A police captain repeated the metallic words. Wood cracked as the cops rammed the door. Jack looped his arm through Cathy's bony elbow. A few dry voices tried to sing "*Venceremos*," but no one knew the Spanish words.

With a sickening crash, the door collapsed. Jack froze. He hadn't expected the police to have such stricken faces, and from the look of them, they hadn't expected the spoiled, disruptive brats to look so frightened. Jack had never opposed the police, and it shocked him to hear them called pigs. In his neighborhood, policemen were respected and feared. No one liked them, but it was an honor to be a cop, and to defy them was unthinkable.

"Okay, you kids," spluttered a burly plainclothesman.

"Oh, fuck," muttered a boy as the police raised their clubs.

In the tense silence, the curse dug like a spur. Enraged by the administration's waffling, the police saw a chance to act. They rushed the student line, yanking and slamming the linked bodies. Some of the students screamed for mercy; others made political appeals.

"You guys, they're usin' you, they're usin' you!" yelled a dark, wiry boy. "Take it easy! We're on the same side!"

"Stop hitting me!" screamed the Vaseline girl. Purplish blood matted her oily brown hair.

Jack clung to Cathy with all his strength.

"Let go, you little cunt!" snarled a big blond cop.

Violently, he jerked her free arm. Cathy turned on him with a voice Jack had never heard.

"Cunt?" she screamed. "Cunt? I bet you never seen one! I bet you fuck your horse every night!"

Appreciative hoots pierced the dark.

"Cathy, shut up!" yelled Jack.

The policeman raised his arm to strike, then paused with his club in midair. He couldn't hit a quivering, hundred-pound girl, no matter what she said. Panic-stricken, Jack dropped her arm, sensing that less harm would come if she resisted less. The policeman's gray eyes caught his move. The solid, male student made a worthier target, and with all his strength, he brought his club down on Jack's shoulder. The room exploded into red, burning pain.

Other policemen joined in, beating and kicking Jack.

"What'd he do to you? Donny, what'd he do?" cut a jagged voice.

Thudding, searing blows came from every direction.

"Stop it!" screamed Cathy. Her voice faded as she was dragged away.

"Stop hitting him!" yelled the Vaseline girl. "I saw it! He didn't do anything!"

The blows stopped, and thick arms hauled Jack to his feet. His legs moved of their own accord. Hot, oozy stickiness blinded him. The ground dropped away beneath his left foot, and he paused.

"Keep movin', asshole," cursed one of the cops with a blow to hustle him down the stairs.

At the foot of the steps, they rushed him forward, then released him so that he went sprawling. Pain turned the world grayish white. Screams sliced the air around him.

"Pigs! Fucking fascist pigs!"

"Hey, get this guy to St. Mark's! He's hurt!"

"Oh, no!" rumbled the policeman. "This guy goes to Central Booking. He's mine."

"I am Professor Randolph Waite!" An old man's voice shook with indignation. "That boy needs medical attention. I have your badge number, Officer Lund."

"All right, sew the bastard up," muttered the cop. "Then he goes in the wagon."

Jack was lowered to a stretcher by stiff, clumsy hands and then carried a long way. Twice his carriers dropped him, and they kept changing direction to avoid pounding steps. Jack called for Cathy, and voices claimed she was fine, but he didn't believe them. How could they know?

"Oh, Jesus," moaned a frightened young man. "Jesus, this one's bad."

"Jack!" The bright female voice was familiar.

"Cathy?" he cried.

"No, Jack, it's Bea. It's all right. You're going to be okay."

A cool hand caught his and squeezed it.

The high male voice he'd heard tightened. "Shit, this guy needs to go to St. Mark's. We can't take care of him here."

"They're not taking students," said Bea.

"What? They can't do that!"

"They're doing it," she snapped. "I just called. No students, except between nine and five."

"Fascists!"

Her companion groped Jack, trying to feel what was broken. Stiff fingers dug his shoulder, and he screamed.

"Oh, Jesus!"

"Look," said Bea, "what if he weren't a student? I mean, he's a big guy. His face is so beat up, he could be eighteen or eighty. How would they know?"

"What do you—"

"We need a volunteer, man!" cried Bea. "We need a professor or a lecturer or something! C'mon, help this guy out!"

A wave of noise washed up a taker. Bill Simmons, a radical young classics professor, offered to swap identities with Jack. Bea's slim hand slipped into his back pocket.

"No—" he gasped.

"I'm glad to do it, man," said Simmons. "It's the least I can do."

So the two switched wallets: IDs, money, and all.

"Hey, what's happenin' with this guy? Ain't you got him ready yet?" Donny Lund's deep voice rolled. Jack tensed at the determined tone. This cop wasn't going to forget him, no matter how badly hurt he was.

"We're taking Professor Simmons to St. Mark's," said Bea.

For the first time, Lund's assurance seemed to waver.

"Professor? That guy's no professor—he's a kid! I saw him! He was with all those other kids in there! Shit, he can't be a professor—can he? They said the faculty were all outside. How could he—"

"Well, maybe you should have thought of that before you bashed his face in," shot Bea.

"Hey, you watch your mouth, nursey," returned Lund. "Just because you're playin' Florence Nightingale don't mean we ain't got room for you in the wagon."

This time Bea held her tongue.

"Okay," said Lund. "We'll take him to St. Mark's, but we're comin' back for him. Professor or no professor, he don't get away with resistin' arrest."

Two policemen hauled Jack down the street to St. Mark's. His crusted, wet shirt stuck to his chest, and pain gored him with each breath.

"Jaysus!" whispered a low-voiced nurse. "Imagine beating up a professor like that!"

A needle stung his arm, and the noise dimmed. There was a lot of pinching at his shoulder and sponging about his face. The probing died away, but angry voices jabbed the dark. One wanted to take him to Central Booking; another yelled that he needed to stay.

"Professor Simmons," came the nurse's hushed voice. "Professor Simmons, I'm sorry. You'll have to go with these men. We've done our best, but they won't let us keep you."

Women's arms slid him deftly into a wheelchair. Outside, the policemen jerked him to his feet. At Central Booking, they hustled him down a corridor and shoved him into a cage of students.

"Jack!" cried ten voices at once. "What did they do to you, man?"

"Where's Cathy?" he gasped.

They had just released her. She had been asking for him, but no one knew where he was. The police had cleared every building of protesters, and the university had closed. Someone claimed the president was resigning, but another said that was bullshit, that asshole would never resign.

Burning pain oozed through the fading numbness until Jack was sickened by its waves. He never contradicted the judge who addressed him as Bill Simmons. He was charged with criminal trespass and resisting arrest, then released on two hundred dollars bond. As far as he knew, Bill Simmons's criminal record had never hurt him. He was now a full professor at Princeton, known for his Marxist readings of the classics.

At the precinct desk, Jack found his mother waiting. Bea had seen her number in his wallet.

"*Na?*" she asked with amused disgust.

That was the first time.

CHAPTER 9

THE END

JACK RAKED UP MOIST, PLUMP cherries by the handful. That morning, Ellie had defended her thesis. He had wanted to bring champagne, but Ellie didn't drink, so he arrived with cherries sweating and straining against their bulging bag. After a few murky weeks of spring, summer had hit Chicago like a firestorm. The two-block walk left him limp and streaming. Thinking back on their walk home from the December party, he couldn't believe that he lived in the same city.

"*Doctor* LaSalle?" he asked as Ellie pulled open her door.

With a squeal, she sprang at him, and he whirled her around the stifling room. Her hair flew out in a soft brown wave, and she shook with delighted laughter. His overloaded bag burst, and their centrifuge spin sent cherries flying every which way. Ellie seized the bag and threw the rest in handfuls that bounced off her rug in muffled plops. She held the last one to his lips, and he bit it, firm, juicy, and sweet. Jack had never seen anyone so happy.

As they gathered the cherries in a feverish egg hunt, Ellie talked about the car she had bought.

"I did it!" she exclaimed, her brown eyes aglow. "I bought an old Dodge!"

Jack scooped up a handful of cherries from under the coffee table.

"How much did you pay?"

"Five hundred dollars," she giggled.

She took a cherry by its stem and held it up critically. Then she leaned back her head, opened her mouth, and lowered it onto her wriggling tongue as though she were swallowing an eel. Jack had never seen her like this—she was acting like a little girl.

"I can stay for dinner," he said. "I can stay until pretty late. Bea's on call, and she'll be sleeping at the hospital."

"Oh boy!"

Ellie jumped on him, and he laughed good-naturedly as his cherries dropped. She brought her mouth to his, and he invaded it eagerly. He wanted this night, and he was determined to enjoy it. Tonight would be one of their last times together, since Ellie was driving to San Diego. If she was moving to California, she'd said, she wanted to feel the transition, not just step out of a plane. Her school year began in August, and she wanted to explore before she had to teach. In an exhilarating purge, she was going to sell everything and drive off with her books, her clothes, and her computer. Her only quandary had been what car to buy, since she had never owned one and had little money.

"Get a Dodge," said Jack. "Old Dodges never die."

So she had bought a blue, five-hundred-dollar Dodge, and in a week she would be driving away. Already Jack could sense changes in her apartment, gaps left by familiar objects that had been sold. He lowered her tenderly and tried to control his excitement.

"What's for dinner?" he murmured.

"Oh, I don't know," she giggled. "But I can tell you what's for dessert."

She fondled him naughtily, but he pushed her hand back.

"Come on, now, there's plenty of time for that ..."

"I meant the *cherries*," she said in a mock huff.

They resumed their hunt, and she said suddenly, "Oh, by the way, Girish says hi."

Jack stopped, clutching a handful of damp cherries. "Hm, what brought that to mind?"

Ellie called his bluff. "Oh, it must have been *eating*. Mm, cannibalism!" She smacked her lips.

"But how did he know I'd be seeing you?" asked Jack.

"Oh, I must have mentioned it," she said.

"He doesn't know—"

"No, no, he doesn't know anything," muttered Ellie. "Don't worry. Anyway, he doesn't care. He's defending next week. He took that job at Irvine, and in his mind he's already there. He's transcended us. He's becoming a god."

"A real apotheosis, eh?" Jack smiled.

Despite his resentment, he had grown fond of Girish, whose arrogance was somehow endearing. Jack looked forward to hearing of his exploits at Irvine—just ninety minutes away from Ellie. As they foraged for dinner, he tried to suppress thoughts of Girish's mocking eyes. Ellie's refrigerator yielded yogurt, bread, jam, and liverwurst. They ate it half-naked on her living room floor, feeding each other in voluptuous bites.

Jack had forgotten what it meant to live without air-conditioning. In Ellie's apartment, you could open the windows and know that every move was seen, or lower the blinds and risk asphyxiation. Never modest, Ellie had left them gaping, but the heavy air barely moved. Her humming fan sent it scampering along in feverish waves. In bed, the heat only intensified. Fully charged by their dinner, he wanted to lap her juices, to suck her into his hungry mouth. But with the neighbors' windows so close, he feared that they would be watched.

Jack paused. "Should we lower the blind?"

Ellie rocked her hips, and her body slid under his gripping fingers.

"Oh, no," she whispered. "I don't care who sees. Just come inside of me. It's so good, what you do. I want the whole world to see."

With the window wide open, he kissed her breasts and belly, then wriggled his tongue until she erupted. Free to act on his passion, he took his fill, digging and gouging until they were exhausted and could speak only in wet murmurs.

Still the air didn't move.

"I'm so hot," moaned Ellie.

Jack fanned her with the sheet.

On the edge of a dream, she gurgled, "That feelsh good. ... Oh—wait a minute."

She hauled herself to her feet and reeled off toward the kitchen. Jack glanced at the glowing blue digits. 1:16. Oh well. He would stay the night. No one at home would miss him, and he had so little time left with Ellie. So little time ...

She returned with the remains of the cherries, damp and cool from their stay in the refrigerator. In the tropical air of her room, the red orbs gathered crystal beads of sweat. Ellie held a round, firm cherry to his lips, then withdrew it as they parted to devour it. Slowly, softly, she dragged the wet ball over the bump of his chin and down his chest toward his nipple.

"Ohhh ..." He shivered.

On and on it crept, with the steady, unpredictable pace of an insect. It felt like a cursor on a Ouija board, quivering under the pressure of many fingers.

"Jack. I'm going to miss you."

Sadness pooled in Ellie's voice. Her grief must have been lying there all along, under the bubbling silliness. Jack felt ashamed of doubting her pain.

"I'm going to miss you too," he sighed.

"Will you write to me?"

"Every day," he murmured. "Every day I want to see you on my screen."

He shivered as the cherry advanced in slow twitches.

"Will you write me sexy emails?"

"I'll try," he laughed. "It'll be a challenge. The only kind I ever get is old German men asking me to review their books."

"Mine will be different," she whispered. "Very different."

She brought her mouth to the cherry on his inner thigh and kissed him as her lips closed on the fruit.

"Ohhh ..." he moaned.

In a dreamy, delicious game, they ate the last cherries one by one. Slowly, maddeningly, they pulled them along, their mouths following the wet trails. Jack rolled a plump, wet fruit over her eyelids and sent it tumbling down her lips and neck. It teased her nipples with tiny, wet touches.

"Lower," begged Ellie. "Please, lower."

Jack dragged the cherry toward her navel. It spun like a basketball that rolled hesitantly around the rim before dropping into the waiting hollow.

"Mm ..." She arched her back.

Something— What—? The phone!

Ellie clutched him, trembling. In a daze, he glanced at the clock radio. 2:02.

"Probably it's the wrong number," she said. "Happens all the time."

She shook in his arms, and he gripped her groggily.

In the living room, a click sounded, and Ellie's alto voice flowed. "Hi. You've reached 773-643-7764. Please leave a message."

"Ellie."

The black silence breathed. That voice—

"Ellie. Jack. Pick up the phone."

"It's Sam!" hissed Ellie.

They looked at each other, uncertain. Sam's voice rolled inexorably.

"Jack. Ellie. *Pick up the fuckin' phone.*"

"You'd better go talk to him." Jack nudged her.

"No, you go," she begged. "It sounds like he wants to talk to you."

"But how does he have your number?"

Jack's feet met the warm, matted rug. Ellie had an unlisted number. How did Sam—? For an instant, he hovered in a sickening purgatory of suspicion.

"Probably Lucy," she whispered.

Sam's voice came again, calm and deadly. "*Pick—up—the— fuckin'—phone.*"

With a determined push, Ellie propelled him into the darkness. He stabbed angrily at the noisy machine.

"Sam?" he croaked.

"Jack."

"What's going on? It's two in the morning."

"Yeah, that's right. It's two in the mornin'." Sam's voice sounded odd.

"Look," said Jack harshly, "this is going too far. What happens between me and Ellie is our business. I know you don't like it, but you have no right—"

Sam sidestepped the attack so easily he seemed not even to have heard it.

"This isn't about you and Ellie."

"What's happening?" asked Jack, his hand tightening. "Why are—"

"Jack," said Sam wearily. "You need to go home to your wife."

"She's at the hosp—"

Again Sam seemed not to have heard. "Bea called me a few minutes ago. You weren't home, and she wanted to know where you were."

"My God!" Jack gasped. "You didn't—"

Sam cut in with dry disgust. "I told her I knew some places I could try. I told her I'd do my best. You need to go home, Jack. Pull on your pants, kiss her good night, and get your ass home."

"What's happening?" cried Jack. "Has something happened to—? Oh, my God!"

"I can't tell you anything like this," said Sam. "Bea will tell you when you get there. Just *get your ass home,* Jack. Your wife has somethin' to tell you."

Jack rushed into the bedroom and snapped on the light. Ellie let the blind fall with a clatter. In a panic, he dressed as fast as he could. Ellie handed him his clothes, her arms trembling. He raced out of the apartment and quickly forgot her in the hollow streets below. His mind was as black and heavy as the night, absorbing everything and producing nothing. As his hand brushed the cool metal of his doorknob, Bea whipped open the front door. In the yellow light, she was terrifying, her hair ruffled, her eyes puffy and bright.

"Jessie's dead, Jack," said Bea. "Where in hell have you been?"

Senior year, Cathy started shooting up. For Jack, it was the line he couldn't cross. Until then, he had swallowed anything she gave him, but these mind-killing needles were the limit. Cathy's acid revealed hidden designs, but her smack was syrupy nothingness. Jack hated the new drug, and he did everything he could to make her stop using it.

By then they lived on the outskirts of Harlem, since Cathy had convinced her parents to finance a flat. To Jack, the rent seemed like a small fortune, and he asked what argument she had used to win their space.

"Oh, I told them I needed to get away from all the sex and drugs in the dorms," she laughed.

Cathy's parents always gave her what she wanted—as long as she stayed away from them.

In the grubby apartment, Jack and Cathy grappled over his neatness and her drugs. His mother had been right: Cathy was a *Schlampe* of the very worst kind. In German, you couldn't distinguish a slut from a slob, since dirtiness implied promiscuity. Cathy showed glaring signs of both. When she ate, she left streaked, crusted dishes, and she tossed her stained panties on the floor. In a losing battle, Jack resisted her chaos, and she called him an uptight Nazi *Hausfrau*.

Worst of all, Cathy wouldn't study, and Jack fought to keep her from dropping out.

"What do you care?" she asked. "What's the point? What am I learning here that's worth anything? A good hit of acid shows me more about my mind than any book on psychology."

Jack begged her to keep going, just to get the damn piece of paper. Play the establishment's game, then blow them apart with their own weapons. Jack feared what would happen if Cathy left school. She was falling out of the fabric of life, dissolving under his fingers. In angry desperation, he fed her and washed her, smoked with her and fucked her and cleaned her clothes. Sometimes he even wrote her papers, and he squashed cockroaches with sudden splats.

In the spring, Cathy began to disappear. Sometimes she would be gone for days. As Jack read Novalis's dazzling words, he felt poisoned needles pierce her skin. When he couldn't stand it, he sought her in the streets, then trudged home to her smell in their bed. Eventually she returned, dazed and dirty, with fresh track marks on her skinny white arms.

Through all of it, Jack maintained his friendship with Bea, who stuck to politics as she did to science. Jack could never quite read her as she consoled him with her serene alto voice. Did she want him? Did she pity him? He couldn't tell whether their bond emerged from sympathy or calculating desire. After the library occupation, Bea broke up with Robbie, and she told Jack of new lovers as they came and went. He was sure that Cathy disgusted her, but Bea never said a word against her. Was it to protect his feelings, or to make sure that she stayed on his good side?

When Bea learned about Cathy's new drug, she was horrified.

"Do something!" she blurted. "Take her to a clinic, tell her parents, call the police!"

Jack shook his head. Nothing he could say would make her stop, and telling her parents—that would be like turning her in to the Gestapo. To Cathy, her parents were the quintessence of evil, for reasons he never understood.

"Just take care of yourself," said Bea. "She's doing this to you as well as her."

As Jack read and wrote, his professors encouraged him, and he found himself appreciated for the first time. Since his father's death, he hadn't known anyone who thought about poetry, and he spent hours in his professors' offices, sometimes debating the meaning of a single word. His teachers adored him, and they talked to him about "going all the way." The phrase was also a favorite of Cathy's—not for earning a PhD but for enjoying a searingly potent hit.

It happened just a few weeks before graduation, not long after their day in the park. With finals looming, Jack wanted to study, and they were fighting about a party. Jack had a paper on Novalis to write, but Cathy insisted on going.

"What good are you?" she screamed. "What fucking good are you? All you do is tell me what I can't do! You're one big obstacle, one big sign saying 'No.' You're like the fucking Berlin Wall!"

If he was such a drag, she would find someone who wasn't, and that threat tore him from his romantic web. After an hour of screaming, he agreed to go to the goddamn party. As soon as he got there, he found a friend who was staying on in their program for a master's. He and Jack spent the night sipping beer and comparing PhD programs in German. Every now and then Jack looked for Cathy, but she seemed to have vanished. Anyway, he was sick of her stunts. If she wanted to see how hard he would try to keep her from tripping, she would have to find another lab rat. *Fuck her,* he thought as he fingered his brown bottle. Didn't he have a right to live too?

When the party broke up, he found Cathy slumped in a bedroom with a stupid look on her face. She smiled at him weakly, and he gathered her up, cursing her useless limbs. As they staggered home, she could speak only in bubbling gurgles. For Cathy in any state, this was strange, and he worried as he laid her out in bed. How thin she was. He stroked her wasted arms. When he finished writing this paper, he would cook her a piece of red meat. He nuzzled her fondly, but dazed with weariness, he gave up his efforts to enter her. It was no fun with her so limp and clammy. Maybe in the morning. Cathy always liked to wake up that way ...

The light warmed Jack's face, and he nudged her greedily, hot and swollen and hard. He pushed impatiently, but she didn't move.

"Cathy," he grunted. "*Wach auf ...*"

He thrust harder and lifted her hair to kiss her neck.

"Cathy?"

Against his lips, her skin was cold.

"Cathy," he pleaded. "Cathy, *wach auf!*"

He reached for her breast, and his hand froze. Cathy's chest wasn't moving. Her stillness killed his urges, and trembling, he rolled her over.

"Cathy!"

For the first time, her face was perfectly smooth. No ripples, no twitches, no contortions. He grabbed her shoulders and shook her, but she flopped limply under his hands.

"Cathy!" he yelled. "Oh, my God, Cathy!"

She disappeared into a blurring stream. For a sickening eternity he shook her and cursed her and cried.

The police drilled him with whirling questions. "Where did she get the smack? How much did she take? How much was she used to taking?"

No one believed that he didn't know. He lived with her, didn't he?

Who was he trying to kid? Jack showed them his unpricked arms, and they had to agree he was no junkie.

"But who does she buy from, kid?" they demanded.

"I don't know," said Jack.

For the second time, he found himself in jail. This time his mother had to pay for a lawyer, for whom she emptied her savings account.

"I told you that girl was a *dreckige Schlampe*," she growled.

Cathy's parents pushed for his incarceration. They swore that the boy from the Bronx had plied their daughter with drugs, and no one could corroborate his story. Before long, though, the truth emerged. Everyone knew Cathy, and people Jack hardly recognized pled forcefully for his innocence. Most convincing was the A-student Bea, who impressed everyone with her intensity. It was inevitable, she said. Instead of arresting this guy, you should give him a medal for having kept her alive this long. The court ruled that Cathy had died an accidental death and sent Jack home to his mother's reproaches.

Jack amazed everyone by taking his finals, and he graduated with honors, or so his transcript said. He remembered nothing, but his mother still kept a picture of him in his cap and gown. Two months later, Jim Morrison died in Paris. Strangely, this was what "brought Jack around." The phrase came from his favorite professor, the one he had been helping with his research. Noticing new energy in his limp assistant, the old fellow asked what had "brought him around." In German, *umbringen* meant "to kill." The irony delighted Jack, though he doubted the old man knew Morrison.

"It just feels like it's time to get serious." Jack smiled.

He never understood how or why he recovered. Suddenly he felt a beautiful weariness, an acceptance, a relieved surrender. It was time to grow up. If you rejected things, you ended up dead in a bathtub at twenty-seven, or in bed at twenty-one. He didn't want to die like that. There was too much to do. Jack hurried through the stacks seeking his professor's books. Someday, he was going to write his own.

A year later, Jack and Bea married. In their long conversations, he found tranquility, and he warmed to the movements of her reasoning mind. If she had set up the union, he no longer cared. Bea was the perfect companion, the epitome of sympathy, intelligence, and well-meaning action. He stayed at their university for his PhD, where Bea earned her medical degree. In a burst of luck, they found two jobs in Chicago, where they thrived in the tempered, productive life they built. When Jack got tenure, they bought their house and had Jessie. He had grown up quite well, considering—considering—

Bea stood with one lean arm across the doorway, her eyes blazing in the harsh light.

"What happened?" he breathed. "What happened to her? Where is she?"

Bea didn't budge.

Vor dem Gesetz steht ein Türhüter, he thought wildly. *A doorkeeper stands before the law.*

"She's in the hospital morgue," quavered Bea. "Where were you an hour ago, when I was identifying our daughter's body?"

Jack could think of nothing but the truth. "I was with a student," he said.

He looked into the blinding sun of her rage.

"A— You— Oh, God. Oh, my God, Jack." Bea stepped back so that her hand fell from the doorframe. "Oh, God, Jack. Oh, my God."

Her face contorted as her tears flowed. Jack moved to comfort her, but she backed away and covered her face with her hands. He followed her into the living room.

"Oh, God," moaned Bea.

"I'm sorry," murmured Jack. "I'm so sorry. I never meant—"

"You never meant to get caught?" Her shrill voice slit the night. "I guess you didn't know your daughter was going to OD."

"She—" Jack recoiled, unable to speak.

His legs hit the couch, and he sank down.

"She's dead, Jack." Bea's voice careened. "A—a woman named Nancy called me. She-ee's a nurse. She paged me. I—I thought it was a mistake, or Jessie playing some sick joke. A—an old black woman. She was so upset. She said they found Misty, they're bringing her in. God—that voice—I could barely understand her. I said I didn't know— But the-en she said Misty, Misty, your daughter. I—I can still hear that voice! 'Dr. Mannheim, they found your girl Misty! They bringin' her in!'"

Choking and heaving, Bea held her hands to her face. Jack rose to embrace her, but she leaped back as though she had been shocked.

"Don't touch me!" she screamed. "Jesus Christ! You're coming from her bed. You've got her all over you!"

"I'm sorry," he whispered and let his arms drop. "I'm sorry, Bea. Please come and sit with me. Tell me what happened. I—I promise I won't touch you."

Her smile erupted into a brittle laugh. "Oh, Christ! You're so ridiculous!"

"Please," he begged.

Jack sat down, the way you taste a baby's food to show her how good it is. Bea inhaled deeply, controlling urges that he feared to imagine. She settled on the couch as far away from him as she could get.

"She broke out," murmured Bea, and again Jack thought of Kafka.

"What, out of the hospital?" he asked. "You can do that?"

"Yeah," she sighed.

To his relief, Bea was becoming herself again, the steady, competent doctor.

"They think she got out sometime between eight and nine. They won't know until tomorrow when they can interview everyone. The shifts change at eight, and sometimes there's confusion."

Jessie would have studied the patterns, he knew. She would have memorized the schedule and learned its weaknesses with an unfailing eye.

As always, Bea followed his thoughts step for step.

"Someone as smart as she is—as smart as she *was*—" she corrected bitterly.

"So what— How did she—"

"How did she manage to kill herself in two hours? This is the South Side, Jack. Some guy named Hakim found her near an empty house on Indiana. A—a shooting gallery, a crack house, something like that. It was her first time. She didn't know what she was doing. They showed me her arms. All clean, except for a bunch of jabs she made tonight. Whoever was helping her didn't know what he was doing either. It's such a waste, Jack! They won't even take her organs, because she OD'd. Her body—her whole life—just a waste!"

She wrenched violently, as though someone had struck her, and then sat still again.

"Have you called the police?" asked Jack softly.

"Someone already did," she said. "I talked to them at the hospital, and they're looking around the neighborhood. This guy Hakim called someone named Lou-Lou. Jessie had a lot of friends over there—did you know that? This Lou-Lou called the police. And then she called Nancy—oh, God, Jack. Oh, my God ..."

Bea gazed up at him, her red eyes asking an unspeakable question. He looked back sorrowfully, uncertain what to say. Every phrase that emerged promised only to deepen her pain.

"It's just as well that she died this way," she choked. "Once she got going on that stuff, she could have died of worse ..."

"No—" protested Jack.

He couldn't express the feeling that surged in him, a sense that any life was better than no life at all. But how to say it? What was the point of saying it when Jessie was already dead? He looked up into a beam of blistering hate.

"I kept calling you," said Bea tightly. "I kept calling you, over and over and over. I—I thought you were asleep. I couldn't imagine—I couldn't have believed—"

"I—I—" he stammered.

"Jesus Christ!" she erupted. "My daughter's dead of an overdose, and I've been getting injected—with what? For how long? Has this girl been tested, Jack? Have you? Do you even know where you've been sticking your—"

She stopped, heaving with rage and disgust.

"She's been tested," whispered Jack ashamedly. "She got tested last December. It was negative."

Instantly he cursed himself.

"Last December!" shrieked Bea. "Jesus Christ, how long has this been going on? How can you know what she's been doing since December? My God, Jack, a twenty-five-year-old, do you really think you're the only one she's screwing? Have you thought about what you could catch, about what you could give me?"

Jack kept his eyes on hers, determined to take the full hit.

"It started in December," he murmured. "I'm sorry—I—I trust her. I think it's all right."

"And when were you planning on telling me this?" asked Bea. "Or weren't you ever? Did you just want to go on with your nice, middle-aged wife and your hot, horny little mistress?"

"That's not fair!" cried Jack, feeling a visceral urge to defend Ellie. "She's not—"

Bea's face froze his stream of words. She had reverted to a state in which only the interpreting scientist could function. With icy deferred action, she reconstructed the whole history and felt its force in smashing blows.

"That party," she murmured. "That night I switched the cards. I thought something— You were different. Of course— My God, you were in bed with her! That night I called you in New York, you were with her!"

"Yes," he whispered.

He could hold nothing back, no longer seeing any point.

"Jesus! You—"

She raised her hand to strike him, then whipped it against her own contorted face.

"Who is she?" she gurgled.

"Her—her name is Ellie," he began.

"The one from the party?" sobbed Bea. "You brought her here, Jack, you brought her *here*?"

"Yes," he whispered hypnotically.

"The—the one with the maroon sweater, the one with the long brown hair?"

"Yes."

Unbelievably, Bea began to laugh.

"Well, I've got to compliment your taste, Jack. She's a knockout. My residents practically killed themselves trying to get her number. I even liked her. What I want to know is, What does she see in you?"

"I don't know," murmured Jack.

"You know," continued Bea, "it's like an epidemic. The past five years, I can't tell you how many of my friends have had their husbands trade them in for some slut in her twenties."

"She's not—" protested Jack, but Bea lasered him with a glance.

"You let me finish!" she demanded. "You listen to me! All of them, just tossed aside like—like old computers when some sleek new model comes out. That's how these guys see their women, as machines for their interface with the world. And all that time, I comforted myself with the thought that you would never do that. I've resigned myself to a life without passion, Jack, but I thought that at least I had loyalty!"

"Without pass—" echoed Jack stupidly.

Her words spun beyond his grasp.

"My God, Jessie was right. You really are a prick." She laughed miserably. "You think I don't know I've always been your second choice? You think I don't know it's her you've always wanted, that I lucked out and got you by default? My God, there were times I wanted to kill her myself! I was glad when she died, Jack. I was glad! Can't you see what kind of life she would have brought you?"

All the cords stood out on her thin white throat. Bea's memory astounded him. Step by step, she recalled every atrocity Cathy had committed, every time she had humiliated him.

"Please, Bea," he interrupted. "I've always respected you. I've liked living with you. I've always been happy—"

"Yeah, you've been happy," she exploded. "You've been happy like someone who goes to sleep for thirty years! What I didn't count on was that you'd wake up and look for a fucking reincarnation of her!"

"That's not fair!" cried Jack. "Ellie's nothing like—"

He choked on Cathy's name.

"Well, she sure looks better," Bea laughed. "And I guess she's capable of earning an advanced degree. I would like to have heard some of those conversations on Nietzsche."

"She's leaving," Jack heard himself saying.

Bea looked at him in disbelief.

"Jessie's dead," she quavered. "This is supposed to comfort me? Are we just supposed to go back to things as they were?"

"No, no," he said confusedly. "I just thought you should know that. I—"

"Look," Bea cut him off, "I have a funeral to plan."

"Please," he begged. "Let's work on it together. Can't we do it together?"

Shy sunlight was brightening his plants' pale leaves. In the heavy darkness, they planned Jessie's funeral, as they had planned everything for twenty-six years. Tightly, composedly, Bea took him through the details—choosing a coffin, reserving a chapel. There was a death certificate to be signed and something about a coroner. Flattened by shame, Jack accepted every suggestion and inserted himself only where he knew he could help.

"Can I pick out the music?" he asked timidly. "Can I choose some of the texts?"

"Yeah," she said steadily. "You pick out the readings. You're good at that."

"I—I've got to tell my mother," he murmured.

"Right," she said. "Go tell your mother."

Bea stood up.

"Whe-ere are you going?" he wavered.

She looked down at him with what seemed like genuine pity.

"I can't stay here," she said. "Not after what's happened. Not after what you've told me. I—I need time to think. I can stay at the hospital, or with Tom Plevin and his wife. I can't be here for a while."

"No—I'll go!" he said. "It's not right. I'm the one who—"

"What, so you can crawl back in bed with her?" snapped Bea. "No, I don't want you to leave. This is your house. I can feel you all over it—your books, your music, your study. I can feel Jessie. I can see her blood. I can't live through this if I have to stay here."

Jack yielded. Bea always knew what she needed, and he let her go. While she bumped around upstairs, he watched the sunrise gilding his leaves. The light registered most along the edges, fiery blades against the brightening gray. Before the light could be called morning, Bea reappeared with a stuffed black bag.

"I'll call you, Jack." Her voice dipped crazily. "You stay here. The police will be coming—we have to plan—"

She opened the door, and he moved toward her silhouette in the strengthening light.

"Please—" he begged, but Bea had already stepped out into the warm, sticky morning.

"Goodbye, Jack."

The door clicked shut. From the window, he watched her walk steadily down the street, a little more slowly than usual. Then he strode grimly to the kitchen to call his mother.

❧

Nothing Jessie had ever put them through compared to the horror of that funeral. It was her crowning triumph, their ultimate humiliation. Jack wished that she could have watched it from the galleries with her amused, disgusted smirk. Once the police finished with him, he spoke mainly to Bea and made decisions he had never dreamed he would make. Of one thing he was sure. Seeing Jessie in the morgue, so white and still, he couldn't stand the thought of burying her. It made him sick to think of her rotting alone underground.

"Let's cremate her," said Bea. "She would have wanted to go up in flames."

As always, Bea expressed his thoughts exactly. They decided to burn her and scatter her ashes.

"The Neutral Zone," suggested Jack. "She can haunt the park for all eternity."

The real trouble came in planning the funeral. Society didn't accommodate atheists. Jack had no idea what to do, only a vague sense that he had to honor her life and give it some kind of meaning. In desperation, he called the Protestant chaplain and imagined what Jessie would say. She haunted him now as a scoffing presence, ridiculing his Gargoyle Palace with its intellectual machinery for birth and death. Accustomed to unbelievers who needed his services, the chaplain offered tactful words of comfort. He suggested an interfaith memorial at noon on Wednesday. The chapel would be free, and people could honor his daughter during their lunch break. If Jack could just tell him about Jessie, he would be glad to prepare a brief homily. But maybe—maybe since he knew his daughter best, her father would like to remember her himself.

As the ritual approached, it became increasingly clear that Jack would have to stand up and speak. His kitchen became Strike Central as he relayed information and wove plans. The phone harangued him in a dozen voices, each one more tormenting than the last. At least once an hour, Bea checked in. Her voice had regained its smooth alto tones, though the mind emitting them was inaccessible. She never mentioned Ellie, but Jack could feel her anger heaving under the surface of each phrase. His mother would arrive tomorrow, accompanied by Rudi, Doreen, and their boys. In New York, the school year hadn't ended, and Doreen was battling his mother, who thought a funeral was ample reason to miss school. From minute to minute, they changed their plans, maneuvering for a shorter stay and a lower fare.

Sam's voice unsettled Jack the most, with its guilt and overpowering grief. Sam seemed to blame himself for Jessie's death, as he did in all things.

"I was gonna go back," he choked. "I liked her. I was gonna go back and see—but Jerry—"

Jack told Sam that he shouldn't feel bad; there was nothing anyone could have done.

"No—I should've—" Sam gasped, almost speechless with woe.

His sorrow ran so deep that Jack doubted his own, but according to Sam, Rachel was worse. She had been crying all morning and wouldn't leave her bed.

"She never knew anybody who died before," said Sam. "I mean, somebody her own age."

Suddenly inspired, Jack asked whether Rachel would like to speak at the memorial.

"She's such a good speaker," he said. "She's got such—such—"

"Yeah." Sam sighed proudly. "I know what you mean. She could be a cantor, or a rabbi, or somethin'. I'll ask her. I think she'd like that. She can say Kaddish. It'd be an honor."

"It would be an honor to *us*," said Jack. "But only if she wants to."

"Oh, she'll want to," answered Sam. "I just wish—I wish—"

An ocean of pity washed away his dissent.

"Listen," said Sam. "You never heard this from me, but you've gotta call Ellie. I've heard she's takin' this pretty hard. I'm sorry I had to call you like that—there was just no other way."

"She's upset," said Jack measuredly. "But I'm trying— You know, Bea's moved out."

"Aw, geez," moaned Sam. "You got anybody there with you? You need—"

"It's okay," said Jack. "My family will be here tomorrow morning, and between now and then, I've got this phone."

"I'm comin' over," said Sam. "And Ruth, she'll look in on Bea."

On Saturday night, Jack had the maddening comfort of Sam's presence—his self-recriminations, his jokes, his trips to the refrigerator. Late that night, Jack went to bed alone, longing for Ellie and knowing he wouldn't awaken to Bea's cool, slim form any time soon.

Early Sunday, in a blank, gray mist, he drove down the Tube to the airport. For the first time, he turned his head to peer at the cracked streets and the dark figures slogging through them. When had Jessie first come here? Who were BJ and Lou-Lou? With stinging eyes, he wondered what Jessie's last hours had been like. What a waste, Bea said. But that all depended. It all depended.

Facing his family was worse than he had imagined—Doreen's patronizing sympathy, his mother's mournful accusations. The first thing she did was open the windows.

"*Lüften, lüften,*" she commanded, though it was damp and chilly outside.

With strong, clumsy fingers, one of Rudi's boys probed Jack's piano while the other pinched the leaves of his plants. For four days, Jack spent most of his time finding things for them to do. He sent Rudi and his sons to the science museum, but his mother couldn't walk well and wanted to stay close. Spotting dust, she muttered about *Dreck* and *Schlamperei*, so finally he let her clean. When she saw Jessie's room, her indignation exploded. What kind of father was he, to let Misty live like that? She didn't blame Jack for the *Dreck*; she blamed the absent Bea, and from the moment of her arrival, she demanded to see her. With agitation that must have been painfully clear, Jack tried to explain her absence. Bea held him accountable for Jessie's death. She was so upset she couldn't stand to see him.

His mother studied him with an ironic look.

"Nah," she said. "That ain't it. Maybe she don't want to see *me*, but that ain't it either. A mother has to have a better reason than that to stay away when her daughter dies. You done somethin'. You guys gettin' a divorce now, is that it? You done somethin', Jackie? What did you do?"

As his mother cleaned, she wouldn't stop muttering. Jack listened as she ransacked Jessie's room, washed her clothes, and fumigated the air with sprays. Jack read through every slip of paper she uncovered and dropped them only when the phone summoned him. Jessie had left no written records. It pleased him that she had taken her secrets with her, leaving no lines to be misunderstood.

In those battering days, Ellie never called him. To the end, she upheld their taboo. When he could, he reached out to her from his kitchen, listening anxiously to his mother's thumps above.

"Ellie."

"Oh, wow, Jack! It's you! Oh, God!"

Like Sam, Ellie blamed herself. She had never recovered from the sight of Jessie bleeding out her angry accusations. When Jack told her that Jessie was dead, she sobbed in desperate heaves. The image of Ellie suffering in her stripped apartment was more than he could bear. To distract her, he asked her about packing. With effort, she told him everything she could, and he gladly absorbed her stories.

"This Asian family bought my dishes today," she laughed. "After they paid for them, the wife bowed. It was the craziest thing—this happy, polite woman, smiling and bowing with a frying pan in her hand."

"That must have been funny," murmured Jack.

It had been days since he had seen anyone smile.

"Hey," exclaimed Ellie, "I'm going to New Orleans! I've decided not to cut the corner. I'm going to take I-55 all the way south and find out where it ends."

"Probably some old pier," Jack laughed. "Be careful. Oh—oh, no—I'm sorry. My mother's calling. I have to go."

"Oh, I'm sorry," said Ellie quickly.

It was something new in her, this fear of giving offense.

"No, no, it's okay," he assured her. "I just wish I could be with you today."

"Me too," she sighed. "You have an open invitation."

"I like that," he murmured. "I'll think about that. Oh—"

His mother waddled into the kitchen, and ashamedly, he hung up the phone.

All through those excruciating days, Jack pictured Jessie looking down and laughing. When Wednesday came, not even the chaplain could have imagined the crowd that filled the chapel. At the end of the semester, everyone was on campus, and the scandal of Jack's daughter's death brought a distraction from grading. Except for his colleagues who had children at the Experimental School, few had known that Jack Mannheim had a daughter. After the ill-fated party, rumors had sped. The existence—well, extinction—of Jack Mannheim's daughter had exposed his unknown human core. The entire academic community had turned out to attend her funeral.

Maybe, thought Jack as he looked out at them, maybe there was more to it than that. Sorrow, not schadenfreude, darkened their faces. Before him sat all of his colleagues and a few grim deans. Next to the grizzled man who cleaned his building sat his department secretary, dabbing her eyes. Over the wooden pews floated the faces of almost every student he had taught for the past five years. With anguish, Jack recognized the ones from his seminar—Girish and Carol, Mariko and Corinne. In the front row, Sam wrapped his arm around Rachel, and Ruth was consoling a despondent Jerry. Only Ellie was missing, having conceded that she should stay away. He couldn't place the large group of black women watching him sadly from the right. They sat somberly in their fanciful black hats, fanned themselves, and waited.

"Wer sind die Schwarzen?" hissed his mother.

Jack told her they were friends of Jessie's. According to Bea, Nancy had asked about the funeral. Maybe she was one of them, she and Lou-Lou, who had called the police that night.

The service began with Bach's F major toccata. In a soft bass, the chaplain mourned the incomprehensible tragedy of losing a young life. Rachel's chanting and graceful elegy resonated more deeply.

"We loved her," she said. "At school, she always challenged everything. We all wished we were brave enough to be like her."

Bea astonished Jack by speaking of Jessie's birth. She had delivered so many babies, but she had never forgotten the joy of having her own. She told funny stories about Jessie's early years, incidents he had long forgotten. Now it was his turn, and he stood before them, a cool, dry page under his hands.

"A reading," he began, "from Friedrich Nietzsche."

Among the black women, a ripple spread. Jack breathed deeply and felt the air rush into his lungs so that his diaphragm pressed against his belly.

"*Das größte Schwergewicht*—The Greatest Weight," he pronounced a little too loudly.

"What, if some day or night a demon were to steal after you into your loneliest loneliness and say to you: 'This life as you now live it and have lived it, you will have to live once more and innumerable times more; and there will be nothing new in it, but every pain and every joy and every thought and sigh and everything unutterably small or great in your life will have to return to you, all in the same succession and sequence—even this spider and this moonlight between the trees, and even this moment and I myself. The eternal hourglass of existence is turned upside down again and again, and you with it, speck of dust!'"

"Huh!"

One of the grieving women made an affirmative noise. Another shushed her, but she refused to be stilled. Jack smiled and went on with his parable.

"Would you not throw yourself down and gnash your teeth and curse the demon who spoke thus? Or have you once experienced a tremendous moment when you would have answered him: 'You are a god and never have I heard anything more divine.' If this thought gained possession of you, it would change you as you are or perhaps crush you. The question in each and every thing, 'Do you desire this once more and innumerable times more?' would lie upon your actions as the greatest weight. Or how well disposed would you have to become to yourself and to life *to crave nothing more fervently* than this ultimate confirmation and seal?"

"Yes!" called the woman, fanning herself energetically.

Until this moment, Jack had had no idea what he was going to say. He glanced down at Rachel. In the plump, smooth-haired girl he saw profound comprehension, wisdom rich in emotion and good sense. Sam's shadowed eyes revealed hope mixed with fear. Amid deep respect swam a suspicion that Jack would do something madder than Jessie had done.

"I've dedicated my life to interpreting texts," said Jack. "And now I've been asked to create a text about a life."

"Yes, Lord!" called a woman in a veiled black hat.

For the first time ever, he was addressing five hundred people, and none of them were taking notes.

"My daughter died of a heroin overdose."

Below him, Sam sucked in his breath. Rachel squirmed as her father's fingers dug her shoulder. Sam leaned forward, his eyes burning into Jack's. He must have been fearing a confession, and the idea struck Jack as funny. Luckily he had resisted reading Morrison's poems, or the tortured valves of Sam's heart might have blown.

"That's the truth," he said. "And there's no evading the truth."

"Amen. You tell 'em, brother!"

"I have seen too much death in my life." Jack's voice rose. "I have seen so much death, sometimes it hurts to go on living."

"Yes, Lord! Yes, Jesus!"

His daughter's friends wiped their eyes and nodded. One girl with a stiff brown ponytail swayed back and forth, soothing her baby. As Jack struggled, these women from beyond the park inspired him more than any audience he had ever known.

"For the rest of my life," he confessed, "I'll be asking myself what I could have done to prevent this. I'll be wondering how I could have convinced her to live—" His voice failed.

A tear glistened on Sam's cheek. His friend leaned back, now that the danger had passed. He seemed to be floating in a sea of grief.

"I applaud my daughter's life!" proclaimed Jack. "I applaud her audacity. I applaud her curiosity. I applaud her defiance. I deplore only her self-destructiveness, her disrespect for her body, her disrespect for her life."

He faltered but went on, his voice careening.

"Life is sacred. Life defies order. Life is the only truth worth pursuing."

"Yeah!" cried Corinne.

Beside her, Girish was trying to maintain what he must have thought was a grave expression.

"When I'm asked to produce a text about life," said Jack, "this is the only one I can offer: the eternal return. Too often, this passage is read as a curse, but it's a test, a challenge, a wake-up call. Nietzsche asks us, at the worst moments of our lives, to consider whether we would dare to live them again—and again, and again, and again for all eternity. Each moment the same—the most glorious"—he smiled down at Sam—"the most terrible, and worst of all, the most banal, the most meaningless."

The audience looked up at him expectantly.

"Well," he said, "I would do it. I have known tremendous moments like that. Even now, looking at the worst there is, I have to say yes to this life. I have known a lot of people who wouldn't, and I mourn for them. I respect them. But their lives are not wasted." He glanced quickly at Bea. "The only wasted life is the one that isn't lived."

"Uh-huh! Yes, Lord!" came the chorus.

"As for me," he concluded, "I want to go on living, as long as I have that privilege—and I urge you to do the same."

"Amen!"

The murmurs had grown to shouts. As he nodded to the organist to start the hymn, he almost regretted extinguishing them. They believed him. They shared his thoughts. He choked as he visualized Jessie. The organ thundered the affirmative chords of "What My God Will, May That Be Done." Jack sank down onto the hard pew and doubled over as grief took him.

With Bea beside him, he allowed his hand to be crushed by five hundred awkward grips.

"You done good, Jack," muttered Sam, embracing him tightly.

Jack's students looked at him with new appreciation.

"I'm sorry," whispered Girish, his black eyes nearly empty of irony.

One by one, Jack clasped the black women's hands.

"We're so sorry, Professor Mannheim," they said.

One of them paused and looked into his eyes—a battered old woman with an anguished face.

"Professor Mannheim," she said, "I'm Louise Lamont. Your daughter, Misty, she used to come see us. She was a nice girl. I don't know how she could have ended up in a place like that. She didn't use no drugs. She was a good girl. She done a lot for us, helped my grandniece Tanesha with her baby. If there's anything we can do—"

"We knew Misty from church," interrupted a stringy woman behind her. "We liked havin' her there. She was always so pretty an' so sweet."

Jack's eyes filled with tears, but he was restored by the spectacle of Louise Lamont hugging his mother. The girl with the ponytail handed her baby to Rachel, who had been asking to hold him. In unknown arms, the infant flailed and screamed, and Sam laughed as the girl took him from his crestfallen daughter.

"We'll call you, Jack!" Sam waved. "You gotta come over for dinner." His brow wrinkled, and his face assumed a look of thoughtful anticipation. "Hey, Ruth, what's for dinner?"

Ruth shook her head and laughed, and Jack returned to the mourners. He and Bea performed so well that no one dreamed they had separated. Bea moved off in a swirl of sympathetic doctors, and Jack took his family to dinner, then to their plane.

Late Thursday night, he appeared at Ellie's door. Sweaty and exhausted from packing, she burst into tears.

"Come on," he murmured. "It's going to be okay. We still have a whole night together."

Right after she had confirmed her defense date, Ellie had chosen that Friday for her departure. She told Jack she wanted a tight timeline: she would defend, pass, and pack, then leave Chicago a week later. After that terrible night at Jack's, part of her had wanted to flee. Now there was no going back. With fearless stubbornness, she was vowing to make Memphis by nightfall and New Orleans by Saturday night. The moment Jack had thought would never come was now eight hours away.

"I didn't think you were going to come!" she sobbed. "I didn't think I'd see you—"

"Shsh ..."

There was barely a bed to take her to, but Jack nudged her toward the shell of her bedroom. She had left a nest of sheets, and he pulled her down into their softness. She was still crying softly as he raised her filthy T-shirt and kissed her warm breasts.

"Mm, salty," he murmured.

Ellie laughed through her tears. Conscious of his movements, he strained to record every delicious touch. Systematically, hungrily, he surveyed every inch of her and tried to store the movements of his mind. As he nuzzled her ribs, she laughed.

"I feel like I'm being scanned!"

"You are," he growled in a mock-sinister voice. "With my mnemonic replicator beam, I'm storing you in my brain so I can taste you forever."

Ellie giggled and wrapped her strong, skinny legs around him. "Let's stay up, Jack. Let's talk all night."

"No, no," he murmured. "You've got to sleep. You'll be driving ten hours tomorrow."

"I can do it," she said with youthful assurance. "Just talk to me. I'm not tired. I swear."

She wriggled out from under him and grabbed the remaining pillow. She propped it so that she could lean against the wall, her lovely legs extended toward him. She invited him to rest his head in her lap, and he arranged himself between her legs. Her slender thighs caused a rushing sound as they pressed against his ears. With gentle fingers, she massaged his head, and for the first time in a week, he relaxed.

Ellie spread his earmuffs so he could hear her voice. "I'm so sorry I couldn't be there. I heard that what you said was wonderful."

"Who said that?" he asked, although he knew the answer.

"Girish." His head shifted as she shook with an embarrassed giggle. "He—he was here. He helped me take my boxes down to the post office."

Girish didn't seem like the type to perform manual labor, and probably he had had ulterior motives. Somehow Jack didn't care. A salty female scent was wafting from under his head, and arousal overcame his exhaustion.

"Ohh …" he moaned as her fingers pressed the vessels in his head.

He breathed in the darkness and felt the blood pulse through every tight passage in his body.

"Jack—" Ellie's voice caught on the pain of a jagged thought. "I want you to promise me something."

He reached out. "What is it?"

"Promise me you'll never do what your father did. I—I'm so sorry—about everything. I'm just worried I've hurt you. I'm worried I've ruined your life. Please—no matter what happens—tell me that you'll never do that."

Jack rolled over and gripped her.

"You *are* my life. Well—part of it."

He kissed her belly with openmouthed bites.

"But promise!" she begged.

"I promise," he said gutturally, looking down toward the source of that scent. "You haven't ruined anything. You're the most beautiful—the most wonderful—"

She pulled him toward her as though still unsatisfied.

"Why do you think he did it? I mean—I'm sorry—it's not my—"

"It's all right," he murmured. "You have a right to ask. I've never known. I think it's because he couldn't get what he wanted."

She lay silently, and he massaged her breasts.

"And Jessie?" she whispered.

"Same thing. So stupid, so misconceived. Like going on strike, only—forever."

"It's awful," she murmured. "I feel so sorry for them—for anyone who— But you, Jack, have you gotten what you wanted?"

"Just a little—for a little while." He sighed. "But—I mean—even if I—"

She really did want to talk all night. Fearing a wreck, he tried to shush her to sleep. Ellie seemed anxious about the months ahead when she could no longer revive him. Heeding the slow, insistent pull of desire, Jack tried nature's invitation to sleep. He moved his mouth softly down into the heart of that saltiness. Proudly he relished her excited breaths. He loved that he could bring her to such a state— trembling, writhing, heaving. When she came, every muscle in her body contracted, and she rose with a sharp, wrenching cry. Sticky and exhausted, she slept dreamlessly in her disordered pink nest.

When Jack awoke, Ellie was gone, and he looked sadly at the barren room. The furniture would stay, having come with the apartment, but all signs of her lambent personality had flown. The Botticelli angels had been stripped from the wall, and the bear had left his perch on her dresser. There remained only the clock radio, whose blue digits said 6:02.

The living room door rattled, and Ellie appeared with muffins and coffee. He gathered her in his arms, and they ate them in bed, leaning against each other. They spent their last hour loading her car. On their feet and vibrating with caffeine, they worked like a pair of engineers. Ellie had stacked her last possessions in a corner, so it was only a matter of carrying them down. In multiple trips down the creaky stairs, Jack ferried everything that remained of Ellie—her clothes, her computer, the sweet-smelling bottles from her bathroom, and her light, scratchy brown bear.

By seven, the five-hundred-dollar Dodge was packed, an indigo missile aimed toward California. Jack approached Ellie with a laundry bag of shoes and laughed as she strapped the bear into the passenger seat.

"He might get lonely," she explained. "He only speaks French."

"Well, that's a good thing," said Jack. "This is it." He shook the lumpy white bag full of shoes. "You'd better go up and do a final check."

"No, you do it," she pleaded. "I trust you. It's too depressing. I don't want to remember it empty."

Jack performed the final check himself, peering into each cabinet and each drawer. The place was immaculate. She had really left nothing. It looked just as she must have found it five years ago. With a terrible coldness in his middle, he stared at the naked mattress, off of which she had bundled the sheets.

"Don't you want to fold them?" he'd asked.

"No." She'd smiled. "I want to keep your hairs. You shed like a dog. I'm going to take them to a New Age California witch and have her cast a spell on you. Or maybe I'll just clone you—yeah, that's what I'll do. I'll take them to a genetics lab."

The alto ripple of her laugh still echoed through the empty room. As Jack closed the door, he glimpsed the blue velvet couch where he had told her about his father. With stinging eyes, he thought of the generations of students who had lived in that apartment—and of the ones who would occupy it in years to come.

Jack descended to give Ellie the all clear and found her talking to the super. She had pinned up her hair with some kind of claw that gripped it like a determined lobster. The super gave her a lingering hug and returned to his flowers.

"Be careful," said Jack. "Be sure to stop when you need to. You don't have to go all the way to Memphis."

"Oh, I'll make it." Her lips quivered.

With his stomach churning, Jack stepped toward her for one last, succulent kiss. Her lips were warm, wet, and clinging. He drew back, and her eyes reddened.

"Oh, please, Jack," she begged. "Come with me. Please stay with me. I—I don't want to go. You could just ride down with me. You could come to New Orleans!"

Jack reached down to stroke her hair. It was tempting. But tomorrow morning he was going with Bea to scatter Jessie's ashes. And he had to work. Last week, desperate to grasp anything positive, he had signed the contract with Springer. He had to deliver the Dionysus book by summer's end, and there wasn't much time. Every living impulse screamed at him to go with Ellie, but a calm, aged voice told him to hold back, more for her sake than his own.

"I can't," he murmured, his voice gaining strength. "This is your big move. You have to do this yourself. Anyway"—he gestured toward the bear—"you've got company. You've got Monsieur l'Ours over there."

"You're right—I'm sorry," choked Ellie. "We shouldn't drag it out like that."

"I'll see you at the MLA," he promised. "It'll be in San Francisco. In December we'll make up for lost time."

Ellie smiled up at him. "Okay. I'll think about that."

"Don't think too hard, or you'll smash up this fine piece of machinery."

Ellie laughed as she climbed into the driver's seat, gay tones over the engine's bass.

"You—you're beautiful!" he called.

She must not have heard him, since she smiled and nodded with tears in her eyes.

The five-hundred-dollar Dodge began to move. Smiling and waving, Jack stayed planted to the spot. Heading the wrong way, Ellie gathered speed. To escape, she had to circle a beehive building set on an island in Fifty-Fifth Street. Jack raced to the west end of her house, desperate for one last glimpse. To his surprise, she circled back and headed straight for him instead of shooting west. Could she— Did she—

But Ellie didn't slow. With a piercing whoop, she gunned her engine and raised a small fist. Like an accelerated particle, she shot once more around the island, burning through the early-morning air. This time when she emerged, she rocketed off down the Tube toward the expressway to the west.

Jack watched her go until the indigo flash dissolved and the air was still. Slowly he headed back to his house, the co-op shimmering before his eyes. He walked through the stinking tunnel where unknown hands had struck her and emerged into the blinding sun beyond. How long? How long would it be before he got the phone call telling him about the wonderful man she had met? Jack pictured her, streaking south on that sunny morning, and with all his being, he wished her well.

When he reached his front steps, he looked quickly for Jessie, then remembered he would never again have to worry about where she was. His house was emptier than it had ever been, and the silence crept into his ears. He watered the plants until they dripped in slow plops. A red light flashed on the answering machine, and he stabbed the button.

"Hey, Jack," called a friendly voice. "Guess I missed you last night. Bet I know where you were. Can't say I blame you. Listen, if you got any energy left, Ruth wants you to come over for Shabbat. It's a mitzvah—we're supposed to invite people over and make 'em joyous, and you seem like a good candidate. I never could resist a challenge. Oh, yeah, Ruth says to tell you that we're havin' kugel. If you're good, we'll give you the corner piece—*what*?"

The message broke up into chaos as several voices called Sam at once.

Jack smiled. Polished by his mother's hands, his kitchen was comfortingly clean. Even Jessie's room, the canker of the house, had found an order that would never again be disturbed. Outside the kitchen window, a cardinal shot by in a red streak. Humming to himself, Jack turned on the water. Before playing the piano, he always washed his hands.

ACKNOWLEDGMENTS

I AM GRATEFUL TO THE many friends and colleagues whose knowledge and wisdom have helped make *Auf Wiedersehen* a better book. I owe a special debt to my creative writing colleague at Hofstra University, Julia Markus, who encouraged me and took my work seriously enough to offer much-needed criticism. I am thankful to my friends Neil, Fred, and Sandy Bockian, Sander Gilman, and Joseph Skibell, who advised me on Jewish culture and religious services. I thank Isabel Guzmán-Barrón, who offered pointers on the representation of Chicago life. I am grateful to my Emory creative writing colleagues, Jim Grimsley and Lynna Williams, who advised me as I revised the manuscript. I also thank my friends Shlomit Finkelstein, Sander Gilman, Gareth Gollrad, Shawn Kirchner, Howard Kushner, Stephanie Schaertel, Henning Schmidgen, and Rhoda Spinner, who offered input as thinking, feeling human beings.

The quotations of philosophical and literary works in *Auf Wiedersehen* have been taken from the following editions: Johann Wolfgang von Goethe, *Faust*, edited by Erich Trunz (Munich: C. H. Beck, 1986); Friedrich Nietzsche, *The Birth of Tragedy and The Case of Wagner*, translated by Walter Kaufmann (New York: Vintage Books, 1967); *The Bible*, Revised Standard Version (New

York: American Bible Society, 1952); Friedrich Nietzsche, *Die Geburt der Tragödie, Unzeitgemäße Betrachtungen I-IV, und Nachgelassene Schriften 1870–1873,* edited by Giorgio Colli and Mazzino Montinari (Berlin: de Gruyter, 1988); Franz Kafka, "Vor dem Gesetz," *Das Urteil und andere Erzählungen* (Frankfurt: Fischer, 1985); and Friedrich Nietzsche, *The Gay Science,* translated by Walter Kaufmann (New York: Vintage Books, 1974).

The musical pieces mentioned and lyrics quoted were created by the following artists: Eric Clapton and Marcella Detroit, "Lay Down Sally," *Slowhand,* RSO, 1977; Robbie Krieger, "Love Her Madly," The Doors, *L.A. Woman,* Elektra, 1971; Johann Sebastian Bach, *Weihnachts-Oratorium,* BWV 248, edited by Alfred Dürr, Bärenreiter, 1989 [1734]; The Doors, "Break on Through," *The Doors,* Elektra, 1967; Johann Sebastian Bach, *Matthäus-Passion,* BWV 244, edited by Alfred Dürr, Bärenreiter, 1974 [1727]; Johann Sebastian Bach, *Johannes-Passion,* BWV 245, edited by Walter Heinz Bernstein, Bärenreiter, 1981 [1724]; The Doors, "Light My Fire," *The Doors,* Elektra, 1967.

Descriptions of the 1968 student takeover of an administration building draw upon the accounts of friends who took part in protests and upon Jerry L. Avorn's *Up against the Ivy Wall: A History of the Columbia Crisis* (New York: Scribner, 1968).

I am grateful to the iUniverse editorial, design, production, and marketing teams that brought this novel to life, especially Check-In Coordinator Vinnia Alvarez, Editorial Services Associate Courtney Wallace, Line Editor Kelsey Adams, Production Services Associate Reed Samuel, and Marketing Services Associate Nolan Estes.

Printed in the United States
By Bookmasters